Suddenly a shot rang out—then two more! Thurlow put down his coffee cup and sprang to his feet, his eyes and ears alert.

"They got him!" he said. "Rilla, call the station and tell them I'm on the trail. They'll take the river road. Call quick!"

He was out the door and astride his motorcycle before Rilla got to the telephone.

"Oh, Thurlow, my son! Don't go out alone!" called his mother wildly.

But Thurlow was thundering along into the dusk, down the bumpy street and under the railroad bridge toward the river road, after a couple of the most desperate characters in the city.

Tyndale House books by Grace Livingston Hill.
Check with your area bookstore for these best-sellers.

COLLECTOR'S CHOICE SERIES

LIVING BOOKS ®

CLASSICS SERIES

Grace Livingston Hill

APRIL GOLD

LIVING BOOKS ®
Tyndale House Publishers, Inc.
Wheaton, Illinois

This Tyndale House book
by Grace Livingston Hill
contains the complete text
of the original hardcover edition.
NOT ONE WORD
HAS BEEN OMITTED.

Printing History
J. B. Lippincott edition published 1936
Tyndale House edition/ 1992

Living Books is a registered trademark of Tyndale
House Publishers, Inc.

Library of Congress Catalog Card Number 91-67810
ISBN 0-8423-0011-2

99 98 97 96 95 94 93 92
8   7   6   5   4   3   2   1

THE house was low and white and rambling with lemon-colored blinds and a moss green roof. There were frills of daffodils all down the garden walks and around the edges of the white picket fence, and a mist of golden forsythia in a semi-circle at the back.

But the story began away back the summer before.

Rilla was just out of high school and planning to go to college the following fall. Thurl had been in college two years. Mr. and Mrs. Reed felt it would be good for Marilla to have one year at home with her mother before she went away to school, she was still so young. The Reeds had old-fashioned ideas and loved to have their children about them. Thurlow came home every weekend. His college was only a matter of fifty miles away and he could make it on his bicycle in a short time.

The Reeds were comfortably situated. They owned their own home and had saved a tidy little sum every year. They had begun when their babies were in their cradles to save up for their education. They were trying to take life as easily as they could, not rushing into great expense, but looking ahead and providing for the necessities that were likely to come.

The summer was hot and Father Reed had not been up to his usual robust strength. He came home from the office earlier than usual some days and complained of headache. It seemed a strange thing for Father not to be in the best of health, for the family to have to keep quiet on his account, and consider how to save his strength. He had always been the cheerful strong breezy dependence of the family.

Then one day he was brought home unconscious. He roused only to give them a farewell smile, and was gone!

They were dazed at first. They couldn't believe it was true that Father was gone! It didn't seem possible to go on without him.

Thurlow suggested that perhaps he ought to give up college and find a job, but his mother said no, the money was in the bank for that purpose and his father would not like him to change his plans. He and his sister must have their education. The mother was strong and sweet about it, though she looked so frail and appealing when she said it that it sent a pang through both the children's hearts. They resolved to get through their education as swiftly and thoroughly as was possible, and get ready to take care of Mother. Of course there was money enough saved up to keep her in comfort while they were studying. Then they would both get good positions and keep Mother just as she had always been kept, in simple pleasant comfort in her own quiet home.

But again the unexpected stepped in.

Early in the fall the bank where the savings had been confidently put in trust, closed its doors. Things were said to be in bad shape. One of the officials was missing, as also were stocks and bonds and much money. It was appalling. Another official committed suicide, and a cloud of gloom spread over the town. Overnight the whole situation changed for the Reeds. The taxes were coming due and the money in the bank on which they had confidently relied wherewith to pay them, was not. Following hard upon that was the discovery that Mr. Reed, a few months before his death, had put a mortgage upon his house in order to get some money to loan to a fellow-workman in the office, to save the roof being sold from over his head. It appeared that this had been done through a Building and Loan Association which had now gone into the hands of a receiver, and that the mortgage included a personal note which Mr. Reed had signed, binding him to pay double the amount of the mortgage in default of payment at the stated times. The mortgage itself had not been unreasonably large, not to the full value of the house, but when it was doubled it became an amount of alarming proportions.

With Mr. Reed's good salary and his comfortable savings account there had seemed no risk in this, but with the bank closed indefinitely, and nothing where-with to pay the fall installment, things looked pretty black for the Reeds. They knew nothing of business, any of them. Mr. Reed had protected them from care and worry. But when they had passed through an interview with the wily lawyer in charge of the Building and Loan affairs they were wiser, and sadder, too. Thurlow Reed stood by the window staring out at a world that had suddenly gone blank and implacable, appalled at what lay before him, seeing no way around it.

It was very still in the big old-fashioned parlor after the lawyer had gone. Rilla sat staring at her brother's back and trying to visualize the future, aghast at the cloud of trouble that seemed to have settled over them.

But the mother sat there quietly with her hands in her

lap, and slow tears stealing down her soft cheeks. Then suddenly she spoke, as if she were thinking aloud:

"Your father was always almost too soft-hearted," she said, as if admitting a truth grudgingly. "He was always too easy, I suppose, but—" she hesitated, and then brought out her final words with a kind of exultant note in her voice, "but—I'm *glad* he was that way! I'd rather have him that way than the other—hard and stingy and close, like some men!"

"Oh! so would I!" exclaimed Rilla with a sound of relief in her voice. "I'm *glad* Father was that way! I don't mind being poor when it's for a reason like that! I'm glad Father helped that man! Even if he did lose his house after all, I'm glad I had a father like that!"

"Here too!" said Thurlow, whirling away from the window and giving his sister a radiant smile. "We'll make out somehow. Don't worry! The only thing that troubles me is that Mother will have to give up her home that Father planned for her."

"Don't worry about me!" said the mother with a deep breath, and a brave smile shining through her tears. "I'm glad, too! Only Father would have been so troubled to have had this happen to us! But of course there didn't seem to be a bit of risk at the time, he was doing so well, and the money was in the bank. So he wasn't even to blame in his judgment. And we'll just hold up our heads and smile! It isn't going to be forever of course that we have to stay here on this earth, and while this lasts we'll take it smiling. We're going home *forever* sometime, and be in the Father's house. What's a little deprivation by the way? And think how I'm blest in my children! Thank the Lord he's given me such children!"

They bent over her and kissed her tears away, then lifted her to her feet.

"Come, Mother, let's go and get supper, all of us

together, and forget our troubles. There'll be a way, somehow, and you're the best little sport of a mother a fellow ever had!" said Thurlow.

The days that followed were full of discoveries. Someone wanted to buy the Reed place and make an apartment house of it. They wanted to get it cheap. Thurlow found that the purchaser was in league with the lawyer who was settling up the estate. The pressure was very strong to insist upon the full amount of the personal bond, as the date had gone by without the interest being paid and technically they could call it a default.

The wily one from the defunct Building Association made several calls upon the bewildered, defenseless family, tightening the meshes of his net each visit. He quoted law at them, and in their inexperience they did not know that some of the laws he quoted did not apply to their case. He pointed out to them that be could hold them to that personal bond for double the amount of the mortgage, and that he could make it impossible for them ever to hold any property, even an automobile, or a piano, or any valuable furniture, until the full amount was paid. But he intimated that there were ways of compromise. If they were willing to deed over their property root and branch to the Association there would be a way of setting them free from this bond.

Thurlow watched the sly eyes of the man as he talked. He felt the man was dishonest. Yet they could not afford to go to a lawyer. There was only one friend in the town who would have helped and he was out of the question for pride's sake. And anyway, he was just about to take his family for a trip around the world and this was no time to apply for help or advice. He was sailing in three days.

Guerdon Sherwood had been their father's friend since school days. He had always kept his friendship for his boyhood comrade even though he himself had grown rich and influential. He would have done something, the Reeds knew, if the matter had come to his attention. It would be nothing to him to hand over the money that would clear the whole trouble up, and he would probably offer it if he knew.

Yet because they knew this, knew him to be loyal and true to his friend of childhood days, the Reeds would not go to him, would not breathe their trouble to him. They had all agreed on this at once, even that first moment after the fish-eyed lawyer had left them.

"We will not say anything of this to Mr. Sherwood," said the widow firmly, looking toward her son as if she half feared he would have some intention of doing just that thing.

But Thurlow had instantly seconded her.

"Of course not, Mother! That couldn't even be a last resort!" said Thurlow decidedly.

"Certainly not!" said Rilla with a proud little lift of her chin.

The mother looked at her two children with misery in her eyes. That would be another thing that was going to make it hard. Thurl had been very friendly with Barbara Sherwood. As children they had been in the same school together, and Barbara and Thurlow in the same classes in high school. During their senior year they had been inseparable. Rilla had grown fairly intimate with Betty Sherwood and Chandler her brother. College had of course separated Barbara and Thurlow to a degree, though they had corresponded often, and during vacations the friendliness had been renewed, Thurlow often going down to the shore for the week-end while the Sherwoods occupied their summer cottage. Of course there had been nothing like an engagement or understanding between them, for they were both still in college and many miles were between them, but Thurlow's mother had watched the growing look of responsibility and gravity in the eyes of her boy, and she wondered now how things were going to be. Would all these radical changes in their lives bring about a sorrow for her son to carry? She looked at him anxiously.

Rilla's eyes were on her brother, too, and presently in her direct way she asked the question that they all had in their hearts.

"Are you going to New York to see them sail, Thurl?"

She watched the desolation spread suddenly over his grave face and was sorry she had asked him. She had only meant to remind him that he had that question to face, but she might have known he would have thought of it even before she did.

He was still a moment before he answered. Then he said gravely:

"Probably not." It was as if he had considered every phase of the matter before he spoke.

"There wouldn't be any reason why you couldn't," said his mother quickly in her comforting voice. "You know they wouldn't know anything about the change in our circumstances. Your father never told anybody what his banking place was. They wouldn't have heard. And it hasn't got out yet that we are losing our house. I don't see why you shouldn't go and have a pleasant good-by, just as you would have done if all this hadn't happened."

"It will cost something, Mother," he said quietly.

"No, it won't, Thurl," said Rilla eagerly. "Betty said some of the young folk were going to ride down in the second car, and they'll ask you of course."

"Perhaps."

"And anyway, I think you should go. She won't understand it. You've been one of her best friends. *And*

7

anyway, we shan't actually starve any sooner on the little it would take to get you down there, and buy flowers and candy or anything you want to give her. I think you ought to go! We've got to be good sports and smile."

"I'll see," said Thurlow, considering his sister's suggestion with a kindling gleam of appreciation in his eyes.

But the young man drew a long deep breath not wholly of relief as he said it. The heavy burden was not lifted just because his family had been good sports, though he greatly appreciated their attitude. And perhaps they were right. Perhaps he ought to go just as he had planned. But it would not be the lighthearted happy affair that he had expected. His own attitude toward the girl he had been secretly calling his would have to be different. He was a penniless youth now, with a family to support and heavy responsibilities. Life had changed its whole plan for him, and he must look facts in the face.

The next few days were very trying ones for Thurlow.

He went to New York to see Barbara Sherwood off, just as if nothing out of the ordinary had happened. Although that very morning had come the ultimatum giving ten days of grace before the demand must be paid to the uttermost, or the Building Association through its representative would file a claim for the entire amount demanded in the bond.

"He might as well have demanded it today!" said the sorrowful mother despairingly. "We can't pay it any better in ten days than we can now." She wiped away the slow tears that coursed down her face.

"No, Mother," said the son who suddenly seemed to have grown old and serious, "ten days is ten days. You can't tell what might happen in ten days. You know I ought not really to be wasting this one day to go to New York. But I mean to make every hour of the other nine days count for something. I don't mean to let that dirty thief get away with stealing if I can help it. For that's what it is. It's nothing short of robbery. He knows we're in a hole because the bank is closed and he's taking advantage of it. I mean to leave no stone unturned. This having an injunction looming on the horizon every time we want to own a thing, even a little old second-hand flivver, is more than I want hung around my neck the rest of my life. Believe me, I mean to give the old geezer a run for his money, anyway."

"I don't see what you can do!" said the mother hopelessly.

"I'll do plenty!" said the son briskly, although he hadn't an idea in his head of anything that he could do. But he meant to do it just the same.

He did not go in the other car as Rilla had suggested he might be asked to do. The invitation had come, but he had declined on the plea of not having time for so leisurely a trip. The truth was that he could not bear the gay throng of his old friends, and their pleasant raillery, besides, he would not have a chance to talk to Barbara alone and he somehow shrank from seeing her handing out her favors and smiles alike to all the boys. It hadn't mattered so much when he was on the spot, able to take her away from the rest whenever he tried, knowing that she enjoyed his society, looking forward to a day when they might really belong to one another. But now all that was off, and perhaps the less he saw of Barbara before she left the better. It was bound to be a wrench and he would take it as bravely and as swiftly as possible.

So it was with grave inscrutable eyes that he presented himself on the ship a half hour before sailing time and brought his gift with him, an exquisitely mounted and fitted handbag of a unique design, simple but costly. He was glad that he had bought it a week before the bank failed, bought it with a joyous heart, delighting that he knew her tastes. That at least would be perfect, his final gift to her. For it wasn't at all likely that he would be able ever again to give her gifts like that. Also, it was something that would remind her constantly of him while she was traveling—that is, if she chose to carry it instead of any others she might have. Perhaps that wasn't so good, now that things had turned out as they had. Perhaps it wasn't well to remind her of himself, since nothing was ever likely to come of it further. Yet it might for a time provide a protection for her against someone less worthy than the memory of himself. Not that he counted himself worthy, only in the quality of his admiration for her. As yet he had not begun to call it by any tenderer name than admiration, though he knew in his heart it went deeper than that, if he only had the right.

So he carried his gift to the ship, intriguingly but simply wrapped, preserving its exquisite atmosphere even to the quality of its wrapping.

At the last minute he had weakened and grown extravagant, purchasing besides a wealth of the handsomest longstemmed roses, yellow with hearts of gold lit with a ruby light, the kind of roses that went with her red gold hair, her amber-lighted brown eyes, and the warm brown costumes she so loved to wear.

He had sent the roses to her cabin with his card, and a book he wanted her to read, just a little inexpensive book, but one that held great thoughts. He had slipped it under the great green bow of rich satin ribbon with which the luxury-flowers were tied. But the beautiful handbag he carried with him and put into her hands himself, that last five minutes when he drew her away from the rest and made her walk the deck with him away from the crowd. Then, standing with her alone, he found he had nothing to say but commonplaces!

"What's the matter with you, Thurl? You look so

grown up and faraway," challenged Barbara gaily. Her eyes were starry, and her face was lit with the excitement of the day, her first trip abroad!

"I'm fairly old," he said gravely, and tried to smile, but there was something in his eyes that told the girl there was more to his words than he cared to explain or she cared to recognize.

"I wish you were going along!" she said fervently, and showed the dimple in her left cheek that made her smile so alluring. She had said the same to half a dozen other boys, and Thurlow knew it, yet his eyes flashed back an echo to her wish, even while he recognized that there was nothing really personal in her wish. Or was there? He could not be sure, and this was no time to find out. Perhaps there would never be a time to find out, now, any more. It was too late!

No, he couldn't even say that. For honorably, he had had no right to find out before, more than eyes can flash in glances and soft inflections of voices can tell. No, they were not through college yet. At least—! *Stab!* His thoughts brought him back to the stern facts of his life. There would never be any more college for him. More for her perhaps, but none for him. That in itself was a barrier between them. If it had been the other way about, it wouldn't have mattered in the least, for a woman felt no shame if she had not completed her education before she married, but a man was somehow disqualified if he had not as good an education as his girl. Married! What was he thinking about? How could he ever get married? And he was only a kid anyway, not half ready for life as he had been brought up to vision it. Yet here he was, by reason of this sudden financial cataclysm, standing as it were on one side of a great rift in the rock that foundationed them, and seeing it widen and widen into a yawning chasm with an invading sea to separate them.

He stood there speechless looking at her little pretty hands as they fingered his gift lightly, caressing it with one hand that flashed with jewels her father had bought her, exclaiming over its beauties and saying that she would carry it always, that it was the loveliest bag she had ever seen, lifting lovely glances to his grave face. He watched the lights play in and out among the waves of her glorious red gold hair, and suddenly his heart seemed like to burst. He wished he were a child and could put his face down in his hands and cry.

And then into the midst of it came that awful warning: "All ashore that are going ashore!"

For an instant the two young things looked aghast, questioning, into one another's eyes. Then the girl rallied first.

"Oh, for heaven's sake, Thurl! It isn't forever! I'm coming back, you know!" She said it lightly, gaily, and then she reached up her hands and drew his face down and kissed him lightly on his lips, still laughing.

"Now, go quick!" she laughed, "unless you'll go along, you know!" she added mischievously, and pushed him from her toward the gangway.

Thurlow went forward with the surging multitude who were staying on land. He walked as in a daze, his heart dumb with sorrow. The touch of Barbara's lips had been light as a butterfly's wing, just brushing his. The thrill of that kiss remained, and yet he was conscious at once that there was a quality of aloofness about it. It was just a casual good-by kiss, with nothing to distinguish it from the farewell she had given the rest of her friends who had come down to see her off. Perhaps her own maidenliness had demanded that it should be so, he told himself as he stepped from the gangplank to the dock, trying to defend her even as he felt the pain of his conviction. Yet there was to him about that kiss something so final, in spite of the merry words she had spoken about her return, that his heart could not accept any hope. She did not know how she would find him when she came back. She did not know that he would be no longer in her pleasant circle of friends, that he might even be gone from the home town. But there had been no room in her light planning of the future for any such possibility. She had said the words so lightly, as if all things would go right on just as they had been when she was at home, and she would come home to find them as ever, on her return. As if there were plenty of time to settle great questions and eternal friendships! As if it didn't matter any more to her than that! She was off for a good time and of course he would be just as devoted when she returned, and she—well she was not even showing any special tenderness for him, her oldest most intimate friend. Just that gay light acceptance of his devotion as a matter of course.

He did not resent it, but it hurt. Somehow as he stepped back in the crowd where he could get a good view of her as she stood smiling on that upper deck where he had left her, it hurt inexpressibly that she had not sensed that he was passing through seas of trouble, and had not given him at least a look, a tenderer smile than just what she was handing out to every one of her friends.

There would perhaps come times later when he could reason this out more clearly and see that she was excited and did not realize what she was saying or doing; when he could feel that perhaps beneath all her gaiety she was feeling the separation from him even as much as he did himself. Oh, he knew he would try to make himself think that in the lonely days ahead of him. But just now the hurt was too deep and keen for any alleviation.

He found himself a position back of the home crowd who were all standing together in a bunch, the fellows with their arms across one another's shoulders, calling out unheard last messages, throwing now and again a snarl of bright paper ribbons to strike the deck rail before her and unfold in fluttering tribute down the side of the ship, chanting some giddy doggerel of a song familiar to the crowd.

Thurlow stood back of them, grave, sad, his eyes upon the girl's bright face, and could not be sure that any of her signals or smiles were for him.

She held his gift in her hands, and once she held it up, and wafted with her finger tips a kiss toward the land as if she might be saying another thanks for just him alone, but then he saw that the kiss went wide with her lovely gesture, and all the others were flinging back gay kisses. The air was full of them. He turned from it all half sickened, closed his eyes and drew a deep breath. For an instant he felt as if the earth were reeling under his feet. Then quickly he opened his eyes, looking steadily toward that ship again as a siren set up its terrifying farewell. Fool that he was! He must not take this to heart so. He was here to see this thing through, and he was a man!

He managed a grave smile and a wave of the hand at the last, as the ship moved out from shore. Then he stood with lifted hat and watched her lovely figure standing there, moving away from him, out, out—! What a terrible thing a ship's sailing was! The sea separating people who had been a part of one another's lives for long happy years!

He turned away while her face was still visible as she stood there smiling back to shore and waving gaily.

Somehow he could not bear to see it fade to nothing! He had a feeling that she did not see him, was not differentiating between himself and the others, so that it would not matter to her. He would go, with that bright vision of her face stamped upon his memory. And if he never had anything else, he would still have that memory. Not just a wide sea with a vanishing ship in the distance.

He elbowed his way through the crowd and nobody noticed his going unless it were the girl on the ship. There was great bitterness in his heart. He told himself he was sorry he had come! Yet he knew he would not have done otherwise.

Once he thought he heard his name shouted by one of the fellows but he did not turn his head. He did not want to see that ship afar with a great ocean between.

He had an errand to do for his mother, but he hastened with it and caught an early train back home. He tried to read a paper on the way, but the letters blurred before his eyes, and finally he gave up all pretense and sat there sternly lecturing himself, trying to get a bearable attitude of mind before he got home and his mother read his face and suffered with him. His mother was like that. She always knew when he was suffering.

He told himself it was a good thing Barbara had gone before she knew anything about his troubles. At least he would not have that mortification to worry about. She had gone respecting him, maybe caring more for him than she was willing to let him see, and that was just as it should be. Time would turn her heart to other interests, and she would perhaps never have to know how his circumstances had put him into a place in life where he could never hope to have the assurance to try to win her. And he wanted her not to be hurt as he was being hurt. She would not have to know or understand the attitude he would feel obliged to take toward her, for his pride's sake. Because he loved her he hoped—yes, he told himself he really *hoped*—that she had never cared, would never have to feel what he was feeling now. Well, he ought to be glad that her kiss had been light, and there was nothing for either of them to regret in it! He ought to be glad that he could remember her happy, carefree face! Perhaps some day he would come to the place where he could be glad about it, but now there was only an ache in his heart. An ache that seemed unbearable when he thought of it as something he might have to carry all his life.

It was late when he reached home. The train was late. There had been a freight accident ahead of the New York train which delayed them, and he missed one train out to their suburb on the edge of the city, but he saw by the light downstairs that his mother had waited up for him. Mother always would. So as he neared the house be adjusted a monotonous whistle on his lips and went in trying to simulate gay indifference.

But his mother saw through it. She came over and kissed him and looked deep into his eyes, and though he tried to smile naturally and evade her glance, he knew she was not deceived.

"Yes, they got off on time," he answered readily, too readily. "It was quite a gay send-off. I'm glad I went of course," he said, trying to sound quite easy and natural.

"Of course!" said his mother, but her eyes searched him and read further than his words. And then, like a wise mother, instead of pursuing the subject further she gave him something else to think about.

"The lawyer was here again this evening," she said with a sigh, as if it wasn't of much interest. "He said over again all the things he said the last time and a few more. He wanted me to sign the papers right away. He said he had to go west on a business trip and he'd like to get this settled before he leaves tomorrow night. He said he'd give us fifty dollars toward our moving if we'd settle at once."

Her son looked at her startled.

"Fifty dollars!" he said with a puzzled look. "He must want it a lot to let go even that much! He must have a purchaser for it, or else he knows his game is crooked and he wants to get away with it quickly before he gets found out. You didn't give him an answer, did you, Mother?"

"No, I told him I would have to talk it over with you. But he wants his answer before twelve o'clock tomorrow."

"Well, I'll look into it the first thing in the morning, but, Mother, I think we'll keep him guessing. If anybody wants to buy the house *we* are going *to do the selling,* see? It's worth more to us than to anybody else, and we have nine days yet to pay the demand."

"Well, I don't know," said his mother with a sigh. "We might lose even the fifty dollars, you know." But she turned away satisfied that she had given her son something else to think about besides the girl who had sailed away from him.

Thurlow went to bed at once but he did not go to sleep. Neither did he spend all the time thinking about beautiful Barbara Sherwood. Instead he was racking his brain for ways and means to save as much from the wreckage of the family fortunes as he possibly could, and about the middle of the night he arose, turned on his light, and searched through the newspaper he had tried to read on the train until he found a paragraph that he had scarcely noticed when he read it, but which had come back to him with strange significance as he lay thinking. He read it twice through.

"It has been definitely decided to build a new school-house in the Seventeenth Ward. The present school is overcrowded and the capacity of the new school will have to be doubled."

His eyes had skimmed over the page as he read it and it had meant nothing to him, but now it suddenly took on new meaning. Their home was in the Seventeenth Ward, a sort of a suburb, yet counted as in the city. Perhaps there was a way out of this maze of trouble after all!

THURLOW went early the next morning to the president of the Board of Education and presented his suggestion that the site of the Reed home would make a central location for the new school that was proposed.

But he found to his dismay that while his suggestions were received with a degree of interest they were put on file to be laid before the Board at its regular meeting which did not occur until five days later, too near to disaster to be counted upon. And though Thurlow urged haste and a special meeting to consider his proposition, with a ridiculously low price if the cash could be had within the requisite eight days, he found that nothing he could do or say would move that august body, the Board of Education, to come together before their regularly appointed time.

He went on his way sadly disappointed, yet he felt that this incident had given him an idea. There was to be a new post office in the near future. Why not try the government authorities? The Reed lot would be a splendid place. Not centrally located in the business part of the suburb, yet near enough for business to grow that way. He would try.

He spent another busy day hunting up officials, gaining interviews, being sent from this one to that one, making long-distance telephone calls and anxiously watching his small supply of cash dwindle thereby. The wasted day stretched into three at last before he gave up the post office idea, convinced that the closely woven meshes of politics were too much for his inexperience. Perhaps there might have been ways of accomplishing his aim if he had only known how, and had a little more experience and influence, and a little less pride. Mr. Sherwood would have known how to do it, would have had influence enough to bring it about. But Thurlow Reed felt a thrill of almost fierce satisfaction that Guerdon Sherwood was on the high seas, and that there was no way possible for even a morbid conscience to persuade him that perhaps after all for his mother's sake he ought to consult the father of Barbara Sherwood.

He was on a suburban train, coming back from his last fruitless effort to persuade a political boss to take interest in buying the house for the new post office site. He was dogweary and discouraged. He had that same stinging sensation in his eyes and throat that he had experienced the time he had fumbled a ball and lost a game for his college, that first time he had been put on the Varsity team. Of course he hadn't been put off after all, but he had been covered with shame and humiliation, and felt desperate at the time. He had wanted to hide. He had wanted to crawl away and never be seen again.

Just so he felt now, utterly beaten! He had perhaps even been wrong in preventing his mother from signing over the property at once and getting that fifty dollars. But he had been so sure that he could find a purchaser, so sure, even that morning when he had gone forth to find his man, so sure he was on the right track and was going to win. Everybody had told him this man was the king pin, and was easy to approach. But he had found him wily and ungracious, utterly impossible to move. As he settled back in the dusty plush seat and pulled his hat down over his smarting eyes he had a feeling that the whole world was against him.

"Oh, God!" his heart cried out, "I'm up against it! I ought to be able to protect my family! They are all I've got, and I can't do it."

Thurlow Reed believed in God. He had always gone through the outward forms of prayer, though he had never seemed to be in any particular position of need before, either spiritual or physical. But now the habit of his lifetime came to his lips in a kind of despairing prayer, although he didn't really look upon it as prayer. Just a blind crying out of his soul to the universe that things had gone wrong.

He drew a deep sighing breath of defeat and let his weary muscles relax. He had walked a long way in that suburb he had just left, hunting the man who lived in the third big estate from the station, behind twelve-foot iron grillwork, padded with thick impenetrable forests of rhododendron and hemlock and flowering shrubs. He had toiled up one long leisurely drive after another until he found the right place, only to discover the man for whom he searched was at the country club three miles away. He had walked a hole in the sole of his shoe and acquired a pebble or two inside, and he hadn't the money now to purchase new shoes. He lifted one foot across his knee and surveyed the limp sole despairingly. He had never had to consider small things like repairs before. Shoes had always been plenty. But there were going to be a lot of things like this presently. The thought startled across his tired consciousness with amazing revelation. He had grown up overnight, and to this!

It came to him that he was as far from the life that had been his, in name at least, when he had gone down to New York to bid good-by to Barbara, as one could possibly be. He had not yet sensed that there were still depths of life that he had not even imagined.

He drew another deep sighing breath and put the perforated sole quickly down on the floor where he could not see it. He couldn't think about it any more. He couldn't stand another thing till he got rested. He had to get rested before he got home or his mother would suffer just looking at his face. That was the trouble, Mother sensed everything and suffered so. One couldn't hide anything from her. Even if outwardly he seemed to have succeeded in camouflaging the state of things, she sensed it. Smiled with him and tried to let him think he had deceived her, yet all the time she was suffering with him just as if she had known exactly how things stood. What was the use? Why try any farther? There were only four days, and what more could he do than he had done? Oh, God! It was just a weary exclamation, showing his limit of despair. Yet how he hated to give up and let that swine of a lawyer beat him! Let him fix that throttling hold upon him for life unless he paid that enormous sum! His indignation rose, but his weariness rose also, and he sank back in the seat with his eyes closed and wished be might go to sleep and forget it all.

In front of him sat two women garbed in afternoon costumes, white gloves, delicate garments, tricky hats that seemed simple yet made their wearers look years younger than their ages. Their voices were low and well modulated, their speech was cultured and refined. They were talking of social affairs. By their conversation he learned vaguely that they had been to a tea or bridge party or some affair of that sort and were on their way back to their homes in his own part of the city. He paid no more heed to them than if they had been the paneling on the ceiling of the car above him. They were just a part of the place where he was sitting for the time.

Then suddenly with a single sentence their words came alive as astonishingly as if the paneling above him had spoken to him and shown an interest in his problems.

"Oh, and, Mrs. Brent," said the older woman, the one with white hair, "have you heard what Mr. Stanwood has done for our club? You weren't out yesterday, were you? But surely someone has told you! It is too wonderful news to keep silent about."

"Why, no! What's happened? I haven't seen a soul for nearly a week till I went out this afternoon, and you were the only one today from our club."

"Well, I surely am glad to be the first one to tell you," said the older lady. "Mr. Stanwood is giving us a new clubhouse in memory of his wife, because she was the first president of the club, you know. She started it. You knew that, didn't you?"

"Why, no, did she? That was before I moved to the city, you know," said Mrs. Brent. "But she was still president when I first joined. I remember her. She was lovely, wasn't she? And then she was ill a long time before she died, wasn't she?"

"Yes, she was ill for a year, suffered terribly, and kept her part of the work going just as long as possible. She was wonderful! And it seems Mr. Stanwood has just heard that we have been talking about trying to enlarge our clubhouse, and he came forward yesterday just right out of the blue as it were, and offered to give us a new clubhouse, root and branch!"

"Wasn't that wonderful!" exclaimed Mrs. Brent gushingly.

Thurlow Reed held his breath and listened.

"It certainly was! And it wasn't just talk. He had some good suggestions to make. It seems he has felt for a long time that we needed a larger auditorium, and he suggested that we purchase some one of the old residences on Regent Street—" (Thurlow Reed almost shouted aloud then. Regent Street was where the Reeds lived!)

"—and use the residence for club rooms and so on," went on the well-modulated voice of the white-haired lady, "and build the right kind of an auditorium in front of it—"

"How ideal!" said Mrs. Brent. "Wouldn't that Lockwood place be wonderful? It's far enough back from the street to leave plenty of room for a good big auditorium with a terrace in front, which is all the lawn you would want in a clubhouse."

"Exactly," said the older woman complacently, "we thought of that at once of course, being vacant as it is, and I called up the agent who has charge of it, but it seems it was willed to the daughters who live in California and they are not willing to sell. They want to keep the old homestead, as they expect to return someday and live there themselves. We even went to the extent of telegraphing, but their reply was quite decided. They wouldn't sell at any price. In fact they can't till the younger daughter comes of age, which won't be for two years yet, so that was final for us of course. We want to get something right away."

"Oh, Mrs. Steele, isn't that too bad! That would have been ideal! But of course there are other pretty places right along there. There will surely be something on that block."

"Not for sale, I'm afraid," sighed Mrs. Steele, shaking

her head. "We've gone over that whole block. The owners are all living in their homes it seems, and one can't just go and ring a doorbell and ask people if they won't get out and sell you their home. Besides, of course one would have to pay more that way, and we can't really pay much for the property because that would take away too much from the auditorium building. The gift was—" she lowered her voice and mentioned the sum given, under her breath, so that Thurlow couldn't be sure of the exact sum, but he distinctly heard the next sentence, "so that we could scarcely afford to pay more than twelve or fourteen thousand for the lot and whatever buildings it contained. We really ought not to pay more than twelve of course, but we might stretch a point if it was in the right location. In fact I think we would have given more for that Lockwood place if we could have got it. Its location is so central and so desirable."

Thurlow sat there fairly weak with astonishment and fearsome delight. Was he in a dream or was he hearing aright? The Lockwood place was just next door to their own. In many ways not as desirable as the Reed house. Could it be possible that a miracle like this had happened right at his side just when he was in despair?

And what should he do about it? Lean forward and snap it up at once? They were almost at the station now where he should get off. He did not know where this Mrs. Steele lived, though he could probably find out. But—would it be wiser to wait till evening and go to her home? No. She might be going away somewhere, or be having a dinner party. There might be delay, and every minute now counted so desperately. Yet something fine and wise in him told him that in a matter of such great importance he must not act in a hasty childish frenzy. He must go about it in a businesslike way. And it would not do to let her know he had overheard her conversation.

It would prejudice her against him at once and might spoil the whole thing. He tried to be calm, to close his eyes and think. He remembered the figures he had heard the lady quote. It would not do to let her know that he knew what she was willing to pay. No, he must wait, even in his desperation he must be calm and take every step cautiously. He must try to follow her if possible, at least to see in which direction she went. Would she be the Mrs. George Steele of whom there was so much talk, the woman who was so philanthropic? Surely he had heard his mother speak of her.

Then as if in answer to his thought the lady spoke again.

"I am expecting the car to meet me at the station. Couldn't I drop you somewhere on the way? I'm sorry I can't take time to run in and see those etchings at Hatch's you spoke of, but I promised George I'd be home early tonight. He has to leave on the six o'clock train for Chicago and he's as helpless as a child about getting his things together to pack. He likes me to do that for him, instead of a servant, so I like to humor him."

She smiled at her friend as they rose and gathered up their belongings, and the train drew to a full stop.

Thurlow had turned away looking out the opposite window. Just as well she should not see his face and recognize him as one who might have overheard her talk. The two ladies drifted past him out the door without looking in his direction, and he came more slowly behind them, keeping them in sight, without being seen himself, until they disappeared into a handsome limousine that stood waiting. Then he hurried into the drug store and looked up Mr. George Steele's address in the directory. Of course the telephone book might have given it, but so many of those rich people were listed privately that one couldn't be sure of finding everybody there.

Having written the address down carefully Thurlow went whistling home and entered the house with a happier look on his face than he had worn in many a day.

"You've had some good news!" cried his sister joyously.

He looked at her, sobering down.

"No, not exactly," he said with a quick little sigh. "It might not turn out to be anything. I just had a hunch."

"Oh!" said Rilla despondently. "Didn't anything come of that post office affair?"

"Not a thing!" he said emphatically. "But don't give up yet, Rill, we've still four days ahead."

"What's four days! Just like the four days that preceded. Wait and hope and find nothing. I'm going to get a job."

"Hop to it, little sister. But don't give up hope. You know jobs aren't easy to get either!"

"I know!" and Rilla sat down on the hall settee and sighed. "What are we going to do?"

"Something!" said her brother as he went up the stairs two steps at a time. "We've still four days!"

"And tomorrow there will be only three days."

"Exactly so," laughed her brother, swinging into his room and kicking off his worn shoes gaily. He still had one other pair of shoes that with plenty of polishing would carry him through a few interviews without shame. It seemed strange that he should have reached a place where a thing like that was something for which to be profoundly thankful.

Thurlow dressed with haste but as carefully as his wardrobe permitted and hurried downstairs.

"Don't wait dinner for me, Mother," he said to the

anxious mother who was concocting an appetizing dinner at the least expense possible.

"Oh, Thurlow," she said, dismayed. "You'll get sick before this is over. I just know you will. Can't you wait till I get dinner on the table? It won't be half an hour."

"I can't wait five minutes, little Mother," he said, stooping to kiss her tenderly. "I've got a lead and I've got to follow it while the trail is hot. It may lead to nothing, but it's my last chance as far as I can see. I'll get back as soon as I can, but I can't stop now. It's now or never!"

"Then you must drink a glass of milk," pleaded the mother.

He poured the milk down in one breath, accepted a couple of sugar cookies from the plate she handed out, and was gone.

"Oh, dear!" sighed his mother. "To think he has to be hurrying around wildly this way for nothing. Just nothing! What would his father say, after all his careful planning for you both! It's heartbreaking!"

"He thinks he has something," said the sister listlessly, "but he might as well give up and try to hunt a job."

"I'm afraid it will be just the same when he comes to hunting a job," sighed the mother, and the slow tears stole quietly down her cheeks.

"Now, Mother, don't you give up too," said the girl with stormy eyes and set lips, rising and going to look out of the window to hide the sudden tears that blurred into her own eyes.

There was unhappy silence in the room for several seconds, and then the mother answered in a tone of forced cheerfulness:

"No, of course not. I had no thought of giving up. We're going to come through all right. I have no doubt that Thurlow will succeed in something soon and we

shall find everything settling into sane living again.
We've got to keep brave and cheerful."

"Of course!" said Rilla peppily, but she stood a long
time staring out into the evening twilight, her lips set in
that firm determination that showed she was thinking
something through to a finish. Her mother watched her
furtively and thought how much she looked like her
father, and presently she got up and went to the old desk
where a lot of important papers were kept. There were
things there that she had meant to look over when she
could bring herself to doing it, not very important
things, but still she had to do it sometime and this was as
good as any time, since they would of course delay
dinner for a while hoping Thurlow would return to
share it with them. She had shrank long from going over
these papers. They reminded her so of the husband and
father who was gone, that she could hardly bear to
handle them over, but perhaps it was as well to get
through with it. A lot of them must be destroyed. The
house of course was not going to be theirs any longer,
no matter what happened, and she ought to get her
things in order.

So she sat down at the desk, and Rilla continued to
stare into the lengthening shadows out on the grass,
thinking out her seventeen-year-old problems.

Meantime Thurlow was having troubles of his own.
Arrived at the House of Steele he had asked to see Mrs.
Steele and was told that she was very busy just now.
Could he send up a message or would he come again in
the morning?

Thurlow's heart was beating like the proverbial trip-
hammer, and he stood there baffled for an instant.
Should he risk a message or wait until morning? He
decided on the message. He took out one of his fraternity college cards and wrote beneath his name:

"I have been told you can tell me whom to see about a house that the Woman's Club would like to purchase." He looked at it after he had written it and the words seemed to be dancing around his name, hand in hand. How tired he felt, and hungry too! He almost wished he had not come tonight!

The maid took the card, looked at him uncertainly, and finally asked him in and gave him a chair in the reception hall. He saw her vanishing up the stairs studying the card and his heart sank. How blundering he had been to blurt out his business in that abrupt way. Now likely the woman would send him word she knew nothing about it. Perhaps after all she wasn't the right Mrs. Steele. Perhaps George had been her son's name or her brother's. What a fool he had been not to approach her on the train, tell her frankly he had overheard her! Now perhaps he would never get on the track of this chance again!

But then he heard the soft stir of silken skirts, and suddenly he saw the lady herself approaching. There was eagerness in her face, and keen questioning.

"Are you from the Lockwoods' house? Are you the agent?" she asked as she came toward him, his card in her hand.

Thurlow rose deferentially.

"No, but I heard that the club was looking at the Lockwood house, and knowing it was not in the market I came to see if you would be interested in the house next door? I represent that."

"Next door?" asked the lady eagerly. "Which side?"

She studied Thurlow's face with kindling eyes as he explained about the house. He could see it interested her.

"And what is your price?" she asked.

The boy's lips turned white as he opened them to answer, there was so much at stake.

"The price is low," he said eagerly, "but it has to be cash. And it has to be within the next three days or I can't sell it to you at all!"

The woman eyed him interestedly.

"Sit down!" she said. "Tell me about it! Wait! I'll call my husband!"

He heard the man upstairs asserting that he hadn't time to stop and listen to a fool thing about the club, but he heard the low insistent plea of the woman, and then the two came down, the man growling:

"All right. Just for a minute, but you'll have to make it snappy!"

During the seconds while they were walking down the stairs Thurlow did some rapid planning. He would have to be as brief as possible or the man would be gone, and the woman would perhaps not decide in his absence.

He arose with his story on his lips. He lifted honest eyes to the keen business man who searched him with cold eyes, but he spoke with the courage of desperation.

"My father died two months ago. Our house had a mortgage which would have been all right only the Building Association that held the mortgage failed and it got into the hands of a couple of crooks. Then we lost every cent we had in the Franklin Bank crash, and now the crooks are demanding the full amount of the personal bond, which is double the mortgage. We can't pay any of it and we've got to sell the house. We have three days left before they take it away from us. If we can sell the house *for cash* we can let it go at—" Thurlow named the lowest sum that would clear the bond and pay the expenses of the transfer. He felt this was the last chance and he couldn't hope to get enough for any over for themselves. But it had to be done. He swallowed hard and went on.

"After that it goes into the hands of the crooks and they'll want plenty if they sell it at all, though I think they mean to build a large apartment house there and make a lot of money out of it. If they take the house that way they'll have a strangle hold on me for the rest of my life till that bond is paid. I'd like to see them beaten if only just for that!"

The successful business man studied Thurlow earnestly for a full second before he spoke, crisply, sharply.

"What's your name?"

"Thurlow Reed."

"What was your father's name?"

"Joseph Reed. He was with the Carter Company for thirty years."

"H'm! I thought so! You look like him. Well, Anne," turning to his wife with a twisted smile on his face, "it's all right. Go ahead with your purchase if it's what you want. I know the house. That's a bargain on that street! Who are those lawyers, Reed? Cook and Crowell? I thought so. I've had experience with them before. Anne, if you buy, get our lawyer to look into the papers and fix it up good and hard. Don't let those crooks get by with murder or anything. And if you need me get me long distance in Chicago tomorrow at noon. You know where. Good-by! See you Saturday!"

The great man stooped and kissed his white-haired wife, swung into his overcoat and was gone to the car that stood ready outside. Thurlow stood speechless, waiting, looking at the satisfied woman who smiled at him.

"When can I see the house?" she asked, as if she had no question in her mind about wanting to take it.

"Right away, as soon as you wish," said Thurlow, trying to make his voice steady.

She glanced at her wrist watch.

"Now?" she said, looking up. "I have an engagement after dinner, but I'd like to get this thing fairly settled before I see the other club members."

"Of *course* now!" said Thurlow, restraining himself from the desire to shout his joy. "I'm sorry I haven't a car to take you in."

"We have plenty of cars," smiled the lady. "Martha"—to a maid who was moving quietly about the dining room on the other side of the hall—"tell Andrew to get the small car and take us on an errand. Tell him to hurry, please."

The lady left Thurlow waiting in a daze of wonder while she got her wraps, and was back just as the car came purring up to the door.

Just as easy as that it was done. Thurlow couldn't believe but that it would somehow fall through at the last. It was too good to be true. Probably when she saw it she would have some fault to find with it, and that would be that! But while it lasted the hope at least was great!

3

THURLOW sat in the back seat with Mrs. Steele who asked him intelligent questions all the way to the house. How large was the lot? How many rooms did the house have? What kind of heating and lighting? How many bathrooms? Was there a garage? He answered the rapid fire of questions as honestly as he could, and then suddenly they were at the house and he was taking Mrs. Steele up the front walk, hoping his mother had not waited dinner for him, hoping the house would be in its usual beautiful order.

But her son need not have worried. Mrs. Reed was always ready to be seen. Even in her working garb she had a sweet dignity about her. Also the lady he was bringing was a thoroughbred. She met the other woman with a gracious informality that made them at once friendly.

"Are you one of our club members whom I ought to know, but don't?" asked Mrs. Steele with a friendly smile.

"No," said Mrs. Reed. "I've never had time for things like that. I've just lived a quiet home life."

"Perhaps you're to be envied," said Mrs. Steele, studying the other woman's strong sweet face. "But I'm sure the club has been the loser thereby."

Thurlow's heart suddenly swelled with pride and he gave his mother a tender look. He would never forget Mrs. Steele's appreciation of his mother. Neither would Rilla who was standing just within the pantry door, caught before she could slip upstairs.

"And now," said Mrs. Steele, "I feel just like a thief coming here to try to steal your home away. It's lovely. Isn't it going to be too hard for you to leave it?"

A quick look of pain came into Mrs. Reed's eyes but she smiled through it.

"Hard? Yes. But we'll be glad to get the chance to sell it! We've been unfortunate, like a good many others these days."

"Yes, your son has been telling me. But now, since it had to come, I'm glad that we are to profit by it. Will it be all right for me to look the house over? I want to tell the rest of my committee about it before we meet with the man who is giving the property to our club as a memorial to his wife."

Then Mrs. Steele was all practicality, asking questions, exclaiming over this and that pleasant feature of the house.

"I think it's just what we want," she said at last, as, Rilla having been driven forth from her hiding, the Reeds stood finally together and watched for their fate from those pleasant lips. "We'll need another bath perhaps, some few alterations in partitions, but on the whole it is quite well planned for our purpose, and I'm positive the rest of the committee will agree with me. We have our meeting at ten tomorrow morning, and I should say by afternoon, if all goes well, we will be ready to sign the papers. But I would like to bring the rest of the commit-

tee, with Mr. Stanwood, our donor, to see the place
before the papers are signed. Would it be inconvenient
for you if we were to drive around sometime during the
morning, say about half past eleven? Oh, thank you,
then I'm sure we shall find ready response from the other
members!"

"She knows her onions!" said Rilla softly as she turned
from the window where she had been watching the tail
light of the Steele car disappear into the evening.

"Yes," said Thurlow decidedly, "she knows all her
vegetables, Rill, very well indeed."

"Well, who is she?" asked Rilla. "And where did you
pick her up, and what's it all about? Isn't it about time
you told us the whole thing? Come springing a high-
brow like that on us when we were starving to death for
our dinner and never explaining a thing, and me with
my kitchen apron on, caught in the pantry. Sit right
down and explain yourself."

"Not a word," said the mother, laughing, "until dinner is on the table. Thurlow hasn't even had any lunch,
I'm quite sure, and as for the rest of us we'll all be sick if
we get so excited. And, Rilla, quick! I smell the stew
burning! If we have to eat stew day after day it's better
to have it before it burns. You take it up and I'll get the
butter and the coffee on. Hurry. Whatever news there is
will keep, good or bad, till we've started dinner."

So presently they were seated at the table and
Thurlow was telling his story, amid a fire of questions
from his sister, and an interested thoughtful silence from
the mother.

"Well," said Rilla when the tale was finally concluded
and they couldn't think of another question to ask, "I
refuse to believe in it till it happens. This is the third time
Thurl has gotten up an excitement, and it isn't any more
likely to happen this time than it was any of the others.

I for one am glad there aren't many more days before the worst is over."

There were tears behind the challenging voice, and the mother and brother realized that it was going hard with Rilla to give up her home. She had always loved it here so, where she and her father used to roam around the grounds arm in arm in the summer time and watch the trees and flowers grow, and visit their favorite bird's-nests, and feed the pet squirrel. It brought a mist to all their eyes to think about leaving the dear home.

The mother got up at last, breaking the silence. There was a look of victory and peace in her face.

"If it is God's will that those people shall buy this house they will!" she said decidedly. "Or, if it is His will that we should go through humiliation and have our house taken from us, then we must not murmur at that either. Now, let's get these dishes out of the way, children, and then go to bed. We are all pretty well tired out and we don't know what the morrow holds for us, so we had better get some sleep."

Very quietly they all worked, and in a few minutes had the kitchen immaculate. They had talked very little. Each one was realizing what it was going to mean to lose the house even in a respectable way.

"But, Mother," said Rilla as she hung up the last dish towel and turned out the kitchen light, "what are we going to do? Even if we sell the house in the right way, where are we going? We can't just make a bonfire out of our furniture and then go and park on the street."

There was panic in the girl's voice. Things were looming large and sorrowful on her young horizon.

"There will be a place provided," said the mother firmly. "I think perhaps I have an idea, but we won't talk about it yet. We must first see what happens to this house. And tomorrow morning, Rilla, you and I have got to begin looking over things and packing away some of our belongings. When we go we may have to go suddenly. That is, if we should happen to be ejected."

"Mother!" said Rilla, aghast, "nobody could do that, could they?"

"Yes, I guess they could, that is, if they were mean enough. I wouldn't be in the least surprised if that slick lawyer did it."

"Oh, Mother! Why didn't we let Thurlow go to Mr. Sherwood before he left? He would have saved the house for us. I'm sure he would."

"Let?" said Thurlow sharply, appearing in the doorway. "Where did you get that word? Did you suppose you were keeping me from it? I certainly wouldn't have gone to Mr. Sherwood, no matter if you all begged me to."

"Of course not!" said the mother. "Rilla, you are overwrought. You don't realize what you are saying."

"I don't see why it would have been so dreadful," said the girl with troubled brow. "It would only have been borrowing a little money. We could have paid interest on it, and paid it back pretty soon. Thurlow and I could get jobs and pay it back."

"We haven't got the jobs yet, sister, and no telling when we will. Forget it, Rill, and go get yourself a night's sleep. 'You'll be sorry you worried at all tomorrow morning'—" he chanted gaily, and then went up the stairs whistling.

"Trying to keep his courage up!" thought the mother with a sigh as she followed slowly up the stairs.

But in his room at last he whistled no more. Instead he went and stood at his open window looking down into the stillness of the summer night and his heart was heavy. Rilla's question of what they were going to do next confronted him and fell heavily on his heart. He had forgotten that there would be other and perhaps worse problems after the house was disposed of. And what of all his friendships and his college, and Barbara, and the future in general?

Thurlow awoke from a troubled sleep early in the morning, and all the world looked dark to him again. He was afraid that his hopes of selling the house to Mrs. Steele's club were going to be dashed. Somebody would be sure to rise up and object, or there would be delay in some way.

He drank strong coffee for breakfast and wouldn't eat the tempting things his mother had prepared. He was nervous and excitable. Rilla watched him warily.

"You're not so complacent yourself this morning," she mocked her brother as she came upon him staring out the window.

He forced a smile and turned upon her.

"I was just thinking that I'd better go out and cut the lawn before we have that visitation from the townspeople," he announced with elaborate cheerfulness, and hurried out to get the lawnmower.

But even so the hours dragged slowly by.

Then at last they came, staring critically at the house and grounds as they surged up the front walk.

Rilla fled to the attic and wept her heart out into an old haircloth trunk where she was pleased to think she was packing away garments. But she did not escape the interlopers even there.

Mrs. Reed was the gracious hostess, but wondering all the while why it seemed such a terrible thing to her to have strangers going about her beloved house, peering into every cranny and corner and bringing out infinitesimal flaws.

It was Thurlow who answered the questions, going about with the men of the party of whom there were three, Mr. Stanwood the donor, and two husbands of the club committee. He was grave and courteous and seemed to be much older than he really was.

Rilla, escaping from her attic just in time before an influx of women mounted to the top of the house, watched her brother with wonder. Thurlow was growing to be a man. She was proud of him as he stood there in the doorway talking to Mr. Stanwood. Oh, to think he had to leave his home and give up his college course and go into some miserable little minor job, just be an underling all his life, instead of turning out the splendid business man his father had hoped and planned for!

There was no question about whether they liked the house. They stood in admiring groups and exclaimed and whispered and exclaimed. Mr. Stanwood lingered talking a long time with Thurlow. Then they all went away. But Mr. Stanwood came back within the hour bringing his lawyer with him, and suddenly before they had realized that the question was settled it was all over, the papers signed, and the money in the bank! They took Thurlow down to the bank with them, got Mr. Steele's lawyer whom Mr. Reed also had known and trusted, and before three o'clock the money was paid to the Building Association, satisfying all claims, and the deed was handed over to the new owners.

Thurlow came back to his mother and sister triumphant.

"You ought to have been there, Mother. It was a thrill! Our lawyer went with me to make the settlement and you ought to have seen those foxy men cringe when they saw who was with me. Mr. Stanwood came along. He said he wanted to see the thing through. And the questions he asked them! You should have seen how hard they had to backwater to get around some of the things they had done. They finally ended up by charging it all on a stenographer who had been fired because she got letters mixed and took too much upon herself. They said she had written the letter, and when Mr. Stanwood asked him how he came to sign such a threatening letter after it had been written, he said he had been on his way to a train and hadn't stopped to read it over. That was that last insolent letter we got. But say, Mother, that Mr. Stanwood is a peach. He even offered to advance the money to settle up the mortgage and let us pay as we liked if we wanted to keep the house. But I knew you wouldn't think we could do that." He looked at his mother questioningly and sighed. He was tired, poor fellow. And after all the triumph of course they were losing their house, getting nothing in return but a clear conscience and a good name.

"No! Of course not!" said the mother quickly. "But that was wonderful of him! An entire stranger."

"He says he knew Father, or knew of him," said the son tenderly. "Almost everyone seems to have known Father! Or at least known of him!"

The mother smiled and a light came into her eyes.

"You had a good father. Everybody respects a man like your father, even though he was not socially prominent, or financially a great success."

"Of course!" said the son proudly. "Father was most unusual."

"Yes, but it is good to know that there are others too," said the mother, "good that all the world are not crooks."

"Well, at least we'll have enough left over from the settlement to move into a decent apartment and pay the rent a couple of months ahead till I can get a good paying job," said Thurlow with a sigh of relief. "There were almost two hundred dollars over when everything was paid."

"That's grand," said the mother. "But look here, son, just put that idea of an apartment out of your head. We can be thankful for this extra money of course, but it won't do much more than move us, and we've got to husband every cent. You needn't get any notions about comfortable apartments. We're not going to try to live in luxury. Not even what you would call comfort or perhaps even decency. We are going to get along with bare necessities, at least for a while, till we can see ahead. And this extra money is going to be a nest egg for possibilities ahead, until we are sure of getting our money back from that bank—if we ever do. Now, I may as well tell you that I've made my plans, and I guess you'll have to let me manage for a little while yet, anyway. It may be a bit hard for you now, but I think it will work out. At least we're going to try it. Now, come and let us get something to eat and then I'll tell you about it."

"But, Mother!" said both the young people in dismay. "You mustn't get that way! We are going to take care of you, you know."

"Yes, well, that's all right, and you're a pair of dears, but we are going cautiously until the ground gets firmer under our feet again. Now, Rilla, you put the milk and butter and applesauce on the table and, Thurl, slice the cold meat and cut the bread. I'll fry the potatoes and make the coffee and we'll be ready in no time."

Thurlow gave his mother a keen worried look, but did her bidding, and in a short time they sat down to the meal, but they ate silently, the young people keeping a wary eye on their mother. They recognized a set of firmness about her lips that portended a state of mind hard to move. They had had experience before with that look on her face and felt more trouble ahead.

Rilla fairly flew at the dishes when they were done, and very soon everything was in place.

"Now!" said Thurlow, leading his mother to her comfortable chair in the living room. "Let's hear the worst!"

The mother went to her desk and got a long envelope, returning to her chair.

"I've been going over the papers in the desk, getting ready to move," she said as she sat down, "and I found some papers I had forgotten all about."

She opened the envelope and took out a long official-looking document.

"It's a deed," she explained, "a deed to a small property down on the south side of the city. Your father took it over from a man who owed him some money. The man's wife died and he wanted to move away quickly, so your father took the property. It isn't worth very much, but the taxes are paid and it's ours. I know you will not think it is a pleasant place to live, but we can't help that now. It's big enough to house us and it won't cost us anything. There is a barn on the place big enough to store the goods we want to keep. I'm selling some of them, of course. That will bring in a few more dollars to live on till times improve. I called up your Mrs. Steele and she said she thought the ladies would like to purchase a couple of bedroom sets from the guest rooms. We shan't need so many again, and they are not especially interesting to us to keep. We never had any sentiment connected with them. The bookcases, too, won't fit anywhere else."

The son and daughter looked at one another and gasped.

"But, Mother," demurred Thurlow, "you don't realize at all what kind of a neighborhood the south side is.

You wouldn't stand it a day, and it's no place for a girl like Rilla to be."

"I thought you'd say that," said the mother, "so I went down there yesterday while you were off. I sent Rilla to return some books we had borrowed from two or three places and I took the trolley down there. It isn't fashionable, if that's what you mean. I'll admit there are several factories near by and the railroad runs behind the house, but the lot is quite deep, and it's only a siding from the main track, running down to a factory two blocks away. Anyway, I think we should move there for the present."

"But, Mother, why be so economical when we have that extra money?"

"Because, we've got to save every cent. By the time we are moved there will be very little left to live on. You haven't either of you an idea how much it costs just to eat. Of course if we're able to get jobs, all three of us, we can in time catch up and have things a little easier, but at first we've got to be very careful!"

"Mother! Not *you!*" Rilla was aghast and Thurlow rose up sternly.

"Yes, of course I'm going to get a job," said Mrs. Reed. "I'm not too old. I can get plain sewing if I can't get anything else, but I'm getting a *job!* That's settled. And we'll all work with a will this winter—unless"— and a faint gleam of a smile shadowed out—"unless the bank opens again before fall."

"The bank won't open again!" said Thurlow with a sad conviction in his voice. "Mr. Stanwood told me it is in a bad way, and we're just going to have to calculate without that bank. But we'll never consent to have you go to work; no, nor to live down there among the factories."

"It's where we'll have to live, son," insisted the mother. "There's a big yard and a neat little house. I'm sure we can make it quite pleasant. Of course the houses in that locality are very plain, and need fixing up. But we can move later if we have to."

They argued pretty late that night, the mother still determined to move to Meachin Street.

"We can sell it later, perhaps, after we have made it pleasant and attractive." She tried to smile brightly.

"You couldn't sell anything to live in down there for even a song," said the son. "I know that region. And the neighbors would be simply impossible! I'm *not* going to let my mother go into such a neighborhood!"

"They are probably only poor creatures who have lost their money just like ourselves," said the mother calmly.

And then there was the whole argument to go over again.

At last, near midnight, they compromised. They would agree to move down there for a while if their mother would give up the idea of getting a job.

But the next morning it was all to do over again.

"Thurlow, you don't understand," said his mother firmly, with the look in her eye of having lain awake all night thinking about it. "I am determined that you shall finish your college course! I can't have your father's well-laid plans frustrated. I can see how we can do it quite well. And a little later Rilla can go. At least she can attend the university in the city, and that won't cost so much. But you must finish out your course in your college where you have begun."

Thurlow's eyes were misty as he looked at the sweet stubborn little mother, but he set his pleasant lips in a firm line of determination. He was just opening his mouth to say no in no uncertain terms when there came a loud throbbing of a car up the drive, a shout like an army with banners, then a thundering at the front door, mingled with gay young voices.

"Hi, Thurl! Where are you? Come out here, Thurl, old man—!"

Thurlow sprang to his feet with startled delight and his mother looked up fearsomely and exclaimed: "What is it?"

"It's the college!" said Thurlow. "You must have invoked their presence," and he went storming out joyously to meet half a dozen big fellows like himself.

4

THURLOW brought them in to meet his mother and sister, introducing them all around: Pat Halstead, Bill Wishard, Twink Collins, Harding Roberts called in affection "Bertie," Jeff Jilton, and Graham Macaffee.

"Also Whirl Reed," added young Halstead with a flourish toward Thurlow. "We are seven! The Sacred Seven we are called. Surely he has told you about us, Mrs. Reed!"

There was a great deal of laughter and boisterous joking, and Rilla looked on in amazement. Suddenly Thurlow dropped off his solemnity of the last few weeks, and was a boy among them again. She felt a catch in her throat when she looked at her brother. Poor Thurl! To have to give up this pleasant friendly turmoil and start to be a man! It didn't matter so much about herself. She had never had all this. But a young man needed to have young men friends!

The mother felt it for him too, and hurried away to the region of the kitchen to prepare something nice for them to eat. Rilla came too, with very red cheeks, thinking of what that young Halstead had said to her:

"Sweet souls of my great-aunt's garden roses! Whirl Reed, where have you been keeping a sister like this? What's the little old idea, darlin', that you should hide her away all these long years? I choose first chance, sweet lady. I know you won't turn me down. I've been trained by a mother who knew her way about, and I give you my word I'm a favorite. Lady, will you walk with me, at the next Prom? Lady, will you talk with me, out on the lawn under a tree somewhere? What I've missed all these years not seeing your lovely face!"

His Irish tongue rattled on, and his handsome eyes admired her. Oh, she knew he was more than three-quarters in fun. It didn't mean a thing! He was just a rollicking handsome care-free youth having a good time. She had heard her brother talk about Pat. She knew he was irresistible. He knew everybody liked him, and he dared to say anything. Yet she could see there was a real liking behind his words, partly for her brother's sake of course. Yet her cheeks flamed scarlet, her heartbeats quickened just the least bit. It didn't mean a thing, but it was nice to have admiring eyes look into yours and talk nonsense for a few minutes. It lightened the gloom of a day of disaster.

Mrs. Reed had baked a large dark chocolate cake with translucent layers of chocolate jelly between, with the secret intent of taking it to the Woman's Exchange and selling it as a start toward a regular business for herself, unbeknownst to her children. But she brought it forth now, thankful that she had it to give, and Rilla hurriedly rolled lemons and cracked ice and prepared a delightful fruit lemonade.

The seven young men milling around in the living room shouting out nonsense to each other in the sheer joy of being reunited, turned as one man to greet the cake, poured glasses of the delicious drink and made short work of the great cake, cutting unbelievable wedges for themselves and each other. Thurlow sat in their midst and beamed. All the sorrow of the past few weeks, all the fears and the triumph, all the dread of the future fell away, and he was a college boy again, with interests outside the little triangle of his family. Even his bitterness about Barbara Sherwood was forgotten and his face took on a look of at least two whole years ago.

Not till the last crumb of chocolate cake was gone and the pitcher drained of the last drop of the lemonade, did they divulge their errand. It was Pat who unfolded it.

"Now, Whirl," he began, pausing before his host with his empty glass in his hand, "toddle off upstairs and get yourself your noblest garments, a nightie of ample proportions, an extra pair of socks, in fact all your glad rags. We've come to kidnap you for the week-end and you might as well be comfortable. Toothbrush not required unless you wish, but you'd better bring a bathing suit. You see we're off for the shore. Jeff here and Macaffee are giving us a party and it's going to be rare. We'll be glad to have your sister come down tomorrow night on the train for the grand finale. I'll meet her myself at the four-four train and make her my special guest!" Pat bowed low before Rilla with his hand on his heart. "But tonight and tomorrow daytime are sacred to the plans of our respected Alma Mater, no ladies allowed. So toddle off, darlin', and make it snappy! We ought to be on our way. Even Jeff's giant car can't get us there in time for dinner unless we get a move on pretty soon."

Suddenly Thurlow came to earth with a crash. The joy fell away from his face, the youth dropped out like a shadow and disappeared, the sparkle and the abandon and gaiety were gone, and all his burdens dropped down and fitted themselves close upon his back again. Gravity, maturity, stood out startlingly, with responsibility and anxiety like wraiths just behind him.

"Sorry, Pat," he said, as if he were at least a decade ahead of Pat in experience. "I'd be delighted to go, but it's impossible!"

Then arose a clamor, all of them together slapping him on the back, shouting that he must go, that they wouldn't take no for an answer, trying to make him believe that the whole expedition was gotten up with him as a center, yelling what this one and that one said, naming other fellow-students who were to arrive at the shore that night, but Thurlow stood in their midst smiling, pained but obdurate.

"You see, fellows, we're moving!" he said. "I can't be spared!" His mother opened her lips to tell him that they could get along without him perfectly well for a few days. Then she remembered Thurlow was not going back to college! There were other reasons besides the moving that made it undesirable for him to go with his friends. His mother turned and faded away into the background of the kitchen where she stood at the back window wiping away the quick tears that had come.

Rilla stared wistfully at Pat's extravagant invitation, gave a quick little gasp of delight and then went blank, the joy fading out of her eyes.

"Oh! I'm sorry!" she faltered. "I would love to go, but—you see—I have another engagement! No, I can't possibly get out of it!" Then Rilla watched her chance and slipped away up the back stairs.

And while Thurlow's mother and sister wept apart for his disappointment, the young man was gravely telling his friends that what they asked was quite impossible.

It came to a moment when they paused in their eager urging and looked at one another, slightly dismayed, questioning. Then a lifting of eyebrows, an almost imperceptible nodding of heads, and one said to Pat:

"Better tell him what it's all about, Pat. Then he'll understand."

Thurlow looked from one to another with a puzzled, sad expression and waited.

"All right, Whirl. We'll explain. Didn't mean to do it yet till everybody was present, make a grand ceremony of it, see? But since you will be so dumb, perhaps it's better to be out in the open. It's this way, Whirl, see, we wantta put you up for head of the student exec. They don't often take Juniors, but it's allowed, and our fraternity is one in this, to a man. And we wantta make our plans and take counsel together. Work out some of our policies for next winter, and all that, you know. So now I hope you see that you've got to put aside all else and come with us. No question about it!"

Thurlow's face went white with feeling. His eyes grew dark with wonder and pain and swept the little group of college men with tender love, humility, and triumph in their gaze. They were the most outstanding men in his fraternity, and indeed in the whole college, and they had chosen *him* for this great honor. For an instant the greatness of it overwhelmed him with feeling. His voice grew husky and refused to function when he tried to speak, and he felt a sense of great mingled weakness and power go through him. Just for an instant his face blazed forth in the glory of a great joy, and then went grave again. He thanked them all with his eyes, even before he could speak. Then his gaze dropped, and he spoke slowly, hesitantly, drawing deep breaths between his words:

"Fellows—I can't say—what I feel—that you should have wanted to—do this! I think—I shall *always* feel— that this is the biggest honor—that ever came to me! I'm not worthy—of course. There are far better fellows—for this job. That's why it stirs me so deeply. I wish with all my heart—I could accept this—this honor—that you have offered me. I'd try with all my strength to do it well. But—fellows—" his voice broke and he drew another deep breath and went on, *"I can't.* Much as I would like to—I *can't!* Because—" he finished desperately, "you see—I'm *not coming back* to college!"

There was an awful silence, a silence so still that it reached with impressive tensity to the back kitchen window where Mrs. Reed stood wiping her eyes on the corner of her apron, and to Rilla's upstairs room where she had taken refuge in tears.

Then the clamor arose again.

"Whaddya *mean,* Reed? Whatcha givin' us? You're not turned yella, are you? You're not selling your football to another institution?"

"No!" flashed Thurlow, *"never!* I wouldn't go anywhere *else.* This was my father's college, and it would always be my choice even if it hadn't been his. But, fellows, my dad died a month ago today, and the bank went fluey, and I've got *to work!"*

There was instant sympathy in every face, and a hush of deference to disaster.

"Say, old man, that's tough luck!" Pat's voice wore genuine sympathy. There was deep concern expressed in every face, and the voices rang true as each expressed solicitation, while the boys rapidly adjusted their calculations. Then spoke up Twink Collins.

"That won't make any difference, Kid. There'll be ways of getting around that."

"Our Frat'll see you through somehow, fella!" said Jeff.

"There are such things as loans, you know, and scholarships," said Harding Roberts, with a wave of his hand that seemed to disperse all difficulties.

"You don't understand!" said Thurlow, a note almost of weariness in his voice, a note that seemed to set him infinitely apart from them all, in another sphere. "It isn't just a matter of money, you know. The money may come back if the bank reopens. But we've lost our home! *Every*thing is gone! I've got to stick by and carry on."

"You can do that a great deal better with your education properly completed, son!" said Harding Roberts loftily.

"There are sometimes things you have to do without, no matter how much better it would be to have them," said Thurlow with a sad smile. "This happens to be one of them."

"Nonsense, Whirl! We'll fix it all up for you!" said Pat in his cheerful cocksure way. "Get a hustle on you and pack that bag, or we'll take you without it. Education or no education, you've got to come with us and counsel about fraternity matters, and student exec. We won't take no for an answer!"

They all rushed upon him and tried to force him up the stairs, but smiling, resolute, he resisted them and spoke firmly.

"Sorry, fellows, I'd admire to go, but it can't be done!"

And at last they believed him and went reluctantly away.

"This isn't the end!" called back Pat.

"No, Kid, this isn't the end. We'll get you back! Wait till we tell Prexy, and the football coach!" the others chorused.

Thurlow stood at the gate and waved them away,

smiling to the last. And then he stood there staring into a future full of pain and sorrow and perplexity.

Yet there was something exultant about it after all. They had *come after him!* They had planned to give him this *great honor!* It was something to have won that from them before he left.

He looked wistfully for an instant into what might have been if things had been different! What he would have done as president of the student exec! What his standing and associations would have been! What his outlook for the future! He had an instant's breathless thought of telling Barbara about it, and of how great it would have been in her eyes, and then suddenly his landscape darkened. He had had no word from Barbara yet! She might have sent at least a post card back on the pilot. Rilla had one from Chandler and Betty. It had been a sharp hurt in his soul every time that he had thought of it. But perhaps she had waited to write a real letter. Surely, surely she would write him one of her long delightful letters sometime soon. One had so much time on shipboard. He thought of the fitted handbag on which he had spent so much time and thought, yes, and money, for money had to be thought of now. It seemed almost as if it had been purchased with his heart's blood.

Rilla at her upper window watched him standing there, saw him turn back toward the house with bowed head. Poor Thurl! She had heard it all from her vantage point of the upper window just above the porch where they had said their lingering farewells. Poor Thurl! It wasn't fair! It wasn't right! And Father would feel so bad if he knew how his plan had failed. Something ought to be done about it. Surely something could be done! Surely she and her mother could manage somehow and let Thurl finish out his college course!

She washed her face, powdered the signs of weeping

from her nose and hurried down the back stairs to clear up the dishes from their impromptu party. She met her mother coming away from the back window brushing away her tears, and knew that her mother also had heard it all.

"Mother," she began, "I think somehow we ought to *make* Thurl go back to college."

"Yes, of course!" said the mother with a choking sound in her voice. "We *must!*"

And then the door swung open from the butler's pantry and there stood Thurl.

"Now, come on, girls!" he said, trying to sound gay. "Let's take a walk and see our new domicile!"

"Not tonight!" said the mother sharply. "We've got something else to do. A secondhand man is coming early in the morning to look over the things we want to sell, and it will take us from now till midnight to get everything sorted out. You both have to help me. I'm hoping to get enough out of the things we don't need, to pay for the moving."

"Mother!" exclaimed Thurlow in dismay. "Sell? Isn't it enough that we have to part with the house without selling our things too?"

"I'm hoping to get enough from selling what we don't need to pay for the moving," said the mother again firmly. "We've got to save every penny, you know."

"Now, Mother! You're not getting penurious on us, are you? And why the haste? We don't have to move tomorrow."

"The sooner we get out of here the better!" said the mother with a deep-drawn sigh and a sad look in her eyes.

Thurlow cast a quick look at her and signalled to his sister.

"All right, ladies, it's O.K. with me. All set? Let's get to work. Where do we begin? In the attic or the cellar?"

"In the attic!" said the mother, and they all trooped off upstairs.

5

BARBARA Sherwood on shipboard was posing for a series of snapshots. She was wearing one of her prettiest sports costumes with a great woolly coat, furred about the collar. Her lovely hair blew around her face with careless abandon. The wind had wrapped her modish skirt about her in graceful lines, revealing slim ankles and dainty feet. The group of young people who stood with her were provoking her to smiles just at the crucial instant when the picture was being snapped so that her two delightful dimples would register. Barbara was adorable, and one couldn't help wondering if she didn't know it, just the least little bit.

She faced the east, and she faced the west, while a ring of youth surrounded her with cameras. She stood in converse with one and another, laughing and posing and enjoying herself hugely. She caught up a lovely passing baby from its nurse and held it charmingly. She flung off her coat and stood with the new sports dress revealed, looking slim and lovely. She went on the tennis court and posed for several shots playing against different opponents, one at least of whom was a world-renowned player. Barbara was pretty and popular of course. She wore distinguished garments and wore them well. She was graceful as a feather in every motion, and seemingly unconscious that she was the cynosure of all eyes. People were standing about saying to one another: "Who is she?" She had a regular procession of admirers waiting to pose with her. No wonder Barbara Sherwood was not thinking of home just then, nor of any admirers she had left behind.

"Now," said her sister Betty, fluting into a pause while the main camera of the fleet was having a new film adjusted, "why not have one taken with Vinnie Benet! A real count. I think that would be lovely to send home to Thurl Reed. That's one he hasn't had a chance to be jealous of yet!"

Betty was incorrigible at odd moments, though quiet enough for the most part. But now her sister flushed a deep crimson and darted her a lightning glance. Though she laughed it off the next second, with a swift inclusive smile that touched Count Vincent Benet apologetically.

"What on earth do you mean, Betchen?" she caroled lightly, as if the matter were trifling indeed. "Why do you always say such silly things? Of course I'm having a pose with the count. I want it for my collection to show *all* my friends when I get home." She laughed gaily and took her place beside the cynical count, who looked down at her with his great black eyes and lifted his smart black patch of a moustache with a haughty curl of his lip and asked:

"And who is Thurl Reed, may I ask?"

"Oh, just a boy at home I used to go to kindergarten with!" laughed Barbara gaily, with a fine coquettish glance up into the count's face that brought the desired flash of his perfect teeth just in time to register on the film.

Betty flouted off to another part of the boat to stare out at the sea indignantly. She was still young enough to have ideals, young enough to adore her older sister and to revel in the childish romance she had watched from her infancy. She stood now with her heart hot with rage at her sister. Why did Barby want to be so silly with all those horrid stranger-men who were so much older than she was, so much older than Thurl? Oh, why did things have to go and get all mixed up this way in life? Why couldn't Thurl have come along on this nice summer outing—and Rilla! How much she did miss Rilla! Presently she stopped staring off at the endless blue of the sea and went to write a letter to Rilla. It was the first time since they were in rompers that they had been separated for a summer, and she was going to miss Rilla terribly. So she sat down and wrote her a letter.

Dear Rill:

I'm fed up with touring already. I wish you were here. I feel all alone. I played three sets of deck tennis this morning with a girl who couldn't serve a ball. Believe me, it was slow. She acted as if she was shoveling sand when she served, but she would keep on, so I had to. I was just dying to play with Chand, but Mother sent him off with a woman's daughter from somewhere. The woman had asked Mother if Chand wouldn't take her around she was so homesick. It seems she's going over for a year to school, and she doesn't want to go. Chand doesn't like her. He made a face behind her back at me as he walked off. So then I was stuck with the girl at deck tennis till some of the older set came to play and I certainly was glad. I was dying to get away.

I don't get much company from my sister. She is doing things all the time. She's having her picture taken in every attitude you can imagine. It makes me sick! What she sees in some of the young men that come around her! One of them called me "Kid" this morning in such a condescending way, as if I was only about eight or ten. "Kid," he said, "run away and don't bother us!" Can you imagine it, Rilla? And I'm only two years younger than Barbara. I don't think he's much older himself. He has a nasty little misplaced eyebrow on his upper lip and he's training it to be pointed at the ends, just because there's an Italian count on board that wears one. I think they're even worse than the little shoe-brush patches some young men wear, don't you? I don't see why men want to make their faces so ugly. It looks just like a smudge on their upper lips. I think it's pestiferous, don't you?

But say, I wish you'd put it into your brother's head to write real often to Barby. I'm just worried about her. I'm afraid she'll get her head turned with all this flattery they're feeding her. I think it will be good for her to get a letter real often from home. I'm sometimes afraid for my sister! I really am! She's so kind-hearted she can't turn anybody down. Me, I'd stay in my stateroom and pretend I was seasick before I'd walk the deck with some of the people on board. I really would! And that's saying something, for I just adore everything they have to eat on this ship, and I've always been proud of being a good sailor.

But honestly, Rill, I don't see anything in this boy and girl business, do you? I think it's a great deal nicer to just have a good time and not go mushing around holding hands and all that. I hate to have to grow up. Grown-ups do such silly things. Say, Rill, let's take a vow we won't grow up. I believe it's college that makes people grow up so fast. Barby used to be so nice before she went away to school. But what do you think she did last night? Asked me to lend her my perfectly new apple-green taffeta to wear, the one I haven't had on yet! She said I was too young to stay up late and that it really was too old in style for me anyway! I certainly was glad that Mother happened around just then and told her no quite sharply. Mother always hates to have us borrow each other's things you know, and she said positively we weren't to do it. I know why she wanted it. I heard the artist of the ship telling her she would be stunning in green, and she came right away and asked me to lend it to her.

That artist by the way is a sketch! I wish you could see him. He has a wind-blown bob, and wears corduroy pants almost as wide as skirts to match his hair. He has a "fine sensitive face" I heard a woman say on deck today. Chand and I call him "pretty-face." His name is Everett Amory and his mother says he is going to be very famous some day. She told another woman we girls would be awfully proud sometime to think we had been privileged to know him. Barby heard her and just ate it up. I can't think what has come over Barby. Goodness! I wish you and your brother were here. You'd make the ship sit up and take notice.

There's a musician in the mob that gathers around my sister. He told her she ought to be a violinist, she has such long fingers, and he'd love to play her accompaniments. He looks at her by the hour, with a languishing air. I don't see how she stands it. How I would love to fire a good ripe tomato down from the upper deck at him sometime. The only thing is I wouldn't dare to stay and watch how he looked when it hit. Wouldn't Mother be horrified? She thinks he is so kind about playing. She says his technique is marvelous. Well, maybe it is, in more ways than one. But whenever he walks with my sister, Chandler and I get arm in arm and prance behind them, just kind of casual-like, you know. Last night Barby got wise to us and told Chand to stop it! Chand just looked innocent, you know the way he does, and said: "Oh, was that you in front of us? I thought it was some love-sick maiden the way he was carrying on. I didn't think you'd fall for a poor egg like that. He takes himself so seriously he'll fall off the earth some day and never know he didn't take it along with him."

Barby is getting awfully grown-up and orders us around a lot, but we're determined to take care of her, nevertheless. It's probably just a stage, you know. I've read about such things. And we're determined to prevent a disaster in the family, like having Barby fall in love with some silly impecunious count or other.

There goes the dinner gong and I'm frightfully hungry so I'll close. Remember me to anybody who seems to miss me, and keep heaps and heaps of love for yourself.

Your loving lonesome
Betty

P.S. Don't forget to implore Thurl to write often to Barby. Tell him to make it snappy. Even a cablegram might be of some use, or maybe a radiogram.

P.S. the second. I don't know how I'm to endure this long separation-year without you. Be good to yourself and don't do anything frightfully different till I get home.

B.

This letter arrived in the same mail with a fat one for Thurlow. Rilla noticed a light in his eyes when she handed it to him, but he did not leave his work. He just stuck it in his left breast pocket and went on packing books in a box. But Rilla noticed that his face looked happier while he worked, and once or twice he started whistling a bit of a tune. Rilla wondered what was in his letter, and after she had read her own, stood a long time looking out the window trying to decide whether she would let her brother read Betty's letter or not. Finally she decided to wait until he had had time to read his own, and then if he looked at all cheerful perhaps she could venture to let him see hers. Maybe it wasn't going to be so good for Thurl to know that Barbara had a lot of admirers on the ship.

Then Rilla put away her letter and went back downstairs to wrap cups and saucers ready for a barrel.

But there was very little time for either of them to read letters or even think about them that day. The moving was on. It had come unexpectedly soon after all, and before either Rilla or Thurlow had seen their new home.

It was Mrs. Steele who precipitated matters. She had called up just after the secondhand man had left with the last load of goods they were selling.

"I don't want to be disagreeable or insistent," she said with charming graciousness, "and you mustn't mind what I say if it makes things the least little bit inconvenient. But I was just wondering if it would be at all possible for you to vacate the house this week? Of course I know that's awfully short notice for you, but I didn't know but perhaps you would be willing if we helped out by paying for extra helpers for you, and of course giving you more compensation. You see it's this way, Mrs. Reed. Our lease for the old club rooms runs out in five days. We expected to keep the rooms by the week until your house was ready for us, but now it seems the owner has found out we are leaving and is getting disagreeable about it. He says we'll either have to make out a lease for another three years, or get out Monday, and it really seems absurd to move our furniture twice for just a few days' time. Of course we could put it in storage, but the wear and tear on it for two movings is hard, and we just wondered whether the extra we would have to pay for having to move our things twice would be compensation enough for your having to hurry out in a short time? Could you see your way clear to helping us out in any way? And would two hundred dollars be enough to cover your extra trouble? We would so much rather pay it to you than to a mover."

Mrs. Reed gave a little gasp, aghast at the proposal. Then she seemed to face facts an instant, and her lips set in a thin line of self-control. Two hundred dollars was two hundred dollars. That meant a great deal just now.

"What day did you say you would want to move in, Mrs. Steele?" she asked in a steady voice that had nevertheless a little quaver in its finish.

"Why, it would have to be Monday at the latest, Mrs. Reed. Monday afternoon. Though I'm afraid we might have to bring a few things over Saturday perhaps, if we could put them somewhere out of your way." She spoke in an apologetic tone. *"Do* you think you could possibly manage it? Of course we're not insisting, you understand."

Mrs. Reed cast a swift glance about her pleasant room,

took a deep breath and tried to answer graciously, without that sound of tears in her voice.

"Could you give me a few minutes to think it over, Mrs. Steele?"

"Why, of course, Mrs. Reed. Certainly. It's awfully good of you even to consider it and we wouldn't want to seem to be pressing you. But you see how we are situated."

"Yes, I see how you are situated," said Mrs. Reed. "I'll—call you in half an hour."

After she had hung up she went and sat down in a near-by chair and held her hands together to steady them, pursed her lips to keep them from trembling! She felt cold all over, almost as when she knew her husband was gone. She mustn't give way! She mustn't let the children see how she felt about this. She must be brave!

She had come as a bride to this house, and she loved it so! It seemed like tearing off the covering to her family life to give this house up. She wished—she had hoped—that she might finish out her life here where she had been so happy! She had given that up of course, but now to be rushed away in such haste seemed like burying her dear dead past before it was scarcely cold.

She sat there struggling with her tears that would crowd up to her eyes and try to flow, struggling with the lump in her throat. She must not give way or she would be crying every day and that would not do at all. All this was hard enough on the children without her sitting around and mourning! Look how brave Thurlow had been, putting away his wonderful college prospects without even considering them. Could she not be as brave? And, after all, wasn't it better to get out as quickly from the dear environment as could be, since it had to be done at all?

Suddenly Mrs. Reed slipped down upon her knees

and went to the Throne for guidance and strength. Fortunately she had been to this Source of wisdom and enlightenment before, and she arose from her knees with a look of peace in her eyes and purpose in the set of her lips, and went to the telephone.

Rilla came back presently from the store, and Thurlow from answering a "Want" advertisement in the paper, the latter with a discouraged air upon his young shoulders, and when she heard him come into the house with an attempt at a whistle—for her benefit she knew— she went downstairs.

"Well, children," she said, appearing in the door of the sitting room where Thurlow had just dropped down disconsolately in a chair, and Rilla was standing idly at the window looking out, "how soon do you think we can get out of here?"

"Good night, Mother!" said Thurlow, passing an impatient young hand over a weary brow, "why the hurry? We haven't even been down to see that place you have in mind yet, and I'm quite sure it won't do before we see it, so that means we'll have to begin to hunt apartments, and that's a work of time, you know. Why, Mother? What's on your mind? Those people didn't seem to be in a rush for us to get out, did they?"

"They've just called up," said Mrs. Reed quietly, purpose in her eyes. "The owner of the hall where they are now is trying to put them out on the street unless they sign a lease for another three years. Their lease runs out in five days. They called up to ask if there was any possibility we would like to take two hundred dollars more to let them come in by Monday. They are of course in an unpleasant situation. Do you think we could move in five days?"

"Oh, Mother!" gasped Rilla.

"Why, the moving part wouldn't take long of course

if we could afford professional movers!" said Thurlow. "It's the getting ready for them, and finding the right place to move to. We can't just decide our destiny in a moment! Though of course we *could* move in a day if we had to. But I tell you, Mother—"

"I thought you would say so," said his mother quietly, "so I told her we would be out by Monday noon, surely. Saturday morning if possible. They've been so nice about things I think we ought to accommodate them, and then of course we need every extra penny we can get. Besides, it's best to get the worst over and begin living the new life as quickly as possible. Dwelling on the past isn't good for us." She looked up and managed a faint cheerful smile.

"Mother! How *can* we?" cried out Rilla.

"You're a great little old scout, Mother!" said Thurlow, his voice husky with feeling. "But, really, you know, you've undertaken a tremendous task."

"I know." She said it quietly, firmly. "And we're going to do most of the packing ourselves to save the cost of professionals. And that being the case we'd better get to work at once. We mustn't waste a minute. I told them we'd be out as soon as we possibly could."

"Let's go then," said Thurlow with a deep sigh, rising from his chair. "The first step is to go down to your farm or whatever you call it, and prove to you that it won't do at all for us to live in. And then we can really get to work hunting a place."

"No," said the mother decidedly, "we're not going down there at all till we go to stay. I've been, and seen what it is, and I know if you went down there you would think it wouldn't do, and it's *got* to do, for the present *any*way. We haven't any time for argument. I'm sorry to do things in this high-handed way. If we had plenty of money and time you should help in the choice, but for the present there isn't anything to do but to use what we have, and make the best of it. You know we don't have to *stay* if we find it impossible. But we can stand anything for a little while till we find a better place."

"But, Mother!" protested Rilla, "you don't mean we won't go down first and clean the house? Won't it be all dusty?"

"A little dust won't hurt us for a few days. Of course it isn't an ideal way to move," said the mother, "but I consider it is just as well to get our things out of here and get a little more money for doing it, as to move in an ideal way. We'll just have to consider we're pioneers and are building our lives anew. There's a barn down there to camp in while we are cleaning the house, and that's more than our forefathers had when they went in covered wagons with all their worldly goods to establish a new home. Let's make a game out of it, children! It will really be easier that way than going back and forth and making our hearts ache with contrasts."

Thurlow looked at his quiet little mother with amazement, considering her wisdom.

"Perhaps you're right, Mother-Mine!" he said, deeply moved, and stooping to touch his lips to her hair. "Mother-Mine" was what he called her on very special occasions. "Well, where do we go from here? I'm taking orders. We'll stand by you and do our best, until you find it won't work, and then, if that happens, we'll claim our right to hunt up something better."

"All right!" said Rilla, swinging around with grim lips. "I'll stand by if you'll promise to own when you're beaten, Mother, and let us find something better."

"And I'll do that as soon as we are able to pay for something better," said the mother. "Now, let's get to work. Thurlow, you go around every room and take the pictures down. Rilla, you dust them and stack them in the alcove under the stairs where they will be handy to carry out! I'll get together all the ornaments and small things that will need careful packing. After we've had lunch, Thurlow, you'd better take the cellar and get everything in order, throw out and burn any trash, get things that have to go with us near the outside cellar door. Anything you think we ought to give away put in a separate place. If we systematize things it won't take so long. And while you are working in the cellar, Rilla and I will take the attic and sort things out."

The two young people went to work with all their might. It helped in this hard stress to have plenty to do. There wasn't even time to think.

By night of that first day the house had taken on a denuded air almost as if it were reproaching them so that they scarcely dared to look about as they sat down, weary and disheveled, to a hastily prepared dinner. Yet there was a kind of satisfaction in thinking how much they had accomplished in a single day, even if the walls did cry out desolately for the familiar pictures that had hung upon them, and certain cherished bits of bric-a-brac that now stood about on sideboard and tables shrouded with folds of tissue paper. The disarray was almost more than they all could bear. It seemed like the death-bed of their former life. It was so far-reaching, and so final. It seemed a death-knell to everything each one had planned and hoped for. The feeling seemed to surround them, and grip them by the throat, so that they could hardly eat.

That was the beginning of the moving, and at first it seemed to them all that they never could accomplish all that had to be done in the five days allowed them.

Mrs. Reed was wonderful. Her children marveled at her strength and courage and executive ability. They marveled at her firmness, and the way in which she held them to the work in hand. For strange to say, not once yet had they been to see their new abode, and still had only the vaguest idea of its location.

Both the young people had occasional qualms about this as they wrought on under the strenuous supervision of their mother. They felt that they should have had a part in so momentous a decision as selecting a new location. Yet when they approached the subject singly or together she always faced them with that unanswerable argument:

"What's the use of going to see it? We have to get out, don't we? We haven't any time to waste, have we? This is the only place where we have a right to go that will shelter us for the time, and we just can't afford to do anything else. It won't cost any more to move from there later than it would from any temporary place we might select in a hurry, will it? And you know we haven't money to throw away renting expensive apartments."

Then some duty would present itself for immediate action and they would go on their way, silenced, but not satisfied.

Only once did their mother weaken. It was late afternoon of the fourth day of their five. She had just finished sweeping up the living room. Weary, with set lips, and tired agonized eyes she came to stand for a moment looking out the window on all she was about to leave. Her eyes traveled over every dear object in the familiar yard outside, and she spoke aloud, perhaps unaware she was doing so, unaware that both Thurlow and Rilla were in the hall tying up the living room rug to protect it from the dusty new home to which it was going. She didn't realize at all that they heard her.

"I shall miss my April gold!" she said mournfully, lovingly.

Rilla appeared in the doorway aghast.

"What did you say, Mother? What is it you are going to miss?"

The mother turned from the window, instantly alert, tense again, with the mask of efficiency upon her face once more, a quick forced smile upon her lips.

"Oh, are you there? I was just talking to myself, I guess." She even forced herself to laugh a little apologetically. "I was just saying I shall miss my April gold!"

"April gold?" said Rilla, mystified, a kind of consternation in her eyes. Thurlow was standing startled just behind her, his troubled eyes searching his mother's face. Had it all been too much for their mother? Was she losing her reason?

"You know," she said sweetly, "the daffodils all around the fence. The forsythia in a golden mist behind the house, and the other yellow flowers in the spring. Your father used to call them my April gold. That was what he called them the first year he planted them. I was just realizing that I shall miss them next spring. But of course there will be others, and we can plant a garden."

She smiled tenderly and brushed the tears away from her eyes. Then she turned back to her work.

"We must hurry, Rilla! There is the kitchen to clean up, and the other floors to sweep. We're almost done, too. I'm glad we are accomplishing it so soon. There! There comes the man now for those things in the cellar. Thurl, will you see to him?"

Yes, the man was at the door. Thurlow cast a quick glance out, then gave another compassionate look at his mother, registering the look in her eyes, the tear on her cheek that had escaped the quick motion of her hand. He would not soon forget that, nor the quaver in her voice when she spoke so lightly, casually, of her April gold. He would never forget the fleeting wistful sigh as she turned away from the window, back to practical things once more. There was no time now to consider sentiment. He turned sharply from the stab of this new pain to go to the cellar and show the man which things he might take away.

But that evening, making an excuse to go out on an errand, he called upon Mrs. Steele and asked her if she thought they would mind if he took a few of his mother's plants and shrubs from the yard, and she graciously told him to take anything he wanted, even to some of the small evergreens.

"We'll probably put it into the hands of a landscape gardener anyway," she said laughingly, "and they might just be thrown away, so you might as well have them."

So that night, after his mother and sister were asleep, he slipped out of the house and worked half the night. He dug all around each forsythia bush that made the golden mist about the back of the house that his mother loved so well. He did not lift them from the ground, but he had them loose and ready to be raised when he would have help tomorrow. He did the same to several small favorite evergreen trees, and some shrubs. And then in the early morning before the others were awake, and when the sun was just appearing, he slipped out again and dug up all her daffodil bulbs, and a lot of other cherished small plants, placing them in boxes and baskets, behind the house where they would not be seen till the movers came.

The next afternoon Thurlow was on the porch packing some valuable things that had been left until the last. He was hurrying because there was very little time left. The moving vans would arrive in a couple of hours now and there were still many things to be done. And in the midst of it all the postman came up the walk with the last mail that would be delivered to them in their old home. Among it were the two letters bearing foreign post-marks, one for himself and one for Rilla. His heart gave a lurch as he recognized the writing, took cognizance of the fact that his was a nice thick letter, stuffed it into his pocket and went on with his work. He was now and then conscious of that fat envelope in the pocket just over his heart, cheered by its presence, stirred by its nearness, but he had no time to stop and read it, no time even to think about it, as the moving went swiftly on as planned.

They had done it! They were ready for the movers, and they were planning to sleep in the new home tonight, Friday night! Mrs. Reed had telephoned Mrs. Steele that the Woman's Club might start moving their things in Saturday if they chose, as she had been cleaning as she went and would be all out tonight. It had been a herculean task, but it had perhaps been good for them. They had not had opportunity to suffer. They had been too busy to think of themselves.

But there would be no chance to read that letter, Thurlow thought as he nestled his heart against its crisp rustle, until—until— Well, when? Surely that night sometime before he slept he could get time to open it! But he could not stop now. They must if possible get to the new quarters before dark. They had to live, even if they didn't read letters right away!

He opened the letter at last standing in the empty hall, under the blare of the electric light, while he waited for his mother and sister to wash their hands and put on their hats.

The last van was ready, and outside was waiting a little old flivver that he had hired to take his family to their new home.

He had a feeling of utter desolation upon him concerning all that had to do with this earthly life, and yet the thought of that letter in his pocket had so far sustained him. Now he felt as if he could wait no longer. He must get some crumb of comfort before he went on. Everything was changing, the earth was reeling under him, but at least there was a letter from Barbara. She had not forgotten him after all.

So he slit the envelope carefully, almost tenderly, and hungrily took out the contents. But, lo, when he had it in his hands it was but a single sheet of paper with a few words scrawled on one side and wrapped firmly about a dozen photographs that just fitted into the envelope.

He stared at the hurried words blankly:

"Too busy to write! Having the time of my life. The enclosed will tell you all about it better than words can do. Hope you are well. As ever, Barbara."

His heart went fluttering down like a balloon from which the air has suddenly been withdrawn, down, down; a light little trifling thing, that heart, that didn't really matter at all. Just one of the things for the discard.

He rallied after an instant and shuffled through the pictures casually, caught the effect of the troop of admirers, caught Barbara's illuminated expression for somebody else in one picture after another; then through the bunch more slowly, deliberately, frowning with his tired eyes at each one. He discovered that there were inscriptions on the back of each. The name of the happy admirer with whom she was photographed in each case. Some gay word of explanation. Nothing personal at all. Nothing that mattered in the least. Not any more than if he had been some casual acquaintance she had met at

the time of sailing. Not any more than if he were a
stranger to her.

Suddenly he heard his mother coming down the stairs
and he stuffed them all hastily into his pocket.

"Ready, Mother?" His voice was husky, and he tried
to steady it, but he knew he was terribly shaken. Then
he looked up and caught a glimpse of her face, realizing
that this was a crucial moment for her. She was leaving
forever the home to which she had come as a bride.
There was sweet, submissive tragedy in her eyes.

He put out a sympathetic hand and laid it on her arm
tenderly.

"You're—pretty tired—aren't you, Mother?" he said
gently. "You oughtn't to have tried to do it so hurriedly.
It was too much!"

"No!" she said, shaking her head and closing her eyes
as she drew a deep breath. "No! It was better so! And
you and Rilla have been wonderful! Thank God for two
such children!"

He saw she was struggling with her tears, and his own
bitterness was forgotten in his deep compassion for her.

"I—couldn't—have stood it—to go—slow!" she
added with an attempt at a smile.

"Brave little Mother-Mine!" he murmured, patting
her arm shyly. "Come on. This part is about over now,
and we're going to stand by you, remember."

This he said a little louder as he saw Rilla behind his
mother, coming down the stairs with a set haggard look
in her face. Rilla was feeling it terribly, too, of course.
Rilla was leaving everything that she knew, too, and
without any hope ahead of getting away to college. Well,
he was a man and must manage somehow to bring up
their fortunes and give them all the comforts and joys
they needed. That was his job. What did it matter if a
girl that he had loved and trusted did turn out to be a

miserable little flirt? What were girls to him? He had his work cut out for him for life. He would forget Barbara Sherwood, forget all girls, forget college and everything and get him a good job. Just as soon as he got the family comfortably located he would go to work and get rich, so they would have everything that Father would have wanted to provide if he had lived.

So he forced a gay look upon his face and brightened his voice:

"Come on, Rill! No sob-stuff. We'll all be weeping together on the old balustrade if you don't smile. Be game, little sister! Chirk up! We're going out into the world and see things! And this is Mother's Surprise! Remember we're earning money by hurrying off this way. You couldn't earn two hundred dollars in four days any easier, could you? Now cheer up and smile!"

And so, encouraged by the son of the house, the Reed family went forth to try their fortunes in a new world.

6

IT was almost dark when they arrived at Meachin Street. The moving vans were drawn up in front of the shadowy property in a straggling uncertain line, four van loads. Thurlow had got them cheap because he was willing to take them after hours. They were not among the listed professional movers, and he had felt a little nervous about their ability to move Rilla's beloved piano carefully, and handle some of his mother's fine old mahogany pieces that had come to her from her grandmother, but the mother had insisted. Indeed she seemed to have developed an intense desire to save every cent possible. It wasn't like her. Thurlow wondered a little at her. The thought passed through his mind that she was probably filled with a great fear that they would have nothing to depend upon for a possible time of illness. But he had had no time to talk to her about it.

But now, as he stopped the borrowed flivver in front of a sagging gate, he was suddenly filled with a great dismay. How could they ever live here? Even in the dark the sordidness of the street was apparent. Why hadn't he insisted on seeing it before they came? Surely if he had known he could have persuaded her to try and find something better! But now they were here and his mother had flung open the door of the car and was climbing out as if she knew her way about! This awful place! A sudden impulse seized him to cry out against it even yet, to insist on going back to the house and unloading the furniture until they could find a proper home.

Across the street were the great brick buildings of a factory, which gave all evidence of being shut down, for most of the windows were broken, and it was dark and apparently empty.

There was no curbing on the street, and no path in the deep growth of grass and weeds before the fence. The other houses on the block were tumbledown cottages of wood. The one next to theirs had an addition crudely built of corrugated iron with a stovepipe coming out of the roof. It seemed to be surrounded with straggling cabbages in various stages of decay. Perhaps it never had been painted. Theirs was the only house that had even a pretence at a fence, though along the row there was one where a few scraggly barberry tufts showed a former attempt, long since demolished.

All this Thurlow's eyes took in at a glance as the flivver's lights swept the block and then leveled straight ahead down the blackness that seemed to end in a dump partly overgrown with weeds, with one tall late hollyhock standing out pinkly in the unexpected brightness to crown the peak of ashes.

He drew in a sharp breath of protest, glanced toward the house itself, took in its meager proportions, the scattering outhouses, chicken house, woodhouse, the looming barn farther on toward the dump, and his heart went bumping down to the valley of despair. How could they *ever*—? He opened his mouth to protest, and then closed it again. Perhaps it would be easier to bring his mother to reason if she saw for herself how impossible it was. She had agreed to be guided by them in the second search for a home if this one failed. It would be easier just to let her see what it was like when she tried to live in it. They could of course stand anything for one night. He had a wild idea of asking the mover just to leave his vans there till morning, and wait until they found another place before unloading, though he knew that was practically impossible. Then he suddenly realized that his mother was out on the ground and walking toward the mover who stood grimly, impatiently, awaiting directions. So Thurlow swung himself out and went forward beside her.

"Mother, why don't you sit in the car till we get a place fixed for you?"

"Nonsense!" said his mother sharply. "This is no time to sit down and be waited upon. Thurlow, I want the things in this van with the blue and white letters on the side to go in the house. The rest, all but a few large pieces, can go in the barn for tonight. Tell the man to bring in that large clothes basket first, and the big box he put in the last thing. The basket has the lamps in it. Lamps and matches!"

"Lamps?" said Rilla in dismay. "You didn't say *lamps,* did you, Mother? You don't mean there aren't electric lights yet? I should think if you telephoned to the office they might send up someone to turn on the electricity or meter or whatever it is, even now, in an emergency. Couldn't I go next door and telephone to them?"

"There is no electricity!" said Mrs. Reed crisply. "It isn't on the street yet. I investigated that."

"Mother!" said Rilla in a voice of horror. "But— there's a big arc light over at the corner of the factory."

"Yes, but it doesn't come over here. The street isn't wired."

"But, Mother, how did you ever think—"

"There, now, Rilla, we are not discussing lighting tonight. We haven't time. Here's the key to the front door, and here are a couple of candles I brought along in my bag. Go unlock the door and light these candles and we'll soon have it light enough to fill the lamps."

"But lamps—Mother! I wouldn't know how to light them! Kerosene lamps!"

"Well, I would," said her mother serenely. "I was brought up with kerosene lamps. I know all about them. And they're not half so bad as you think. Run along and open that door for the man. Hurry!"

Rilla picked her way daintily over the dewy grass in the darkness and fumbled with the key with unaccustomed fingers till one of the men took it from her and unlocked the door. Then with cold trembling hands she applied one of the matches to the door frame, and lighted the candles. She stood an instant in the doorway, shielding the flame with her hand, a pretty girl, slender and half defiant, looking about her with dread and distaste in her whole attitude.

Her brother caught the vision of her and sighed as he went over toward the barn with the key of its old rusty padlock in his hand.

A dark lurking figure, hovering across the road in the shadow of the old factory, saw her and stood staring furtively in wonder and deadly speculation.

Her mother saw her and set her lips, smothering the mother-sigh that came to her lips, then plunging through the tall grass to the steps of the uninviting little house.

"But, Mother, we can't stay *here!*" murmured the girl

as she stepped within and took in the tiny dimensions of the rooms.

"Can't we? Why not?" said the mother firmly, crossing the small front room and flinging open a door to the left. "We said we must see Thurlow through college, didn't we? Well, this is a way to do it. This house will cost us almost nothing, and will shelter us. It needn't last forever, you know. And of course we can fix it up a little. It won't be half bad when it is cleaned."

"But *lamps!*" sighed the girl with a distasteful little shudder. "Oh, Mother, wouldn't there be some other way?"

"Perhaps, but not that I know of at present. Besides, lamps aren't so bad. I'll show you how to keep them bright and clean. They make a beautiful light."

"Oh, Mother!"

"Be careful! Don't let your brother know what we're doing it for yet, or you know what he will do, and you know how stubborn he can be. There! Don't I hear him coming?"

"No, it's only two of the movers. They are bringing the dining room couch," said the girl drearily.

"Yes, that's right, put it right in here," said Mrs. Reed, "and the beds go in these two rooms." She indicated the open doors to the left.

Rilla walked to the kitchen, staring out the one high little window into the unknown darkness, trying to blink back the tears so that her mother would not see them. She was so tired, and it seemed as if they had wrought so hard all for nothing!

A speck of light down a short distance approached and shot along the high embankment with a roar. The railroad! Hadn't her mother said something about a railroad? They were backed up to a railroad. How distressing! The train thundered by, reminding of heavy feet slatted down upon metal slabs. She turned away to look out the glass of a door that opened toward the barn, and as she looked the light from one of the vans shot out, illumining the open doorway of the barn, and from the back of the square old barn there scuttled forth dark creatures, half a dozen of them, like cockroaches running from a sudden approach. And the light streamed forth in pursuit of them in long thin slants, like gashes in the darkness, till it ended in the blackness of the meadow lot that ran down to the foot of the embankment below the railroad. Rilla looked and rubbed her eyes and looked again, but the sudden dark objects had disappeared, and of course it must have been just a hallucination, a blurring of her eyes with tears. She brushed away the moisture and went back to the front room. She must forget her horror at everything and help.

Her mother was busy with the lamps. She had stood them on the box the man had brought in, nice clean glass lamps of ancient pattern. She had a tiny funnel and was pouring kerosene into them. There were clean cotton wicks running down into the liquid, and up to a brass holder, that turned it up and down by a little screw. There were three shining glass chimneys standing near by, and the flicker of the candlelight fell across Mrs. Reed's tired eager face. Rilla suddenly realized that her mother couldn't be so keen about this little old dirty house either. Her mother was willing to do anything to send Thurlow through his education, and her main concern now was not whether she was going to like living in a cramped little house below the railroad, or filling lamps with nasty smelling kerosene, but whether she was going to be able to get things comfortable and pleasant for her children before they made a fuss about it and tried to drive her away from her plan.

Then Rilla was ashamed and flinging her hat down on

the couch the men had just brought in, tied on the apron her mother had unwrapped and looked about for a job.

There were brooms and mops and cleaning rags and soap and scrub buckets. Her mother had thought of everything. But where did one begin in a dirty little house that had been shut up for so long? And at this time of the night?

Rilla picked up a mop in one hand and a scrubbing brush in the other and looked about aimlessly. To scrub one should have hot water. Was there hot water to be had in a house that had no electric light? She stepped into the kitchen, but in the dimness she could see only a small iron sink, very rusty, and a queer inadequate-looking iron pump whose handle when lifted gave forth a melancholy, raucous croak.

Her heart sank lower yet. Did one have to depend on a thing like that for water? And of course there was no stove yet so it couldn't be heated.

She came back to the front room where her mother had conquered two of the lamps and set them triumphantly on the ugly brown mantel. They showed up clearly every crack in the unpapered plaster of the walls, and every scuttling spider in the corners and on the floor. A pale brown creature like a spectre of a slim beetle slithered out of a crack in the kitchen doorway and flashed out of sight. Rilla suppressed a shudder. She supposed that must be a cockroach. She had heard of roaches but had never seen them. Then she remembered the dark forms that had shot out from under the back of the barn and wondered if she was losing her reason, or perhaps falling asleep on her tired feet?

"What shall *I* do, Mother," she asked helplessly at last.

"Make the beds, Rill, dear," said her mother cheerily. "They just set them up. Never mind about deciding whose room is whose tonight. Make them up just where they are. You'll find the bedding all in the drawers of that bureau they are bringing in now."

"But, Mother, I think I saw a cockroach just now."

"Probably!" said her mother as if that were a pleasant thought. "But we mustn't mind a little thing like that now. Just be careful not to get the sheets or blankets on the floor at all, and we'll be all right. We know our beds are clean. In the morning we'll look after cockroaches and any other intruders. I've got some stuff that will clear them out, and we'll have it all clean and cozy by another night."

Rilla stood and stared at her wonderful mother. She had known all along that they would have all these things to face, and yet she had done this preposterous thing! What courage! Why, Mother stood there wiping off the third lamp with a cloth almost as cheerfully as if she enjoyed filling oil lamps on the top of a packing box in a strange dirty house.

Feeling a sudden rush of more tears Rilla turned and went into the bedroom, approaching the bureau with the key her mother had handed her. Mother had not forgotten one thing, it seemed. She came now with the bright lighted lamp and set it on the bureau.

"We won't bother about bureau covers tonight," she said with an almost impish grin. Poor Mother! She was trying so hard to take everything as a joke. *Dear* Mother!

"But, Mother, where did you get all these lamps? We've never used lamps before."

"I had them packed away in the attic," said the mother. "They were my lamps that I went to house-keeping with when I was married." Her eyes dwelt on the one she had just put down with gravely tender reminiscence.

Rilla felt a sudden lump rising in her throat. She tried to smile, but her lips were stiff with weariness and astonishment. She tried to say something, but found there were no words, and her mother only stood there an instant and then went away leaving her with the clean smooth sheets that smelled of lavender and home, and the familiar beds she had known since childhood. So while she smoothed the sheets neatly, and tried to stuff the pillows into the cases, she was struggling to think life out in wider terms than she had known it before. After all life was something more than things. More than even a clean house to move into. Necessity had sent them here into these very most trying circumstances, and Mother was looking tenderly at her old lamps, and thinking of Father and the dear times they had had together! Rilla knew she was thinking about him. She knew it by the sweet look of her eyes.

Out in the barn things were happening.

The big van had drawn up in front of the door to enter as Thurlow with difficulty unlocked the rusty padlock. It was their idea to drive into the barn and unload close at hand to save carrying. The barn door was wide and high and would easily admit the van, but when the door swung wide and the two great headlights illumined the place there was a sudden stir, whether in the dark corners of the barn itself or underneath the floor, they could not tell. But a cavern yawned ahead of them; boards had been torn loose irregularly in the back wall. A strange acrid smell arose and filled the nostrils of the men as they brought the van to a standstill.

Thurlow, standing within the great grim barn, nearer to the stir than the others, thought he saw a shabby foot disappearing through the opening in the boards, where the light shot through and picked it out again in the grass. And the strong pungent odor was distinct now, and suggestive.

The driver swung off the van, gave a keen look at

Thurlow and came around, peering into the shadows with eyes that were used to seeing many things. Then he sniffed the air.

"Looks as if somebody had been making himself at home in our barn," said Thurlow coolly. "I saw a foot disappearing through that hole."

"Mmmmm!" growled the driver, sniffing off into a corner toward a dim dark shape, and whipping a pocket flash out.

"Some baby's got a still somewhere around here—!"

The other movers, scenting some excitement, appeared on the scene now, and the flashlight showed up various pipes and a good-sized vat.

A quiet consultation in the shadows of the barn, a low direction from Thurlow and the offending machinery disappeared through the opening between the boards out into the lot back of the barn, and presently good strong hammer blows drove strong nails into old warped planks. The last board was in place when Mrs. Reed appeared in the doorway with two old-fashioned tin lanterns lighted and ready for service.

"I meant to give you these the first thing," she apologized to the head mover as she handed them in, "but I got to doing other things and forgot to fill them. I can't seem to think of everything at once."

"At that you're doin' fairly well, ma'am," said the man.

When she got back in the house again she said to Rilla in a low tone:

"There's an awfully queer smell over there at the barn. I do hope those movers aren't drinking men. I thought I got the smell of a whiskey breath when I spoke to the head one. I hope they'll be steady when they bring the piano in. I shan't rest easy until that's placed. I wouldn't have anything happen to your piano for all the world—your father's last gift to you."

"Oh, I'm sure they seem very careful, Mother," soothed Rilla. It seemed to the girl that little things like accidents to their worldly goods at this time did not bulk very large, since their world itself seemed to be destroyed. If they had been suddenly caught off their native continent and flung on an uninhabited island in the sea Rilla could not have been much more dismayed than she was tonight.

And it cannot be denied that her brother was not much behind her in dismay. He did not hear the low-voiced comments between the movers when they heaved the ill-smelling contrivance out behind the barn, nor see the significant glances that passed between the men, the winks with their tongues in their cheeks, but suddenly it was borne in upon Thurlow that it was not a very savory neighborhood to which they had come to camp, even for a night, and he was impressed with the conviction that he ought at any cost to have come down here first and investigated.

He was silent and distraught as the men unloaded the goods and placed them, giving a direction now and again, or lending a hand. He looked at some of his mother's precious furniture dubiously and wondered how safe it would be in this place.

One of the last things to be taken from the last van was the lot of shrubs and plants.

"Where you want these put, Buddy?" asked one of the movers as he lifted a giant forsythia out of the van. "Here, you," he said to his fellow workman, "get busy! I seen a shovel and a pick around here somewheres—dig some holes an' we'll stick 'em in the ground as we go! Where you want 'em, Bud?"

They had called Thurlow "Bud" or "Buddy" all the

evening, he could not be sure whether in derision or condescension, but he had taken it all in good part and gone gravely on with the business of the hour. But he was exceedingly grateful to them for this suggestion, for it would be days perhaps before he would be able to put those great shrubs in the ground and meantime they might die, which would be worse than not having tried to bring them.

So Thurlow took a lantern and walked ahead of the men, placing bushes at random in a general line just as they were placed back of the other house. Perhaps, if they were in the ground Mother wouldn't realize that they had not been native here, he thought.

But he added a generous tip to each man as they prepared to leave, and then turned back to the dim gloomy barn alone.

There were cobwebs looping everywhere, showing up in the weird light of the lantern, and grim spooky shadows on the walls as he walked about making sure that everything was safe as it could be made in a barn that had been recently used for an illicit still.

Then suddenly he dropped into one of the fine old parlor chairs that had been set down in front of everything, looking out of place in that queer surrounding, like a lady in a pigsty. He dropped his weary head down into his hands and sighed.

Then like a garment, all his bitterness and vexation of spirit came and fitted itself down upon him again. He had time now to think about Barbara and her gay indifference, and to let the hurt of it press into his weary spirit like a great thorn. Like many thorns, every one of those pictures being an individual thorn.

He had only glanced them through, but he had caught her expression in each picture, and known it was not for him. He had also noticed that not in one pose had she been carrying the precious handbag that he had taken such pains to get for her. Of course that might have been accidental. The pictures might have been snapped unawares. That did not prove that she did not care for it. But he chose to let it seem a slight to his gift. If she had really cared, would she not have taken pains to get it and have it in evidence in at least one of her pictures?

For a full five minutes he sat there and let the sharpness of his disappointment sink into his heart.

Then suddenly he rose and flung his arms wide:

"Oh, well, that's that!" he said aloud in a despairing tone. College was gone! Home was gone! Barby was gone! He had to live for Mother and Rilla. That was all right of course, and the sooner he got at it the better.

His eye fell upon the spade and pick lying where the men had left them on the barn floor, and suddenly it seemed to him that he could not go into the house and talk, nor could he lie down and sleep. His overwrought nerves could not relax, though he was weary almost to the breaking point. But he must go on. He would go out there and spade up a place around the lot for those bulbs. He would get them in before his mother knew.

But his mother came to the door and called him softly.

"Thurlow! Son! Aren't you almost done? You ought to get to bed."

"Presently, Mother," he said. "I've got a few little things to do yet."

"But you're so tired! Let everything go till morning, can't you?"

"Pretty soon, Mother!"

"I've got your bed all made up on the couch here, and I've heated some soup. Won't you come and get it while it's hot?"

He dropped the spade and the lantern and stepped to the door. Soup sounded good.

He stepped inside the room that already had taken on an air of being inhabited. The clean lamp shone clear on the ugly mantel, the clean sheets and pillow were waiting for him, but he could not lie down yet. He had to think his way through before he stopped.

"Are you all right?" he questioned pitifully, searching her tired courageous face.

"Right as can be," she said cheerfully. "I've sent Rilla to bed and she's asleep already. Can't you come in now?"

"Not just yet. I've got to look around and see that everything is all right," he evaded. "There are a few little things—! You go to sleep. I'll be in presently."

So he slipped away to the yard and sought out his basket of bulbs, determined to get them in the ground before she knew about them.

The moon had risen high in the heaven, a full moon, the harvest moon, and the world was bright as day. It showed up the little barren house and neglected yard, and made the factory across the street loom even larger than it was. Desolation and a desert future it seemed to the weary boy as he plunged his spade into the rank sod and tried with all his tired might to dig a neat foot-wide bed along the fence.

His muscles were so weary that his very shoulders sagged, big football player though he was, and his heart was so heavy that it fairly sagged his body down to earth, but he dug on, thinking through all his troubles bitterly. Bitterly. Why did God let all this happen to him? Well, he wouldn't blame God. He believed in God, though he didn't spend much time thinking about Him. He was just up against it, that was all. He had always had things nice and comfortable and everything had gone so smoothly for him, college and girl and home all satisfactory, and now to have the money and the home gone and college out of the question, and then on the top of it all Barbara off having a good time with a lot of other fellows where he couldn't hold his own, that was the last straw.

Viciously he jammed the spade into the reluctant ground, now and then changing to the pick to subdue a particularly resistant spot, until he had gone all the way across the front fence. Then down upon his knees, sticking bulbs in the soil six inches apart. So much would be accomplished, whether he ever got time to do any more than that or not. Mother would have her April gold at front and back. And perhaps another night or early morning he could get in the rest.

He was sure his mother must be asleep by this time or she would have been out to call him again. He had thrashed out all the bitter thoughts of his girl that he could think of. Of course she wasn't his any more anyway. It was well she didn't care. She wouldn't be hurt. And if he loved her he didn't want her to be hurt by his love, did he? Of course not. All was well. He was out of her class now, probably for life. A young man without a full education, with a family to support and no job, and no possible future, could not consider entering the Sherwood family.

And so at last he dragged his weary feet back to the barn, put away his tools, and the bulb basket, put out the lantern, snapped the rusty padlock shut and went softly into the house.

Mother had left the lamp burning on the mantel, had pinned newspapers up at the windows, had opened the clean inviting bed, had even put a newspaper by his bed for him to stand on, a basin of clean water and a towel on a box near by, a chair on which to put his clothes. There was a glass of water too. Where had she got the water? A big bottle half full on the mantel answered that question.

He undressed wearily, turned out the unfamiliar lamp, and lay down on the heavenly bed, tireder in soul and body than he had ever been before in his life. They were moved to this queer sordid house and what would the morrow bring forth?

7

IT was very quiet there on Meachin Street. The few trains that ran on the little branch railroad ceased at midnight. The sullen dark little houses gave forth no sound of human voice nor even radio. Dark figures stole uncertainly down the street at intervals, quite late, and straggled into their abodes. The moon shone on, making sharp shadows of the factory walls across the humpy road. Dim far bullfrogs from the pond across the dump gave forth dispassionate thudding noises occasionally. The city seemed a far vision against the sky, almost like a painted thing in silver and blue. And if there were stealthy footsteps passing like phantoms down behind the barn, they did not rouse the sleepers in the dusty cottage where they slept, worn out with their labors of the day.

But in the morning, when Thurlow went to look behind the barn to see what the contrivance was like he had helped to fling out from the opening in the barn wall, there was nothing there save a trampled place in the dewy grass, and a trace of footsteps back to the tumbled-down fence, that vanished in the cinder path below the embankment.

Thurlow paused and studied the trampled place where the heavy object had lain. His eye traveled down the trail to the fence in speculation, and he knit his brows, studying presently the whole miserable little back street where he had come to live, for a time at least. Then his eyes dwelt on the house which sheltered his mother and sister. He had stolen forth to investigate this still business and do away with it somehow before they should discover it. He hoped they might never know about it. He hoped they were still asleep.

Comparing their house with the others on the street it seemed slightly better, more in repair, not quite so forlorn and decrepit as the one next door for instance, with its patched walls, corrugated iron roof, and broken window panes.

The Reed house was whole at least. His father had probably kept it in repair. The gable of the roof faced the street with one window, meaning there must be a room upstairs, perhaps two, one front, one back. There was a lean-to next to the unpleasant neighbor's house that explained the two downstairs bedrooms, the main part of the house consisting of two rooms, parlor and kitchen.

He studied the possibilities. If they had to stay here a few weeks perhaps he could manage to build on another wing on the other side for kitchen and dining room and use the old kitchen for another bedroom so that they could all be downstairs together at night. He was quite sure his nervous mother, when she got to know her neighborhood well, would not enjoy being downstairs, with her son in the second story. The presence of that still in the empty barn might or might not denote lawlessness in the neighborhood, but Thurlow decided that he would feel much easier in his mind for the present at least if his mother and sister were protected.

Back of the house, and midway between the barn and dwelling there was a sort of shed, perhaps a woodshed, standing at an odd angle, made of boards upright, with cleats over their joinings and a board roof. It seemed so casual and irregular and fitted so illy with the rest of the layout of the place that Thurlow was almost annoyed by it. It was long and narrow, and wouldn't make a bad offset on the side of the house, balancing the ell on the other side. There was a great pile of stones down at the back of the lot. Perhaps, when they got things somewhat straightened inside he could build a crude foundation and set that woodshed on top of it for a dining room and kitchen. And the curious formation that must have been meant for a chicken house in a former scheme of things, loitering at the back of the lot as if it had just happened there, perhaps that could be moved up and used as a sort of porch, or annex or something. Perhaps even a woodhouse. It occurred to him to wonder how this house was heated? Would they have to have wood stoves? Did his mother realize what she was up against in coming here?

Well, it wasn't winter yet, and meanwhile he could quietly be looking around for the right place to move to. Let his mother try her experiment. In his odd hours after work—when he got a job—he would be fixing up this place so they could rent or sell it, and then Mother would be willing to move to a plain decent place somewhere.

So he comforted himself, and then went in softly to see if his family had wakened.

Mrs. Reed was up and dressed, and down on her knees before the meager little fireplace in the front room starting a blaze. She had a newspaper twisted up in small bundles, and a few sticks.

"I brought them with me from our cellar," she said in answer to the question in his eyes. "I tried to think of all the things we might need these first few hours, but I see I've forgotten some kind of a framework to set the coffee pot on. I wonder if you could get me a couple of stones out in the yard?"

Thurlow got the stones and placed them, meanwhile marveling once more at his mother's adaptability. And when he turned about he saw his mother holding out a long-handled fork toasting a slice of bread.

"Where's Rilla?" he asked.

"I'm letting her sleep," said her mother tenderly. "She was very much broken up last night, worn out."

"She ought to be letting you sleep!" said her brother harshly.

"Thurlow, don't be hard on your sister," said his mother pitifully. "She feels as if her world is broken."

"It is," said the brother with set lips. "So is mine. So is yours. But staying in bed isn't going to mend it. Come on out, Rill, and play the game!" he cried out, lifting his voice.

"I'm coming!" said Rilla in a small dreary voice. "I'm almost ready."

Rilla came out of the bedroom in a moment more. She had been powdering her nose vigorously but there were traces of recent tears behind the powder. Thurlow gave her a quick keen look.

"Call the butler, won't you, little sister, and tell him to set the table. We are breakfasting in the living room this morning." He grinned at her and provoked a tiny flutter of a smile.

Thurlow set out the little folding table and Rilla graced it with a white cloth. Her mother had remembered that, too! There were even three cups and plates and spoons and knives. There was a basket with bread and butter, and strangely enough they found themselves hungry. Then came Mother with a bottle of orange juice she had prepared the day before. They looked at her lovingly for all her care and thoughtfulness to make good cheer in the midst of the dirt and desolation. And after all it proved quite a festive occasion.

When the meal was concluded Thurlow got up and gathered up an armful of dishes, taking them to the kitchen. After he had set them down on the question-able-looking shelf by the sink he stepped over scowling and surveyed the funny little old rusty pump.

"Do you mean to tell me," he said, straightening up and looking at his mother as she came bringing more dishes, "do you mean to tell me that all the water we have has to be coaxed out of that lousy pump? Why, its throat is as dry as a desert!"

"Oh, no," said his mother coolly, "I brought along ten Mason jars full of drinking water, besides two big old jugs full for washing. I thought we'd have enough till we got the pump primed."

"Primed! What's primed? You don't mean painted up? You couldn't make me believe that that little old runt of a rusty pump would give forth water even if you painted it all the colors in the rainbow!"

The mother set her armful of dishes down and laughed.

"Is it possible that you don't know what priming a pump means? Here, pour some of the water from that jug slowly in at the top, Rill. And, Thurl, you pump! Steady now! You've got to take a pump seriously and pump as if you expected something out of it, and, Rilla, you mustn't pour the water in too fast. There, now, it's beginning to catch!"

The pump meanwhile began to wheeze and gasp, and catch as if it were choking, and the young people grew excited over it, giggling and watching and making jokes about it. It coughed and gurgled, and at last began to wheeze in a kind of rhythm.

"It's coming," said Mother confidently.

"What's coming, Mother?" demanded Thurlow desperately, ceasing his efforts for the moment, to the entire discouragement of the pump which suddenly gurgled despairingly like a lost hope and grew unresponsive again.

"Oh, now you've let it run down. You must keep on pumping! A pump is a very temperamental creature when it's been dry for a long time. More water, Rilla. Keep on steadily, Thurlow!" The mother was as excited as a boy watching a dog fight.

Thurlow returned to the fray till the pump was back at its coy gurgling again, and at last a little stream of rusty water trickled forth from its rusty mouth.

"Do you mean to tell me, Mother, that we've got to take this lousy pump in our arms and fondle it every time we want a drop of water to scrub with? I'll be switched if I will. I'm going out and get a plumber. I'm going out and get a permit. I'm going out and look around and see how far the water main is from here. Even if we only stay here through the day, I'm going to have something to show this little old lousy pump that it can't get the better of me! That it can't expect the whole family to wait on it hand and foot every time we need a drop of water!"

Yet Thurlow as he talked on wildly showed that he had at least learned one lesson about pumps, for as he talked he kept on pumping, and now a good stream of muddy rust-red water was gushing out in good shape.

"Isn't there some way we can put a motor on this beast and keep it working? There isn't any meter on it anyway, is there? We could perhaps train it to be a perpetual fountain and water the yard and the garden when we get one, couldn't we?"

They were all laughing now till the tears were running down their faces. Tired and sad, with nerves taut as fiddle strings, the laughter relaxed them. They were making a game out of their sadness, and each was glad for the sake of the others.

Rilla brought a couple of tubs and some pails and pans from the box of kitchen things and filled them, and at last Thurlow cautiously ceased his ministrations with the pump handle.

"There! Now you be a good child and act a little human and we'll give you almost anything you want!" he said, bending over the pump and patting it on its unresponsive cold shoulder. "Here! Perhaps it's coddling you want." And he seized his mother's apron and gravely wrapped it about the narrow iron shoulders, tying the apron strings around and fastening them in a large awkward bow.

Then he seized a dish towel that his mother had produced from somewhere and wrapped it about for a bonnet, leaving only the rusty spout of the pump sticking sulkily out.

"Now, sister," said Thurlow, leaning over as if to look it in the face beneath the bonnet, "if you'll just be good and not get the croup again, we'll treat you like a brother, and you'll find this is really a better home than you'd think. You really will!"

He gave it a final pat on the top of the hump backed handle and Rilla sat down and bent double with hysterical mirth.

Even the mother was laughing and crying at once. But it did them all good, and they smiled bravely as they wiped away the tears and prepared to go to work. The house was just as dirty and discouraged-looking in the garish morning light as it had been the night before in candle light, but somehow a cloud had been lifted and their hearts were not quite so heavy.

"Now," said Thurlow, "what's first, Mom? You're the boss today."

"Hot water first," said Mrs. Reed. "Plenty of it. If you'll lift that large preserve kettle of water over the fire, that will do to begin on. I wonder if that mover brought the sticks of wood from our cellar that I told him about?"

"I'll rustle some wood," said the young man. "I saw a dead tree in the lot, and I know where the axe is, too. Perhaps I could even locate the sticks of wood."

Thurlow went out and the two women set to work.

"Spread up the beds, Rilla, and lay our hats and coats and clean things on the beds. We know they are clean. Get everything you can out of this living room and we'll begin cleaning here. Did you see the stepladder? I thought I told the man to bring it over here."

"It's in the kitchen, Mother."

Rilla caught up her brother's coat that had slipped from the chair to the floor, gave it a careful shake to free it from its contaminating touch on the floor, and out of the pocket came a shower of small photographs, slithering across the floor in shining order. Barbara Sherwood doing deck tennis. Barbara Sherwood in bathing costume about to dive in the ship's pool. Barbara Sherwood in lively converse with one young man after another, smiling up into their faces and apparently having the grandest time!

It was just as if some little demon had arranged them out in order so that one could not but see each one, even if one had no intention of looking. And it certainly never occurred to Rilla that there was anything in a handful of snapshots that was prohibitory. Thurlow would of course show them to her when he got time. She had seen the nice fat letter with the foreign stamp in his hand when he gave her her own, and had rejoiced in it for him. Her sisterly heart had ached for him when none had come all those long days after Barbara had sailed. But there was something sinister in this row of shining faces, so contented, so complacent. Rilla sensed it even in the quick hurried glance she permitted herself.

She gave a little hurt gasp and then, stooping, gathered up the pictures to restore them to the pocket. But her mother had heard the exclamation, caught the look of compassion on her face.

"What is it?" she asked, sensing some disaster. She put out her hand and took the pictures, studying them an instant, Rilla with half-averted eyes getting another glimpse over her shoulder. This mother and son had no secrets, yet there were fine reserves that the sister especially felt she had no right to cross. This was something that affected the deepest interests of her son, and the mother, after an instant's study of the top picture, deliberately looked carefully at each one. Then with a quick motion she swept them all together again and handed them to Rilla.

"Put them back in his pocket," she said, without comment.

Rilla slid them into the pocket, feeling the rattle of the single sheet they had come in as she put them away. Her heart was sorrowful for her brother. Was that all that Barbara had written?

But she hung the coat up circumspectly over the back of a nice freshly dusted chair and went about her work.

An instant later Thurlow came in, his arms full of wood.

The fire was soon snapping and blazing briskly and the water began to send up a prosperous-looking steam.

"Now," said Mrs. Reed, "Thurlow, put enough hot

water into that smallest tub of pump water, to make it good and hot, and then fill up the kettle and put it to heat again. Here are three scrubbing brushes. I'll take this wall, and the front. Rilla, you take the back wall and the other side. Thurlow your part is the ceiling and about a yard down, because you have the stepladder. You begin first and do a little way so we can go on from there and won't be undoing each other's work. Here are soap and cloths. Don't be afraid to use plenty of water. Rinse out your cloths and scrubbing brushes often, and when you've done about a square yard, rinse it off and dry it with this big cloth. We'll fill our scrub buckets from the tub. Rilla, we'll wash windows and paint as we go. Do a yard or two at a time all the way down."

They were off at the game of cleaning house, and found it wasn't half as bad as they had anticipated. Thurlow made comical remarks continually and kept them laughing, though now and then when he was silent and grave, sloshing on water and scrubbing vigorously, his sister would glance furtively toward him and wonder how he could be so gay when she was sure all the time he had a heavy heart. That look of bitterness that sat in his eyes when he was silent and thought they were not watching him, must mean that he was not happy. Her heart swelled with pride at the brave front he was putting up, and she resolved not to be behind him in courage.

So, presently, when the work began to assume serious form, and arms and shoulders began to tire with the unaccustomed labor, Rilla piped up a tune. It was only an old hymn, "Work for the night is coming," and sung half in derision to provoke another laugh, but it led to other hymns, favorite ones of their mother, and they all joined in, Mother taking the alto, and Thurlow rolling his rich baritone in, blending with Rilla's sweet high notes. So presently, Meachin Street heard the gospel in song. Ears that had been accustomed only to blasphemy and cursing, or at best to the latest popular whine from the one radio the street boasted, now caught the strains of "There is a fountain filled with blood," "For God so loved the world," "Abide with me," "Face to face with Christ my Saviour," "Glad day," and many others. The morning passed on and the room grew cleaner and cleaner, though it seemed to stretch into unsuspected proportions as unaccustomed arms and backs and knees grew weary.

"Good night, Mom!" said Thurlow, climbing down from the ladder to change the water in his bucket. "I never suspected this room was so large. I would have said I could do the whole thing in an hour. But then, I never knew it was so bloomin' dirty. Say, Mom, you're a great little mother to have the dare to move down here the way you did, knowing there would be all this to do! I expect Mrs. Beddow, our old neighbor, is even now saying you are no lady for doing it."

Mrs. Reed laughed lightly.

"Mrs. Beddow is not so hot herself, as a housekeeper!" she said nonchalantly, and sent them both into peals of laughter over her unexpected slang.

"Now, Mother," protested Rilla, "I never expected you to get your English corrupted the first day in Meachin Street. I'm afraid I shall have to reform my speech to set you a good example."

"Okay with me!" said Mother, rubbing a pane of glass till it shone in surprise over its bath after all these years of neglect.

The morning went rapidly, and when a factory whistle from the neighborhood blew a heart-searching blast that startled them all, they stopped and looked at one another.

"Now, think of that!" said Thurlow comically. "We

get that service free! We shan't have the expense of keeping the clocks wound any more. We can just take our time from the whistles from now on the rest of the day. There might be even two a day, one at six at night, and likely one at six in the morning. Midnight, too. We ought to be able to keep up with the times with four whistles a day."

> *"Four whistles a day,*
> *Tell the time of day,*
> *Let us all be gay——!"*

chanted the young man.

They stopped work for a bowl of the delicious soup Mrs. Reed had found time to make amid the throes of moving at the old house, and while they ate they admired their work, and compared notes on the number of spiders each had killed.

Even inexperienced workmen can accomplish a lot when they have an experienced manager, and so, not long after they returned to their work, the walls and ceiling were finished, and the place began to take on a subdued, cleansed look. It was still ugly, and the cracks in the plaster were just as plain to be seen as before, but somehow they were not so offensive when one knew they were clean. Even some of the penciled decoration, and family accounts which were evidently kept on the walls by the last occupant, were somewhat dimmer.

"We'll have to try our hands at paper hanging as soon as we really get cleaned," said Mrs. Reed as she stood back to survey the wall. "I used to be pretty good at papering when I was a girl!"

"Mother! You couldn't put on paper!" said Rilla, aghast.

"Why not?" asked Mother. "I can put it on, and I can teach you how to put it on, too."

Thurlow bowed low before her with his hand on his heart.

"Mother-Mine, you are discovering to us so many heretofore unsuspected talents that you frighten us. We never realized that we had a paper-hanging mother in our midst."

They were very tired but they laughed again and it rested them, and then the mother and sister were sobered with the memory of those snapshots they had seen. Oh, perhaps Thurlow wasn't so hurt after all as they had feared. Maybe there had been a letter too, and he had it hidden in an inner pocket over his heart, and was just letting his satisfaction run out in this dear funny way.

"Well, now," said the mother, "if you aren't too tired, perhaps you'll put up the shades and the rods for the curtains."

"Curtains? Do we get curtains already?" demanded the young man. "I supposed they were articles that didn't come till sometime in the dim and misty future after everything else was done."

"We can't live behind newspapers long," said his mother. "You're sure you are not too tired?"

"Tired? Why should I be tired, woman? You insult my former football career! *Me* tired? I'm fresh as a lily!"

So the work went rapidly on.

By half past four the room was shining clean, smelling of soap and water. The shades were up and the white muslin curtains from a guest room at home hung at the windows, and for a wonder just fitted! Then Thurlow and Rilla went scurrying back and forth to the barn, bringing a few more chairs, a small table or two and the hall mirror. Thurlow hung that on the wall at once and the room began to take on a friendly homelike attitude.

But when he turned around from hanging the mirror to see what his mother thought of it she wasn't there, and they found her in the kitchen filling a queer contrivance with kerosene.

"What on earth is that?" demanded Rilla with new qualms.

"An oil stove," said her mother serenely. "I'm glad I kept it. I almost gave it away once, and then I decided to put it away in the attic, and now it has come in useful. I think it will work all right. I oiled it when I put it away and it was well wrapped up. There wasn't a spot of rust on it anywhere."

"Do you mean to tell me there isn't any gas connection in this dump?" asked the son, scanning the wall for an outlet.

"No gas on this street!" said his mother, still serene.

"And yet you thought you could come down here and live! Now, Mother-Mine, just turn around here and look at me! I'm not going to stand for this, do you understand? There isn't a bit of need of your economizing like this. There are at least three hundred dollars we can use for necessities, and Rilla and I are both going to have jobs, and what is the point anyway? Now, Mother, tell me? Surely you've got sense enough to see that this isn't true economy!"

Mrs. Reed calmly washed the oil off her hands, adjusted and lighted a broad cotton wick, set a teakettle to boil over its flame and then turned around.

"Well, if you must know, my son," she said, turning her pleasant tired eyes toward Thurlow, "this perhaps is as good a time as any to tell you. The reason is that you are going back to college! Of course you'll protest. I expect that. But Rilla and I have talked it over and we're not going to stand for your stopping now. You've got to finish your course and get your diploma. Rilla is going to get a job to help out, and we'll have plenty to live on and see you through, if we are careful. I'm only being careful, son!"

Thurlow stood dumfounded.

"Well, I'll be lambasted!" Thurlow exclaimed, dropping down on the kitchen chair he had just brought over from the barn. "Is that what you've got up your sleeve? I thought there was something in the wind, the way you two have been carrying on the last week. Well, you don't expect me to settle down and take that on the chin, do you? Me? A great big husky giant? Well, if you do you've got another guess coming, and you might as well understand now as later that that is *final!* I'm not letting any two women support me and send me through college, now or any other time, so that's that!"

Thurlow brought the front legs of the wooden chair down with a thump and rising stalked out of the kitchen door and down to the barn. There were tears stinging in his eyes and a lump in his throat and anger and a frenzy of tenderness welling within him so that his heart was like to burst. So he went to the barn, and tired as he was began pulling things around and doing a lot of utterly unnecessary work. And in the midst of it he took off his coat which he had put on with the half intention of going down to the store to find a special kind of screw he felt he ought to have to fasten those boards on the back of the barn. For to tell the truth in spite of the stout nailing of the night before he had found that three boards were loose again, and there were wet footprints on the barn floor from the muddy place back of the barn where the drainings from the still had dripped. He didn't mean his mother to know, nor Rilla either, but he was morally certain somebody had been in the barn in the night after he went to bed, perhaps ransacking their things, though he hadn't yet discovered that anything was missing. So now, as he was pulling around the chairs and the old dining table to make a barricade that would not easily be pulled apart without making some noise at least, he swung off his coat to protect it, and as he flung it down on a chair a shower of photographs fell at his feet. Barbara Sherwood again had projected herself into this strenuous day, and cast a light honeyed smile at him that filled him with pain.

He stood staring at the pictures a moment and then stooping swept them up in his hand and sat down on the chair deliberately to look them over once and for all. Scowling as he would never have scowled at Barbara Sherwood in the flesh, he faced her pictured face and hardened his heart; studied her expression of utter delight in first one pose and then another, and gave particular attention to the men who were her companions.

"What she sees in that egg!" he apostrophized. Then he turned to another.

"That poor fish hasn't anything but a smile and a set of good teeth!" he declared disgustedly, "and that one looks like a half-witted ape! If that's the kind of men she likes, let her have 'em!" he murmured as he rose and took the whole bunch of pictures, feeling in his pocket for the written sheet in which they had been wrapped. He read the gay message over again contemptuously, folded it about the pictures, searched until he located his own desk behind other furniture, and carefully hid the packet in the secret drawer. Then he piled up the chairs in front of it again, locked the barn and stamped back to the house.

Over in the kitchen where the two women were left with the strangely docile oil stove, which beamed with a bright flame much to the young girl's amazement, there was silence for a space after the son had gone out. At last the mother lifted her head from bending down to be sure the flame was just high enough and not too high, and spoke.

"I expect we're going to have a pretty hard time making him see it," she said with a weary sigh.

"Yes," said the girl thoughtfully, "I guess we are." Then she added after a pause, "But I don't know but I like him better because he feels that way, after all. He's pretty sweet, Mother!"

"He is, isn't he?" said his mother. "I do hope he is not going to feel it much about that girl."

"He will," said his sister with conviction. "He's keen. You can't fool him. She wouldn't need to write a thing, just send him those pictures, to show him how little she cares he isn't there!"

"Well," sighed the mother, "if she's that way perhaps it's just as well to have him find it out now as later."

"It makes me furious!" said Rilla. "She ought to have better sense! Doesn't she know what Thurl is? Can't she see how he's away above all those poor simps on the ship? And now, just because she's sent those pictures, it'll be just like Thurl to get his nose up in the air and not write to her at all."

"Perhaps it's just as well that he should not," said Mrs. Reed sadly. "Perhaps that's one reason all this had to happen, to test out things and people. You know even Thurlow may have some lessons to learn. I guess the Lord knows what He's doing, and why!"

Rilla was silent. Discontented. She wouldn't say in so many words that she doubted this, but she thought it. Her eyes were smoldering. Her mother took note of her expression.

"Well, I wouldn't worry about it," she said soothingly. "Perhaps there isn't anything to it at all."

"Yes, there is! I'm sure there is. Betty's letter showed

she realized it. She wanted me to tell Thurl to write to Barby, to write often."

"Well, it will all come out some day," sighed the mother, "but if I were you, I wouldn't say anything about Betty's letter. Not yet awhile."

"Of course not," said Rilla. "I didn't mean to anyway. He'd never write if I did that. And anyway I don't know as I want him to write if she's going highhat! Thurl is just as good as she is any day, and some day she'll find out."

"Perhaps she will. But—there he comes! Let's look cheerful!"

That night the little house that had been so long vacant, shone cheerful and bright in the sordid neighborhood of Meachin Street, and furtive figures stole from the other cabins and peered at it curiously, even strolling by toward the dump to study it, and wonder what it might portend for each and every one. Were these some squatters who ought to be ousted by fair means or foul? Were they some swells who would be snooty and have to be taught sharp lessons? With their lighted windows and curtains? *Curtains!* Imagine it, on the second night in!

Yet they looked wistfully at the brightness as if it were a distant star come near enough to be watched, and something stirred in breasts long callous to holy things, some memories of homes that one or another had had in the dim sad past.

But if any furtive visitors tried the back wall of the barn they failed to find entrance, for Thurlow had slipped out to the store before dark and got his screws and applied them to the boards ingeniously from inside, so that efforts from outside were ineffectual.

8

THE first Sunday in the new home was a very quiet one. They were all extremely tired after their unaccustomed hard work, and had agreed to sleep late. Breakfast and the noonday meal became one and the same, and was quite simple in its menu. Roasted potatoes, to try the oil stove oven, concerning which both son and daughter were most incredulous, cold ham, bread and butter and ripe peaches. It didn't take long to assemble.

There was none of the hilarity of the day before. There had been a bit of restraint in them all since the subject of Thurlow's going to college again had been broached, and he had repulsed the idea so wrathfully. It was as if he had suddenly grown up and felt his maturity had been belittled. He wanted to make them understand that it was utterly out of the question. He was not angry, only very grave and thoughtful.

After the meal was cleared away Thurlow went out to the barn and brought back an armful of books and papers he had taken from one of the boxes, and they all read for a little while. Mrs. Reed, sitting in her big comfortable chair by the bright little curtained window, her back toward the window so she wouldn't look out and catch a glimpse of the new surroundings, read her Bible. The young people read restlessly for a little while, their minds scarcely on what they were scanning with their eyes. By and by when their mother went to lie down for a nap they took a little walk outside. Not that it was inviting in the neighborhood. Not that they really wanted to see what it was like. But they had an urge to get the worst over with and sound their new surroundings to the depths.

It was pretty bad. They hadn't realized before how very bad it was, they had been so busy. That first glimpse in the semi-darkness, while it had shocked them, had given them very little idea of the place as it really was, and they had not looked around much since. But now in the late afternoon sunshine, with the comparative quiet of the Sabbath over even the dump, it stood out in all its ugliness.

The house next door seemed a blot on the face of the landscape. There was a little old woman with straggling hair and indiscriminate garments, lounging with her elbows on the sagging gate and staring curiously after them as they came out to their own gate. And just to escape her inspection they turned by common consent in the opposite direction and walked out toward the dump, thinking to find privacy in which to scan the vicinity.

They walked slowly, side by side, in the thick over-grown grass by the roadside, till it ended suddenly in a scattering growth of burdock and thistles that merged into mounds of ashes and tin cans.

"Oh!" said Rilla pitifully, halting and looking about her, "is it really like this, or am I dreaming?"

"It's certainly no dream of loveliness!" said Thurlow with sternly set lips and frowning brow.

They mounted a little eminence of ashes ahead of them and looked down a slope, the whole side of which was covered with dump, ashes and cans and old weathered newspapers, too discouraged by long exposure even to flutter. Odds and ends of old furniture were scattered among the refuse. Legs of tables, an old carpet-covered sofa with its springs bursting forth, rusty kitchen utensils, and high and dry on the tallest point of the dump, an old pretentious rocking chair with its seat broken through and hanging in tatters. It looked as if it might be the devil's playground and he had a surprising sense of humor, the way inanimate articles were scattered about promiscuously.

They stepped up a little higher on the ash pile, looking down below them and off to the right, their gaze attracted by angry voices which suddenly rose in a startling crescendo of profanity. There were four disreputable-looking men down there, sitting on boxes and stones, and one cross-legged on the ground, just outside a ramshackle little structure of corrugated iron, crazily put together. The crude doorway faced toward the two young people, and there seemed to be a fifth man sitting just inside the shelter. All of them held cards in their hands and they were angry. Two of them were very drunk, and one was waving a gun about.

They gazed in horror at such a scene almost in their very dooryard, and then Thurlow quickly drew his sister back and walked with her down into the meadow that ran behind the barn.

"Now," he said sternly when they had reached a sufficient distance so that they could no longer be seen nor heard by their unpleasant neighbors, "I hope you see why I couldn't under any consideration go away to college and leave you and Mother in such a neighborhood alone all the week, even if I had all the money in the world, even if there was no need for me to get a job. It isn't necessary for you to scare Mother, of course, but I'm glad you saw that. I want you to be awfully careful about going out alone at night, and even in the daytime dress very plainly and don't look at anybody or speak to anybody you don't know. I mean to get you and Mother out of here as soon as possible, but while we stay you must be terribly careful. You don't know what we're neighboring with. They might even be gangsters of a sort, though I suspect they're merely common scum of the earth."

Rilla was a little frightened, but she was very silent and wide-eyed. At last she said: "Why do you think God let this happen to us, Thurl? I don't mean just to you and me, for our sakes, but to all of us? Mother? She's always been so sweet and dear and good. Why do you think God let it come to her?"

Thurlow was still a long time and then he said:

"I sometimes wonder if He really cares. You know at college hardly anybody believes that there is a personal God. I haven't paid much attention to all their big phrases about it, but these last few days I've wondered, now and then when I've had time, if perhaps after all they are not right."

Rilla cast a startled look up at him.

"Oh, Thurl! Don't get like that! You know that would hurt Mother more than all the rest, money or college, or having to live down here or anything."

"I know," he said sadly. "I don't want to feel that way. I've tried not to think such thoughts but they keep coming. It's horribly desolate not to believe things, the good old things that you've been taught, even though they've never seemed very important to you before. But when you get into trouble you think things."

"Yes!" said Rilla, looking off toward the impish black

speck that was a train shooting at them along that high track above the cinder embankment that girded their back fence, and would presently thunder by and spit out noises and shrieks as it went.

"Maybe that's what it's for," she said meditatively after a pause.

"What? What's what for?"

"To make us think. Maybe that's why God let it happen. Maybe it's to make us think. Maybe there is something we ought to be thinking about in life that we don't think, and it was the only way God could get us to do it."

He looked at her with thoughtful surprise, studied her delicate lovely young face, sweet young womanhood just beginning to bud, here on the edge of a dump! and sighed deeply.

"Maybe you're right," he said quietly after a long time. "I wish I knew. I'd think about it quick, I know that. Come, let's go back to Mother. We mustn't let her get blue. She's been awfully brave. Let's go in and have a little music. She'll like that."

"Yes," said Rilla, brightening, and slipping her hand within her brother's arm as they walked back to the cottage.

Rilla sat down at the piano and began to play hymns softly. They could hear their mother moving about in her room, and almost at once she came out smiling. How hard they were all trying to be brave for one another! It was really beautiful as they struggled together not to mind the terrible changes that death and loss had brought.

And then presently the brother and sister began to sing, their voices blending sweetly. The windows were open and the song stole out.

> *"Rock of ages cleft for me.*
> *Let me hide myself in Thee!"*

The words sounded forth clearly, and crept through the sunset-colored air, floating out even over the dump that had taken on a reflected glory now with the "quiet colored end of evening," and dropped down like a personal message on that little shack of rusty iron on the side of the dump, speaking with startling sweet distinctness.

The old woman by the sagging gate lifted her bleared eyes full of sorrow and bitterness and hate, and was shaken by a memory, church bells in a faraway land, ivy-clad entrance, words from an old book. And down in the doorway of the shack on the dump, her son, who was a thief, suddenly started to his feet, flung down his dirty cards on the ash heap, and looked up toward the rim of the dumpside.

"Hell! What's that?" he said sharply, and drew out his gun, alert, listening, his wary eyes studying his horizon.

But the singing went softly on, one old hymn after another, till the stars pricked out in the amethyst sky one by one, and the dark came slowly down like a veil and dropped into place about the earth, like the draperies of a great couch.

> *"Abide with me; fast falls the eventide;*
> *The darkness deepens; Lord, with me abide!*
> *When other helpers fail, and comforts flee,*
> *Help of the helpless, oh, abide with me!"*

Dark figures stole from the side of the dump and crept in the shadow of the great dead factory wall to watch and listen and speculate as to what all this meant to their world, and their activities.

Suddenly around the corner of the factory spun a small trig roadster. Its bright headlights shot out yellow paths down the rough road and startled the slinking creatures in the shadow of the brick walls. They faded into the darkness like wraiths. One instant the lights picked them out with clear distinctness, gaunt figures with blinking frightened eyes, the next they simply were not, mere creatures of imagination.

"Why don't you ask those men if this is the right street, Sandra? I don't see any sense in coursing about here blindly and getting all turned around."

"What men, Cousin Caroline? I don't see any men."

"Why, those men on the sidewalk! I saw five of them there as we turned the corner."

The girl at the wheel turned the trim little car till its lights illuminated the whole side of the old factory.

"There aren't any men there, Cousin Caroline," said the girl at the wheel. "There isn't even any sidewalk, just an irregular path in the grass."

"Why, how strange, Sandra," said the older voice, "I am perfectly certain I saw five figures standing there as we turned the corner. There! What is that over there by the corner of the building?"

"Just shadows!" said the girl a bit patronizingly.

"No! I saw something move! See! It looks like a hat brim!"

"Nonsense, Cousin Caroline," laughed the girl lightly, "you really ought to do something about your glasses. Or your nerves. You know it is easy to think you see a tree move in the dark."

"Now, look here, Sandra! I can see as well as anybody and you know it, and as for nerves, who wouldn't be jittery after careering around in this part of the city where you don't know what you may come on any minute? You know I never approved of your coming down to that Mission to work, even just to the services, and as for your going poking around in the slummiest kind of slums hunting after some reprobate girl who is probably parading the streets with a crowd of rowdy men, I certainly can't uphold you in it. Your father left you in my charge and I intend to look after you even if I get kidnapped in the attempt. If you insist on coming to the slums every Sunday afternoon, why, I shall have to sacrifice myself and come too."

"But, Cousin Caroline, I'm not in the least afraid, and Father thoroughly approves of what I am doing."

"Your father has no idea in the world what kind of places you go poking into. And anyway he has his head in the clouds just as you have, and is no fit judge. Sandra, I'm quite positive I saw the brim of a disreputable old felt hat then, peeking out around that corner. Why don't you call out and say, 'Who's there?' in a good loud tone, and ask if they know the way back to Cantor Street?"

"I'd rather not do that, Cousin Caroline. I'll just stop the car over this other side of the road and run and tap at a door. There's a light over in that cottage, see?"

She suited the action to the word, by running the car over in front of the Reed property.

"No, Sandra! I beg you won't get out and leave me here alone. Someone might jump in the car and ride away with me and then what would become of you? You don't know what kind of people live in that terrible little dark hovel!"

"But it isn't a hovel, Cousin Caroline! See, there are white curtains at the windows."

"Curtains at the windows! What difference does that make? They may only put them up to lure people in. You don't know what they are. If they open the door they might snatch you in and lock you up and then what would I do? Oh, why did we come down this terrible street?"

Sandra stopped her engine and suddenly the soft strains of the old hymn took the place of the throbbing of machinery.

"They are all right, Cousin Caroline. Listen!" said the girl. "They are singing hymns! What a gorgeous voice!"

"It's probably not a voice at all. It's probably only a cheap little radio left going. Or else they are singing some terrible words to an old tune! They do that now, you know—on the radio!"

"Or some terrible tune to sacred words," laughed the girl. "No, Cousin Caroline, that's a genuine voice sing-ing 'Abide with me.' Listen! Hear how clear and distinct the words are!"

> *"I need Thy presence every passing hour:*
> *What but Thy grace can foil the tempter's power?*
> *Who like Thyself my guide and stay can be?—"*

"I'm going in," said the girl. "There's nothing to be afraid of where they sing those words that way!" and she sprang from the car.

"Well, then, lock the car and take the key with you! Yes, I *insist!* I'm not going to be left here to be kid-napped—!"

But the girl was halfway up the walk, thrilling with wonder at finding a voice like that down in this quarter of the world.

She waited till the last line was finished before she tapped at the door, and looked interestedly through the white curtained window into the attractive room while she waited. Across from her she could see a woman who reminded her of her own dear mother who was gone home to heaven. A young girl with lovely lights in her hair from the bright lamp on the mantel, swung around on the piano stool as Sandra tapped at the door and the lingering chords of music died suddenly.

The anxious cousin in the car saw the door swing wide, letting out a flood of light, and a good-looking young giant, trimly dressed, was standing in the doorway.

Sandra stood looking up at the young man in astonishment. At best she had hoped to find a decent family of factory hands in the little house with the bright windows, but here was an attractive young man who might have moved in any society she had ever known and graced it. For the instant she was speechless with surprise. Then she summoned her faculties to speak.

"I'm lost," she said lightly. "I wonder if you could tell me how to get back to where I came from? I was hunting a pupil from the Mission and I've gone around and around so many little strange streets that I'm completely turned around. Where is this, anyway?"

Thurlow looked at her with interest, took in with another glance the neat little runabout at the door, and smiled.

"This is the South Side," he said, "and this street rejoices in the name of Meachin Street. Where did you want to go? I'm rather new here myself. We just moved in a day or so ago."

"Why, if you can show me where Grace Chapel is, I can find my way home from there."

"Grace Chapel? What street is that on?"

"Sandra! Sandra! Don't stop to talk any longer. These people wouldn't know where we want to go. Come on! I'm sure we can find our way back the way we came—!" came the plaintive wail of Cousin Caroline in the car. "Come on, Sandra! This is a dreadful place! I've seen some more men in the shadows. It's so awfully dark here—!"

Thurlow shot a keen glance out to the car, and then smiled into the blue eyes of the girl.

"It is a dark street," he said, "but I can show you the way out, I think. Get into your car and drive slowly and my sister and I will walk out a little way with you, till you've turned a couple of corners and got your bearings again. Come on, Rilla! Mother, we won't be but a short time. You won't be afraid, will you? It's early yet, you know."

"Not a bit of it!" said Mrs. Reed, coming to the door and smiling down at the stranger. "I'm never afraid anywhere. Go as far as you need to go to make her feel safe and sure," she smiled.

"Oh, thank you!" said Sandra, and then wistfully: "You look a lot like my dear mother who went to heaven over a year ago."

"Oh, my dear!" said Mrs. Reed, stepping out the door and reaching over to put a tender kiss on the girl's forehead. "Come again and see us, won't you? I'd like to know you."

"Why, I'd love to," said the girl with a catch in her breath. "Perhaps you'll come over to our Mission some-time. It can't be far from here."

"Why, yes, perhaps we will. We can't go to our own church any more, it's too far away, and we haven't any car any more. My son will find out where it is. I'm Mrs. Reed and this is my daughter Marilla and my son Thurlow."

"Well, I'm Sandra Cameron," said the girl half shyly. "I teach in the Mission. It would be wonderful if you would come and help us with the music."

She turned to Thurlow and Rilla wistfully. "I heard you singing hymns or I wouldn't have dared come in.

You have a wonderful voice." She looked at Thurlow. "I know the rest would be so glad if you would come and sing for us sometimes. And"—she turned to Rilla— "we're terribly in need of a pianist just now. My talents don't lie in the line of the piano. I play the violin and sing a little but that won't take the place of a piano, and the girl they sometimes get to play is awful. She flats everything that ought to be sharp, and sharps all the flats."

"Perhaps we could get together on something sometime," said Rilla.

"Wouldn't that be fun?" said the stranger-girl.

"Sandra! Sandra!" came the voice of Cousin Caroline, "I must *insist*—"

"Yes, Cousin Caroline, I'm coming!" called Sandra patiently. "These people are going to show us the way out—"

"I think that won't be necessary," called Cousin Caroline coldly. "I've figured out the way in my mind. I always had a very good sense of direction—"

They were walking down to the car now, and Thurlow swung open the car door as courteously as any of Cousin Caroline's friends could have done.

"This is Mr. Reed, Cousin Caroline. Miss Cradock, Mr. Reed."

Cousin Caroline stared at Thurlow, but he did not seem to mind. He smiled and bowed, and then turning closed the car door.

"Now," he said, "if you'll just drive slowly, we'll walk along and guide you till you can find the main highway leading to the other side of the city."

"It wouldn't have been at all necessary if Sandra hadn't been so headstrong," said Miss Cradock ungraciously. "She would come down to search for some wild young girl who was absent from Sunday School. I told her if she hadn't the gratitude to come without being gone after she wasn't worthy of her effort. I don't believe in coddling vagrants."

Sandra's eyes were looking speculatively down the street at the sordid little houses.

"I was sure they told me she lived down this way. I don't suppose you would know where she lives, would you, Mr. Reed? She is named O'Hennessy. Rose O'Hennessy. And her brother has such a curious name. It is Bat. They told me if I would just ask for Bat O'Hennessy's sister I wouldn't have any trouble locating her. They said anyone down this way could tell me where Bat lives."

"Sorry, I don't know my neighbors yet," said Thurlow with a bit of dignity in his tone, ignoring the sordidness of his surroundings. "But I'll keep an eye out for him if you'd like, and try to locate his sister for you."

"Thank you so much."

Rilla came down the path with a light scarf about her shoulders, looking like a fairy out of place in that surrounding, and was duly introduced to Cousin Cradock. Then the little procession started, Rilla slipping a hand in her brother's arm.

They halted a few blocks farther on, after several devious turnings, Sandra thanked her guide and said she knew her way now, reminded her new acquaintances that they must come to the Mission, and they parted, Rilla and Thurlow hurrying back because their mother was alone.

"She's a darling, isn't she?" said Rilla, after they had gone the first block in silence.

"Oh, well, I don't know that I would go quite so far as that on so short acquaintance," grinned Thurlow. But she knew he had liked the stranger, and when a little later she asked him if he would take her to that Mission sometime, he said he guessed he knew where it was. He had seen a place such as the girl had described when he went to the hardware store for his screws.

Sandra turned her car up the familiar avenue and her cousin drew a breath of relief.

"Well, I'm sure I'm thankful we got out of there alive! I never expected it!" And then a moment later: "What on earth did you let that horrid woman kiss you for? I declare I never saw such forwardness. Kissing *you!* Be sure to wash your face in antiseptic soap when you get home. You can't tell what germs you may have picked up! I do hope this night's experience will teach you not to take up slumming any more as a fad! I really can't stand the nervous strain. Who was that young man? Had you ever seen him before? And that girl? Are they people who belong to the Mission? How did you dare trust a stranger to guide you? He might have directed us to some gang of kidnappers. Having money as I have makes one cautious. You know they all know who has money. And I couldn't survive being kidnapped at my age."

Sandra did not answer. She was thinking what nice eyes the stranger had, and hearing again the thrill of his voice as he sang "Abide with me."

"And I shall insist," babbled on Cousin Caroline, "that you do not go down to that awful Mission again until my brother comes back and can accompany you."

But Sandra was thinking of other things and still did not answer.

9

A little over a week later the cottage was clean from the
speck of a cellar to the tiny hole of an attic up a ladder
from the second floor. Everything was in as apple-pie
order as could be, although half their goods were still
stored in the old barn. So Thurlow started out to get a
job. He hadn't gone before because there was so much
to be done, and he knew if he left even for a little while
it would be the signal for his mother to undertake more
than she was able.

The work and the change from her old home was
beginning to tell on Mrs. Reed. It had been many years
since she had had to do actual physical labor, like scrubbing and housecleaning, and while she had plenty of zeal
and skill, her physical powers were not what they had
been in her early years. So her children watched her
carefully, and tried to take all the burdens they could
from her, and to anticipate what she might be tempted
to undertake.

They had not been to the Mission yet, although all
three of them had spoken of it with interest. The only
Sunday that had passed since the attractive girl had

stopped at their door and told them of it had been cold and rainy, a presage of the fall that was rapidly hastening on. Also Mrs. Reed had contracted a heavy cold, so they stayed housed, promising themselves that next Sunday they would hunt up the Mission and attend regularly if it was at all a suitable place to worship.

"We can't give up going to church," sighed the mother, "and of course it's entirely out of the question for us to try to go back to our old church every Sunday. It's much too far. Besides, I don't think I would care to. Everybody would be commiserating and sympathizing and I'd rather just drop out of sight, at least for a while."

But now, as Thurlow started out in the early morning, confident that when he should return he would be the proud owner of a good paying job which would soon enable him to take his mother and sister to a more attractive neighborhood, he thought of the blue-eyed girl who had stood at their door and invited him to come to that Mission. Involuntarily he turned his steps in the direction where he thought the chapel was located.

It was a little old church, tucked in between a row of miscellaneous houses of an ancient period, all of them more or less drab and dreary. But the church, though exceedingly plain and simple, had recently been painted white, and glistened freshly in contrast to its surroundings. It bore a sign over the door in good clear letters, "JESUS SAVES." It somehow gave Thurlow the idea that it was a haven in the midst of the storm and strife of earth, so sure and cheerful and peaceful there in the grime of the city. It made him think of the girl with the clear eyes. He wondered as he went on his way whether he would ever see her again, and whether she would really be as interesting in the light of day as she had seemed in the lamplight of the doorway against the darkness of the evening. He registered a vow to go to the Mission next Sunday if possible.

Thurlow had gone out with a high held head that morning, but he returned gravely, with a humbled look upon him. He had discovered that jobs were not as easy to get as he had hoped. The day had practically wiped out of the picture every opportunity that he had thought a possibility when he went forth in the morning. He had to begin all over again.

But he brought with him a sheaf of daily papers, and a determined look upon his face. He put on his overalls, went out to the barn for his tools, and began to dig a cellar out on the side of the house opposite the present lean-to. His mother and sister came out to question what he was doing.

"I'm digging the cellar for a new dining room and kitchen," he said gaily, as if they were things he could manufacture overnight.

"But where? How?" began Rilla.

His mother eyed him with a half-proud, half-worried look. She was hoping that he would yet yield and go back to college when the time came. There were still two weeks before college opened, and she had been secretly mending up his clothes and preparing him if the way should open.

Thurlow grinned. "I'm using the woodshed over there for the addition. It has three good walls and will be about the right size to balance this end when I get through with it. I can perhaps get a man or two around here to help me move it when I get the foundation ready. Do you object, Mother? It's your house of course."

"No more mine than yours," she said quickly. "No, I don't object. But—" She dared not mention college again. There was a look in his eyes that anticipated her thought and forbade it. "But—it's hardly necessary, is it? We'll get along this winter."

"I need the exercise," said the son, "and besides, I thought it would improve the looks of things a little. Not so many messy little buildings strung along without rhyme or reason."

"Perhaps," said the mother, looking about. "It won't do any harm."

"Make it more valuable when we go to sell it pretty soon," said Thurlow.

"Oh, you couldn't sell this," said his mother. "I tried. I had a couple of agents look at it. They said the location was against it. Only factory hands would apply, and now that this factory was closed it was out of the question."

"Well, we'll see. Anyhow I need the exercise, and besides I want to get the furniture under one roof, and get rid of that old barn—part of it anyway. It's a menace as it stands, all coming apart, and we can take care of the things better if we have them around us."

"But why a dining room and kitchen, Thurl?" questioned Rilla, staring up at the house. "Why not another bedroom for you? That attic is going to be awfully cold in winter and hot in summer."

"Oh, I'm going to take the kitchen for mine," he said lightly. "I thought it would be better for me to be downstairs near you both. I thought Mother would feel better if we were all near together."

Rilla gave him a knowing glance, realizing that her brother felt the neighborhood was such that they might need protection, but she only said, "Oh! Yes, that would be nice."

So Thurlow went into the city every morning to search for a job, and returned every afternoon about four o'clock to work on his foundation till dark. The evenings he spent studying the want columns in the newspapers, and writing letters applying for jobs. But day after day went by and still no work was in sight, and the foundation grew apace. One day he came home early with a couple of strong men in a truck, and some rollers, and by night the woodshed had been promoted to stand on the new foundation alongside of the cottage.

"It has very good lines," said Mrs. Reed, coming out with a sweater around her shoulders to look at it. "That line of the roof is almost as if it were made for the place, and as you say it does make the house look better balanced."

Meachin Street had come out en masse to watch the proceedings. The old woman next door was hanging over the fence, and her disreputable son whom Thurlow had recently discovered to be the famous "Bat," hung around the open doorway of the hovel with a little vicious-looking black pipe in his teeth and watched, while pretending to be doing something to the old stove pipe that sallied forth from the corrugated tin end of his dwelling and issued up at an uncertain angle bearing a thin stream of smoke.

Three men who lived in the next house below hurried around their own shack several times, casting frowning furtive glances toward the invasion, muttering words about strangers who brought alien labor into a neighborhood, instead of hiring help already on the spot.

Down at the corner a scrawny middle-aged woman who "boarded" seven little boys for a living, in a four-roomed dwelling, came out with all her household and drew up frankly along the dilapidated fence to watch proceedings.

Stray men came up singly from the way of the dump and strolled by, looking long at the new building. It was plain that Thurlow's reconstruction act was causing no small consternation in the neighborhood.

Thurlow watched this inspection without seeming to do so, while he worked, and tried to figure out just what it meant. Finally he heard one of the seven little boys who had loitered about in the yard ask Rilla, "What youall a gonta do? Keep peegs in that there end?" and he and his sister suddenly broke down and laughed long and loud.

But the woodshed was finally in place and firmly nailed to the house, the helpers departed, the family withdrew to privacy, and the neighborhood had a conclave in the farthest house to decide what it was all about and what should be done about it, if anything. It was the general consensus of opinion that the Reeds were setting up some sort of illicit liquor business and must be watched. Meachin Street could not afford rivals.

The next morning Mrs. O'Hennessy, the old woman next door, tapped at the door, a cracked teacup in her hand.

"Cud ya lind me a bit pinch o' sugar to put in me sup o' tay? There ain't ben a grain o' sugar in the house fer a week, an' I'm that hungered fer it I can't go no longer."

"Why, of course. Come in," said Mother Reed, who had opened the door.

The old woman shuffled in and slid down on an upholstered chair near the door, sitting on its edge, one hand spread out on the cushion, as a child might do, and stared down at the upholstery and then around the room.

Mrs. Reed took the cup, filling it with sugar, and brought it back.

"You live next door?" she said pleasantly. "I haven't had time yet to look around and know my neighbors' faces, but I shall expect to get acquainted soon."

The old woman lifted bleared eyes to Mother Reed's kindly face and stared.

"Sure, I lives next door, but what wud the loikes uv you do bein' acquainted wi' me? You with yer pianna an' yer stuffed chairs! We ain't got but two chairs in our house. The rest are broke. My ole man broke 'em las' toime he was took away with the tremuns. So when they're both to hum, an' Bat wants ta set—Bat's my son—*I* gotta stan' up!"

"Why, that's too bad!" said Mother Reed sympathetically, suppressing an inward shudder at a neighbor who made a habit of delirium tremens. "Are they so badly broken your son couldn't mend them? I have some very fine glue I can lend him if he wants to try."

"Who? Bat? He wouldn't bother. He never does nothin', only jes' eat. Oh, we'll make out. We're use to it! What all you goin' ta do with the new end ta the house? Little Davy Macgargle said you was goin' ta raise pigs in it. Ef tha's so I'm glad ya didn't put yer addition on my soide the house. I never could stand schwine, they make such a terrible noise alla toime, an' a stench too. But o' course some don't mind that. It's all in how you was raised. Me, I was raised respectable. We never let the schwine run like some do, right inta the house. Only the hens, o' course, they cum in ta pick up scraps. It saves a heap o' trouble ta let the hens run in an' out. They always clean up after we've et. But if you're useta pigs, why I 'spose it's the same like."

Mrs. Reed barely suppressed another shudder, but she maintained a partial smile as she said pleasantly, "Oh, no. We don't keep pigs. I wouldn't care for pigs in the house either."

Rilla behind the kitchen door was bent double with suppressed laughter, and then her eyes filled with tears to think of her lady-mother companioning as a neighbor with such, the very scum of the earth!

"Youse gonta keep hens?"

"Well, no, I don't think we shall. Not now anyway. I've never kept hens. I spend a lot of time in my garden."

"H'm! Can't do much with a garden in winter!" said the old woman, taking up a pinch of the sugar and running it slowly through her dirty fingers. "Well, thin, whut's the new place fer ef 'taint fer hens ur pigs?"

"Oh, just another room," said Mrs. Reed with a smile. "These rooms are smaller than our old home and we can't get all our furniture in. My son thought it would make the house look better, too. He likes to fix up things for us."

"He does? Well, he ain't much like my Bat. But your son'll be gettin' tied up ta some gal cum another year likely, an' thin whar'll you be? Ain't you got no man?"

"No," said Mrs. Reed steadily, gravely, with a sweet light of sorrow in her eyes. "My husband went to heaven a few months ago. It's been hard to get along without him."

"*Heav'n!*" cackled the old crone. "How d'ya know that?"

"Because he was a Christian." Mrs. Reed spoke gently as to a little child. "Because he had accepted the Lord Jesus as his Saviour and was trusting in His blood shed on the cross to save him from sin."

Mrs. Reed spoke slowly, deliberately, determined that if the woman had never heard salvation before she should hear it now. But the woman only stared, and then cackled again.

"You musta had a mighty good man ef you're that sure, just a little reason loike that! Me, I'd know my ole man was goneta the other place sure 'nough!" And she cackled loudly as if it were a great joke.

"My husband was a very good man," said Mrs. Reed gravely, "but it isn't being good that takes us to heaven."

"It ain't? Whut is ut thin?"

"It's believing on the Lord Jesus, the Son of God, who died on the cross to take the punishment for all of us sinners."

The woman stared.

"Be you a sinner? Ya don't look it."

"We are all sinners in God's eyes. You and I and everybody."

"*I* ain't sa bad!" said the poor creature, lifting her sagging chin. "I don't steal like some. But God—! I don't know's I'd b'lieve on Him! He's got it in fer me! I ain't had nuthin' but bad luck since I cum ta this dingblasted country. God don't loike the loikes uv me!"

"Oh, yes, He does!" said Mrs. Reed earnestly. "He loves you!"

"Oh, yeah?" said the old woman, rising contemptuously. "Me, with that Bat fer a son, an' that louse fer a husband? Ya think He loves *me?* Ya got anuther guess acomin'!"

"But He does. He sent His Son to die for you." Mrs. Reed was very much in earnest now. She felt somehow as if she just must get the truth across to this poor sin-darkened mind. "Listen! These are Jesus' own words for you: 'God so loved the world that He gave His only begotten Son that *whosoever* believeth on Him, should not perish but have everlasting life.'"

The old woman stared.

"Where did ye get the loikes of that?"

"In the Bible."

"You think God loves *me?* Well, you don't know me, that's all!" and she laughed a wild hilarious cackle. Then suddenly sobering she looked around and caught sight of Rilla's photograph on the mantel. Her mother had just found it in the bureau drawer that morning and put it up.

"That your gal?"

"Yes," said Rilla's mother.

"She married yit?"

"Oh, no!" said the mother quickly. "She's very young. She hasn't finished her schooling yet."

"Ho, ho! School! Nobody don't need no schooling down here on this street. She'll get married. You see! Funny if she an' my boy Bat would get tied up, wouldn't it? Happens that way sometimes."

The mother barely restrained a desire to strike the poor toothless old hag and drive her from the house.

"My daughter will not be married for a long time yet," said Rilla's mother with dignity.

"Girls grow up quick down here!" said the caller significantly.

"Not if their mothers take care of them," said Mrs. Reed, and suddenly felt that she could bear no more.

After the woman had left Rilla found her mother in a paroxysm of weeping.

"Now, Mumsie," she comforted, "you didn't mind what an ignorant old woman like that said!"

"I suppose not," said her mother, smiling through her tears, "but somehow she got terribly on my nerves. The impertinent old hag! But I know I'm wrong. She's probably one of the reasons why God sent us down here. Did you see how ignorant she was? Did you hear the poor thing say God didn't care for her?"

"I'm not at all sure God sent us here, Mumsie," said Rilla seriously. "I think it was maybe that you couldn't trust Him to send us work and you got penurious and wanted to save money."

"No, dear, I think we should have come. Only"—she shivered—"that *Bat!* Have you seen him, dear?"

"I should say I have, and he's all and more than you think. But you don't need to worry about him. He won't bother me any."

"Well, don't go outdoors when he's around. I can't bear to think of his looking at you, a creature like that! I never realized it might be as bad as this. I never thought of the neighbors at all."

Rilla kissed her mother and laughed.

"You'll be Christianizing the whole street pretty soon," she said. "You'll be teaching them how to make over their houses and plant April gold around them by spring, if we stay that long. Personally I'm going to try to sell this house before that time, and get you into a better neighborhood. Mother, just think how perfectly dreadful it would be if Thurlow and I should come home some day and find you over at Bat's mother's house playing bridge with the ladies of Meachin Street!"

So they laughed it off, but nevertheless the mother had a new anxiety, which did not decrease as the days passed by, and new phases of the street were revealed to her.

But Thurlow went on with his improvements, and before long had several pleasant windows and doors cut in the woodshed addition. It was slow work of course because he spent every morning downtown searching diligently for a job. But as soon as the new wing was open to the rest of the house, Rilla and her mother came in with paint brushes and curtains and glorified the place till it shone—whitewashed walls with a little delicate green stenciled border. Rilla did that, perched on the top of the stepladder. Luckily the ceilings were not high. White curtains at the windows, rugs on the dining room floor, linoleum on the kitchen, bright pans and dishes ranged on hooks along the wall and shelves that Thurlow put up. It was good they had plenty of nice things to make the inside of their home pleasant and thus make up for the desolation on the outside.

Then the cold weather set in, creeping slowly upon

them, and Thurlow searched the secondhand stores for little wood stoves, to heat the house more adequately. He cut down two dead trees at the back of the lot, cut up the wood and housed it close to the back kitchen door, sheltered by a crude lattice and a roof, so they would not need to go out in a storm to get it.

But all the time as he worked his face grew graver and more troubled. For it was beginning to be serious now. He hadn't got a job yet, and he had to own to himself at least that there wasn't a shred of a prospect in sight for one.

Also he had letters from his college friends beseeching him to return, offering him jobs galore to finance his winter expenses, and even one from a small group of his fraternity friends, offering to lend him money which he could repay after he was done his education and had a good position in life. But he had steadily refused every offer. He could not bring himself to live on his friends, nor to borrow money without any prospect of repaying it for years perhaps. Moreover he dared not leave his mother and sister without protection.

He had not told his mother about these letters, but Rilla had seen the postmarks, forwarded from the old home address, and guessed what was going on. She and her mother often talked it over, and at last they broached the subject of college again to Thurlow.

His mother showed him how she had prepared his things ready to pack, she told him they were all cosily fixed and that she felt he owed a duty to his father to finish out the education he had started him on. She said a great many other things and Thurlow threw down the saw and hammer wherewith he was fashioning another shelf in the kitchen and just looked at her. He did not attempt to speak, just let her talk until she had said her say. His arms were folded and his face was grave and quiet. And when she was quite done and could not think of another argument, he just said:

"No, Mother, I can't do it." And then he walked out of the kitchen and took his hat and went into the gathering twilight, leaving the two women worried and breathless.

Later in the evening he returned to them wearing the uniform of a city policeman. He had got a job at last, and he walked into the house grimly and stood before his waiting mother and sister.

They looked at him and their eyes grew wide with horror.

"Oh, Thurlow! What have you done, my son?" his mother cried.

"I've got a job at last, thank the Lord," said Thurlow Reed fervently, "and now I can hold up my head with a little self-respect. Don't take it that way, Mother! It's perfectly respectable to be a policeman, and believe me I'm going to be a good policeman!"

"But, Thurl, what will Barby say?" broke out Rilla with lips white with apprehension.

"What the heck do I care what Barbara Sherwood says? It's none of her business anyway, and besides she isn't here to see."

"But she will be sometime, my son!"

"She's nothing to me any more, Mother. Put that out of the picture. I'm done with that life. I'm going to make good in this one. Now, tell me if I make a good-looking cop—and *smile!*"

Out in the road a shadowy group of loiterers coming back from a rendezvous around a bonfire by the dump, caught sight of one of their enemies going in the door, and huddled together to discuss it, then stole in single file across the road and stood at an advantageous point where they had often stood before to peer within a window and make sure that their eyes had not betrayed them. Was that really a cop living in that house? Was that what his game was after all, camouflaging his movements by bringing his women folks down and pretending to live there, just so he could watch their movements? And now what were they going to do about it?

10

THE next Sunday they went to the Mission to church.

Thurlow had almost forgotten the blue-eyed girl in the meanwhile. His mind had been engaged in watching for a letter from Barbara Sherwood—a real letter, not just a scrawl around some pictures of herself and his rivals. He had brooded not a little over the subject and had told himself bitterly that he would not write her a word until he had a real letter from her, the kind of letter she used to write when he first went away to college.

There had been good reasons, every Sunday since the stranger had knocked at the door asking the way, why the Reeds could not go to the little church, but now Thurlow could evade it no longer, and they went.

The girl, what was her name?—Oh, yes, Sandra Cameron—came toward them with a smile as they entered.

"You have come at last," she said. "I'm go glad. Here I've been telling everybody down here what a musical find I had discovered, and then you never came!"

"We couldn't come sooner, my dear," said Mrs. Reed, looking about her on the neat little audience room with pleasure. "We had so much to do getting settled. But we've been meaning to come."

"Well, it couldn't be more opportune," said Sandra, "for the man who leads the singing is down with the grippe, and there isn't a soul to play the little old tinpanny piano."

"Oh, but you're not going to put us to work the first day out, are you?" objected Thurlow in a panic, almost ready to turn and flee.

There was something in the blue eyes as the girl looked up at him wistfully that made him yield after all, and stalk up to the front following her. Rilla had already succumbed and was being led to the piano. So they settled down as naturally as if it had been their home church.

Sandra found a comfortable place for Mrs. Reed near the front, provided her with a hymn book and Bible— there were plenty of Bibles for everybody, scattered all over the room—and then settled down with a flock of young girls.

"But don't you play yourself?" Rilla had asked when besought to do the playing.

"Why, yes, a little," said Sandra, "but you see it's important for me to sit with those girls. They are so young and full of spirits, and they will whisper and giggle in the midst of the very most interesting part of the service unless someone is there to keep them quiet. Besides, my playing isn't so great. I haven't got that leading quality that I recognized in you. You're used to playing for singing."

"Only for my brother, and a little at school," said Rilla.

"Well, then you have a lot of talent." Sandra smiled and there came a glow into Rilla's sad young heart. She had felt so separated from all her kind, and from the life she had known in the old home, and somehow it seemed especially desolate on Meachin Street on Sundays. But here, given something real to do, being a part of a service that had a spirit of worship right from the start, new hope sprang up within her, so she turned to the page in the hymn book with pleasure.

The place was filling rapidly. They were not stylish people, but there were many that were refined looking. They wore simple clothes but Rilla's keen young eyes detected a certain air of being to the manner born that rested her. Perhaps she was a snob, she thought to herself, but she would have hated it if all the people down here had been like that awful O'Hennessy woman, Bat's mother. Yet there were some of the poorer class, too. Not quite so far down in the social scale as Bat's mother, not dirty, nor ragged, not quite so ignorant, but plenty of very plain decent people, with clean but mended garments, old-fashioned, and odd, some of them, but most of them with that look of eagerness in their eyes, that hunger for what they evidently found in this house of God.

If Rilla had been given her choice she would not have selected this plain little chapel in this out-of-the-way corner of the city for her regular place of worship, but since they were aliens from their own natural environment, and since her sore young heart longed to hide from her old associates, she was glad that so tolerable a place had been found, for she knew her mother would never have been satisfied to stay away perpetually from church as they had been doing since they moved. So Rilla was pleased and interested, and struck the first chords of the opening hymn with her firm true touch, making the little congregation sit up and take notice of the sweet-faced girl who was at the piano.

And there was Thurlow standing up on the platform

quite at his ease, conducting the music. His rich full voice rang out thrilling on the little church and filled the listeners with a joyous astonishment, making everybody, whether they could sing or not, join in. Of course Thurlow had sung a lot at college. He had been leader of the Glee Club last winter. Of course he wouldn't mind conducting a little crowd of plain people like this. Rilla's heart swelled with pride. She was proud of her brother, and her brother's lovely voice.

The singing went well. The people took hold with a will. Thurlow sang a solo, and his mother sat there with tears in her eyes which she would not let fall, and thought of her boy, her dear boy, going to be *a policeman!* Oh, if his father could know, how unhappy he would be—even in heaven! Or would he? Did a heavenly point of view show up reasons that earthly minds could not foresee? Was God directing this summary move of Thurlow's, or was it the devil, as she had been thinking? She watched her boy as he sang the tender words of the hymn the minister had requested.

> "'Man of sorrows,' what a name
> For the Son of God who came
> Ruined sinners to reclaim!
> Halellujah! what a Saviour!"

She was proud of her boy. But she wondered if he was really a child of that Saviour! Oh, he was a church member. Both of her children had united with the church when they were quite young, but did they really trust her God? She wished she knew. The future loomed dark for both of them and she felt so weary sometimes, and so unable to guide them. It seemed a hard way ahead in spite of her indomitable spirit.

They lingered to talk a few minutes with some of the

people. The minister was most cordial and friendly, and said he and his wife would come and see them. The girl Sandra smiled upon them as if they were old acquaintances. It was all very pleasant.

They walked home slowly through the dark little streets. The pavements were very rough and the young man held his mother's arm and guided her over the bad places.

"Well, what did you think of it?" asked the mother fearfully. If Thurlow didn't like it she would have trouble in getting him to go again. He hadn't been liking their regular minister at all lately.

"Why, I thought it was all very pleasant," he said, "didn't you? They seem a lot friendlier than back at our old church. I liked that preacher. He isn't high-hat, he seems human. And he made the Bible a lot clearer than anybody I ever heard preach before."

"Yes," said Rilla. "I liked him. I'm going up to join that Bible class they say he has. He's asked me to play every Sunday. The woman they had has gone away for the winter to teach somewhere. They say she wasn't very good anyway. And they asked you to sing again, didn't they, Thurl? Did you tell him you would?"

"I told him I wasn't sure what times I would have off yet," said Thurlow with a reserve in his tone, and they suddenly fell silent, thinking about Thurlow as a policeman. He went on duty for the first time tomorrow morning, and it was like a heavy weight on their hearts as they thought of it. It was respectable of course, and it was grand of him to insist on working and being on his own and protecting them. But—*a policeman!* They had always thought of him as winning honors in college, and then turning out a professor, or a specialist of some kind, either in machinery, or medicine, or some really intellectual job.

Slowly they walked through dark narrow streets with lumpy brick pavements of ancient setting never repaired, streets where people huddled in corners, two or three together, and conversed furtively, streets where the only lights were brilliant red names of different liquors set forth in weird picture-letters. Life was set for them hereafter in sordid places, and the only bright thought seemed to be the plain little friendly chapel where God was honored. What was it all for? they wondered, each in his or her own separate thoughts. Was it some lesson to be learned, some punishment—for what? Was it for always or would the weird unhappy dream pass and they wake up again happy in the right kind of a home?

But when they turned into Meachin Street there was their light burning clearly from the mantel in the little parlor. Queer to think that little drab cottage with the unfinished lean-to was their only home! The mother looked ahead with troubled eyes. Perhaps she ought not to have brought them down here. Perhaps she was all wrong and ought to have put her pride away and insisted that they go to some of their father's friends and borrow some money. Or insisted that Thurlow take it from his fraternity brothers. Anything rather than to let him give up altogether his connection with the world of letters. How his father would have grieved if he had known!

As they passed the O'Hennessy homestead there were sounds of loud altercation, oaths flung back and forth in high screaming tones and deep vindictive roars, a smart stinging slap with outcry, and the crashing of some article of furniture as it came into collision with an old-fashioned iron stove. The sounds were so definite that one could identify them almost as if seeing them. There likely went Mrs. O'Hennessy's second chair. Now both Bat and his mother would have to stand whenever the old man was at home. Mrs. Reed shuddered as she went by. Stealthy shadows seemed to move crazily away from the front of the shack and fade into darkness. What a neighborhood to have to live in! Oh, why didn't she realize how impossible it was going to be? But it was too late now to do anything. It would cost too much to move, even if there was a place they could possibly afford.

The brightness from the cottage shone out and made a path of light toward them as they arrived in front of their own place, and Mrs. Reed hastened up the walk, glad that here at least was a refuge from the night and the dirt and the unwholesomeness. The house they had managed to clean up till its interior at least was bearable. When spring came they might be able to do something with the outside of the house also, and the yard. But they couldn't be expected to clean up the neighborhood. Even if their neighbors made an attempt to clean up their filthy yards and houses a little, following their example, that wouldn't clean up the moral atmosphere! Oh, God, did you send us down here to do that? To teach these people how to be saved? How to live better lives? It didn't seem as if it could be any worse, nor as bad over in Africa, or China, or India, or any of the God-forgetting countries where people went to be missionaries. Could it be that because they had failed to take an interest in spreading His gospel through the world, He had put what was left of the Reeds' happy family, down into this terrible place to shine for Him? To witness for Him in this, one of the darkest places she had ever seen? Could there be darker places than this yet upon the earth?

Mother Reed went quickly up the steps and waited fearsomely while Thurlow unlocked the door, in sudden panic to get out of this dark strange night that was all about her and seemed so infested with shadowy presences, and wild angry noises, mingled with drunken curses.

So they stepped inside the cottage and talked cheerfully to one another. Thurlow lighted two more lamps.

"Let's have a try at some of those hymns, Rilla," he said as he set one of the lamps where its light fell upon the music rack. "My! I'm thirsty! I'll get a pitcher of water."

He took one of the smaller lamps and went through the new dining room to the kitchen. They had only moved their furniture into it a couple of days before, and it still looked pleasant and interesting to them. But as he passed through he noticed that both doors of the sideboard were standing wide open, and three of the drawers were part way pulled out. It struck him absent-mindedly as strange that Rilla had been so careless, but he was thirsty and went on into the kitchen to get the water.

But as he set the lamp down on the kitchen table its light fell in a half circle on the neat oilcloth of the floor, and there right in the midst of the radius of light he saw a big muddy footprint!

He stooped down in horror and studied it. Yes, it was mud! A real footprint. He couldn't explain it. Then he felt a draught of air and looking up he found that the back kitchen window was up half-way! And he had left it carefully locked! That was the last thing he did before he went out to church, lock every window!

Examination of the window catch showed that it had been jimmied open, and that the window fastener was broken, snapped in two! Someone had been breaking in! He went swiftly back into the dining room, glancing into the open doors and drawers, but at a hasty glance could not seem to find that anything was missing. He closed the drawers and doors quietly and went back to the kitchen, giving a quick look around. Someone had been in here! What for?

He put the window down softly, setting the broken catch in place. Mother mustn't know about this. He must manage somehow to make things safe without startling her and Rilla. Not tonight anyway. They wouldn't sleep.

While he was getting the pitcher of water he was thinking what to do. Then he went to his tool box which was under the kitchen table, took out his brace and bit, and quickly drilled a hole straight through the window sashes to within a quarter of an inch of the outside, and in this he inserted a stout spike of a nail, drawing the white curtain in place over it, and gathering up the chips from the hole. The window was firmly fastened now and could not be opened from outside unless they used dynamite.

"What on earth are you doing, Thurlow," called Rilla. "I thought you wanted to sing."

"Coming!" sang Thurlow cheerfully. "I'm bringing you a pitcher of water. There aren't any apples, are there, Mother?"

"Why, no, child," said his mother, appearing in the door, "you aren't hungry again, are you? Would you like a sandwich? I'll get you one."

Thurlow swept his handkerchief over the footprint, gathering up the mud. He swiftly stowed it in his pocket, then taking the lamp in one hand and the pitcher in the other, he hurried back to the living room, saying the first crazy thing that came into his head so that his mother should not suspect how troubled he was.

"Lamps and pitchers!" he laughed. "You haven't either of you got a trumpet, have you? Wasn't there some old guy in the Bible did something with lamps, pitchers and trumpets?"

"That was Gideon," laughed Rilla. "You don't suppose we're put here to surround Meachin Street, and smash our pitchers and blow our trumpets and let our light shine and take Meachin Street, do you?"

"Well, there might be worse duties then taking Meachin Street for the Lord," said the mother.

"Yes, let's take Meachin Street!" said Thurlow grimly. "Which song shall we sing in place of blowing our trumpets? Here, how will this one do?"

Rilla sat down at the piano, and presently their blended voices rang out in a queer little jig of a chorus neither of them ever heard before. They sang it half laughing, but the words were quite distinct out there in the shadows where were listening ears:

> "Oh, yes, my friend, there's something more,
> Something more than gold;
> To know your sins are all forgiven
> Is something more than gold!"

They sang it through several times, the last time almost gravely as the meaning of the words stole into their own hearts, and certainly if there were listeners outside they would never forget those words, linked as they were to that unforgettable rhythm.

Then suddenly the rhythm changed, the voices grew more serious as they poured forth like a message:

> "Nor silver nor gold hath obtained my redemption,
> Nor riches of earth could have saved my poor soul;
> The blood of the cross is my only foundation,
> The death of my Saviour now maketh me whole.
> I am redeemed, but not with silver;
>
> I am bought, but not with gold;

> *Bought with a price,—the blood of Jesus,*
> *Precious price of love untold."*

They sang for almost an hour, and the melodies linked to priceless words went forth into the silent night, to souls in the darkness, bitter, sin-laden souls. For Meachin Street had stopped fighting and cursing and was listening. Sodden hearts were suddenly arrested by strange new thoughts borne on the wings of song.

At last Mother Reed, soothed and somehow strangely comforted by hearing her children sing, herded them to bed. Tomorrow would be another day, but at least she could sleep tonight, and tomorrow there would be new strength.

So mother and daughter soon slept, but Thurlow lay and thought about that footprint, and how he could guard his family, and what he ought to do. Listening to every stealthy footstep, every stir of creature and snapping of twig, even almost hearing the courses of the stars on their mighty way through the ages, he slept almost none at all.

And tomorrow he was going to be a policeman!

II

RILLA went out one day and got herself a job in a bank, in the older part of the city from which modern business had grown away. It was not a big job, just a beginner's job as an assistant, but it had possibilities of a rise later when one of the other girls got married, and it wasn't too far from Meachin Street. She could even walk it in pleasant weather, though her mother objected to the neighborhood through which she had to pass and insisted that she take a bus which came within four blocks of home, or the trolley which was half a block farther away.

Rilla was very proud of the minute salary she was to get. It wasn't much, but it was something and she was helping. Moreover the hours were easy.

Thurlow was a little worried about her leaving her mother alone, but the mother laughed at the idea. She was not keen on having Rilla working at her age, but almost anything was better than staying around Meachin Street all day long. It wasn't a good atmosphere for a young girl. She would get to moping. And the work in the bank was pleasant and respectable. Besides there was a woman working there, an elderly woman, whom Mrs. Reed had known for years, and she felt Rilla would be safe there.

So Rilla in a simple dark blue dress with white collar and cuffs, and muffled to the ears, for the weather was cold, started off the next Monday morning to her job, happy to be doing something real. Mother Reed watched her out of sight, and then flew back to her kitchen where she secretly baked and brewed delicious things to eat all the morning, and in the early afternoon packed them carefully in a basket and took the bus downtown to the Woman's Exchange where she entered her name as a regular baker from whom various edibles could be ordered. Then she went home and made doughnuts all the afternoon, packing them into neat pasteboard boxes that she had purchased for the purpose, stowing them safely in the closet till morning, and saving out a big stone jarful for the family, to explain the delicious odor of them they would find when they reached home. The big pot of soup that had been getting itself cooked all day on the lowest burner of the oilstove made the dinner, with doughnuts and apples for dessert, and the children never suspected how their mother had gone into business.

But the same cannot be said of the neighbors.

Mrs. O'Hennessy appeared on the scene the next morning, just as Mrs. Reed was about to go out to take her doughnuts to the Exchange.

"I come over ta see what was it I smelled last night. It smelled like Christmas when I was a kid."

"Oh, that was doughnuts I was frying," smiled Mrs. Reed. "Would you like to taste them? I'll get you some," and she vanished into the pantry, coming back with a generous plateful.

She found Mrs. O'Hennessy standing in front of Rilla's picture, looking wistfully at it.

"I had a gal oncet," she said mournfully, and then with a sigh, "but she went to the bad. She couldn't stand the old man an' she jes' went to the bad. She hated the ugly shack, and the dump an' everythin', an' she wanted pretty cloes, so she jes' went away one day an' never come back."

The mother sighed sentimentally, and there was a waft of alcoholic odor from her breath. Then she turned and caught sight of the doughnuts and seized one avidly.

"They're turrible good," she mumbled with her mouth full, and sugar all over her grimy chin. "I ain't tasted anythin' so good sence I was a kid. You all must be turrible rich havin' such wealthy cookin'! Me, I don't get such loike food. Not ner less it's a death in the fambly ur Bat makes a big haul on sweepstakes. Oncet he won over two hunnerd bucks an' we had roast pig. But I don't look fer that ta happen agin. You all must be wealthy. Havin' such loike this ta eat."

"Oh, no," smiled Mrs. Reed. "We never were wealthy, but we lost what little we did have not long ago when the bank failed. No, I make these for sale."

The heavy jaws suddenly stopped halfway in a chew, and the dirty hand slowly handed over the small portion of doughnut still remaining between thumb and finger.

"You chargin' me fer this?" she asked, her eyes growing small and malicious. "I ain't got no money, not a cent!"

"Oh, no!" laughed Mrs. Reed. "I'm not charging you for these. I sell them downtown, but I'm not so poor I can't give a neighbor a bit of my cooking now and then. Here, take this plateful over to the family, maybe they'll enjoy them too!" and she handed out the whole plateful.

The old woman looked at her wonderingly.

"All them?" she said, incredulously.

Then slowly she held out her apron—it was such a dirty apron—as if she expected them to be dumped into it, and there was a kind of awe in her voice.

"Oh, take the plate right along," urged Mrs. Reed pleasantly. "You can bring it back next time you come to call, you know."

"Take that plate? That purty plate? My, I wisht my Rosie was here ta see it! Say, you *mean* it?"

"Of course!" said Mrs. Reed, feeling a sudden sting of tears to her eyes at the thought of what this was meaning to the old woman. What a great thing it was in her barren life to have a neighbor offer a bite of something nice on a pretty plate. Oh, God, was perhaps this old woman's soul a prize to be won for heaven?

Then a sudden crafty look came into the old woman's face, and made her look like an old squirrel who was going to venture all for a nut held out by a friendly hand. She reached out an excited hand, took the plate, and with a stealthy look behind her she stole out of the door and hurried to her own abode. When she reached the shelter of her own yard she paused a moment and looked back. Mrs. Reed was just coming out of the door with her boxes of doughnuts in her arms, and the old woman waited until she was in front of her house before she called out:

"I thank 'e!" And then as Mrs. Reed smiled she added, "D'ye mind ef I keep the plate till termorra? I'd like ta show it ta me old man!"

Mrs. Reed's impulse was to tell the woman she could have the plate. It was only an odd one that she did not value highly. Then it occurred to her that perhaps she would get too much the reputation of being wealthy if she began by giving everything that was admired. Perhaps she would be wiser not to do too much. Some of these people were perhaps beggars by nature. And moreover, she must not seem to be above them in possessions if she would hope to win them and give them a message of better things. So she only smiled again and said: "Certainly, that will be all right. I shall not need the plate until tomorrow. Bring it at your convenience."

It is doubtful if Mrs. O'Hennessy knew what convenience meant, but she stood in the shelter of her old shack with the plate of doughnuts in her hand until Mrs. Reed went out of sight around the corner.

Mrs. Reed certainly would have been surprised if she could have seen the reception that Mrs. O'Hennessy presently had, uninvited, from the street. One after the other neighbors came even from up the next block, with cups or pans to beg the loan of salt or sugar or baking powder, or an onion. One came with a hammer borrowed over a month ago that was never intended to be returned, till this sudden desire to have curiosity satisfied made it a necessity. It could always be borrowed again of course. And to each and every comer the flattered Mrs. O'Hennessy exhibited the rapidly diminishing pile of doughnuts, wiping off the sugar from her chin, and adding many details of the house next door that certainly would have surprised the Reeds could they have heard them. Mrs. O'Hennessy had not been so much in the limelight since her Rosie had finally left home three years before.

At last there were only three doughnuts left, and with regret she put away two of them for Bat, and his father. She dared not make away with them all, since the knowledge of them had become public property. The third one she left on the plate for further exhibit should any from around the corner hear of her treasure and come to see it. But when they came she sent them all away with their mouths watering and plenty to talk about.

The next morning while Mrs. Reed was making little apple turnovers, all lovely cinnamon and sugar and thick syrupy juice, she heard a knock at the door, and opening it she saw a row of seven dirty little boys, all about the same age—the small "Welfare boarders" of one Mrs. Butts who lived the second door below.

They stood in a procession, each with different degrees of uncouthness, soiled hands and faces, soiled garments such as they were, eager hungry looks in their eyes, and each held up a penny. They did not state that they had stolen the pennies out of Mrs. Butts' pocket-book while her back was turned. They merely held up the pennies.

"We-we-we—wanta—buy—*cakes!*" stated the oldest boy, who stuttered.

Mrs. Reed looked at them in astonishment.

"You want what?" she said kindly, her eyes kindling with pity at the forlorn little procession of mere babies, cast on Meachin Street for mercy. Hungry, eager little eyes looked up into hers confidently.

"We—wanta—buy—*cakes!*" stated the stutterer again.

"Don't you all sell cakes, with sugar like on outside?" spoke up the second in the procession. He had deep blue eyes and thin straw-colored hair, falling down over them so that he had acquired a strange habit of tossing back his head every time he wanted to look out from under his thatch.

"We got pennies," said the third one anxiously, holding his up to view.

"Oh, my dears!" said Mrs. Reed. "Yes, I'll get you some cakes."

She hurried back to her stone jar. Thurlow had taken

two when he started off to work, and Rilla another when she went to her bank. There were only a few left, but they were enough to go around. She would have to make another batch of course, so her own children shouldn't wonder why the ones they had left were all gone, but she could not deny those poor hungry little boys. It went against her to take their pennies, but of course if she did not she would be swamped with such customers. And even so, she would be playing a losing game if this kept up. Next time she would have to tell them she had none, for she just couldn't bring herself to tell them that a penny would not cover the cost of the cake.

But she took the seven doughnuts out and her heart swelled with love and pity again as she saw the eagerness with which they fell upon the delectable cake.

The little boys settled down on the ground in front of the house to eat their treat, and Mrs. Reed lingered a moment watching them, asking their names, and where they lived, and getting various bits of gossip and much insight into human history thereby. Then one small urchin spoke up suddenly with his mouth filled so he could scarcely articulate.

"Where is it buried?"

"Where is what buried? What do you mean, Jack?"

"Your gold!" said Jack, pausing in his mastication to speak impressively. "You got gold buried out here in your yard. Where is it? We wantta see it."

"Gold?" said Mrs. Reed. "I have no gold."

"Yes, you got gold buried," insisted Jack. "Them mens what lives tother side of our house saw the man 'at lives with you buryin' it in the night. Out in the yard he saw him buryin' it. They all seen him. The night you all come they seen him buryin' it. They stood out there by the fact'ry an' seen him bury it in the yard. I heard 'em tell about it."

"Oh," said Mrs. Reed, sudden enlightenment coming to her, and her face breaking into amused smiles, "that must have been my April gold you mean."

Several weeks before, Mrs. Reed, wandering about the place investigating the whole yard, had discovered what Thurlow had been doing that first night when he stayed out nearly the whole night. But she had kept his secret, and intended to be fully surprised when April came.

"What's April gold?" asked a little redhead with an evil eye. "You can't kid us. We heard them mens talkin'."

"No, I'm not kidding you," smiled the woman, talking like a mother to the belligerent little band. They had eaten her cakes, and their mouths were still sugary with them, but they were ready to fight her now for a sight of her gold. How she longed to take them and wash their hostile little faces and comb their hair and make them happy and comfortable, but she knew she mustn't. Even now her turnovers were in danger of burning in the oven, and she had much to do before night, but she had to linger a moment and answer their furious young questions.

"No, I'm not kidding you, dear children. April gold is flowers. Beautiful bright yellow flowers, yellow as gold. And what my son buried was bulbs, seeds and bulbs of flowers. He put them into the ground all around the edge of the fence and behind the house and in the garden everywhere, and they will lie there all winter and die, but in the spring they will come to life again. You watch when April comes and you will see little green shoots begin to come up through the ground, and by and by there will come buds, lovely big yellow buds, and then one morning when the rain has fallen, and the sun is bright again you will see a burst of bright yellow flowers, all golden in the morning like sunshine. My April gold! That's what I call my April gold! Lovely golden flowers! You wait, and you watch, and then some morning you'll see a row of lovely golden flowers all about my yard, and then you come over to visit me and I'll give you each a golden flower to carry home with you."

"And will there be cakes, too?" asked the youngest one, licking his pitiful puny lips.

"Why—yes, there'll be cakes that day, cakes for all of you. As many cakes as you can eat," she promised recklessly. "You be good boys and wait and watch till April."

The hostility died out of the eyes and they grew round with wonder. The faces grew wistful and strangely innocent. They were all still for a minute and then one said:

"How can they come up and live again if they are dead? You said they have to die. My daddy died. He won't come up and be a flower, will he?"

Mrs. Reed's face was strangely tender.

"Yes, he will come up again at God's resurrection day," she said reverently. "He won't be a flower, but he'll be a living man, your father. And perhaps he'll be one of those who will be all golden with the glory of the Lord. Things die, but they live again! Jesus died and rose again from the dead. Don't you know about Jesus, how He died on the cross to save you from sin, and how He rose from the dead?"

"He's just a name," said the oldest boy contemptuously. "Just a name you say when you get mad. A name you curse with! I heard 'em say so!"

"He's the Name above every name," said the woman, watching the wise little sinners earnestly. "He's the King of Kings and Lord of Lords. He is the Saviour of the world. His name is the only name in all the world that can save people from everlasting death."

They looked at her solemnly, while she tried to tell them how He loved them enough to die for them, and then when she had to go because she smelled her baking burning, they straggled away, saying they would be back in time for the April gold.

And Mother Reed went back to her work, wondering again if this was part of the reason why she had had to come down here and live, and whether there was really any hope for those puny contaminated little souls who were the offspring of the scum of the earth. Wondering whether they were worth so much to the Heavenly Father, that He had thought it right to deprive her own two bright good beautiful children of their natural birthright on this earth in order that a message might be brought to Meachin Street.

All the morning she thought about it, and prayed about it as she turned out delicious turnovers and tarts and more doughnuts, and prayed for her two, even as she prayed for the little Welfare children.

And then strangely enough she thought of Barbara Sherwood, Thurlow's bright beautiful girl with the witching ways, the delicate manner, and the careful upbringing. What was Barbara going to think of them all when she got back? It was all quite irrelevant to what she had been thinking, but it came to her how far they seemed to have come into another world, quite another world, since Barbara said good-by and sailed away. She wondered if Thurlow felt it too?

12

A FEW days later Rilla, having decided to walk to her bank because it was so pleasant that morning, suddenly became aware of the shuffling gait of some person behind her, keeping pace with her.

At first she only quickened her gait, but the steps behind got no farther away. Nervously she turned to see who it was, and recognized Bat O'Hennessy. He leered at her triumphantly, and with a sudden stride was beside her.

"Didn't know who was trailin' ya, didya?" he said in an intimate tone.

Rilla looked up at him, and found to her astonishment that he was taller than she was. At a distance he had seemed such a little insignificant creature. Then she paused and gave him a cool stare.

"I'm sorry," she said coldly, "I don't believe I know you."

Bat grinned.

"Aw! High-hat, are ya? Well, you've met me all righty, and you'll meet me plenty yet. I live next door to ya, and I watched ya move in."

"Oh, I beg your pardon!" Rilla's tone was quite polite but there was a queer little catch in her throat that sounded frightened. "We're—neighbors then. That's—different!"

She tried to smile, but her lips were stiff and refused anything but a wry little shadow of her usual smile.

"Ya needn't get scared. I'm gonta walk a piece with ya. I thought it was time you an' me got acquainted." He was grinning into her face and his look chilled her to the soul.

"Yes?" she said faintly, still a quiver of a smile at the corner of her mouth. "But you know men don't usually speak to girls or walk with them until they have been introduced."

He grinned derisively.

"They do down on Meachin Street," he said. "I guess we'll make out 'thout an interduction. Where you goin' to?"

Rilla was too frightened to do much thinking. The streets were almost deserted. She wanted to dart away from him and run, but she couldn't tell what that long loose gait slouching along beside her could not do in the way of sprinting if she should, and she didn't know her way about these narrow devious streets as well as he did. It might be he would chase her into some blind alley and get her in a trap. She had read of such things. Instinctively she felt that her only safety lay in keeping cool, so, though her voice trembled the least little bit, she answered quite brightly, as if she were conversing with a child:

"Why, I'm going to my work. Are you on your way to your work?"

"Work?" he laughed. *"Me? Work?* Haw, haw! No, ma'am, I don't do no work. I jes' loaf. There's easier ways of livin' than workin', don't you know that? A good looker like you shouldn't oughtta work. I can put you wise to a way to get a lotta money ef you know how ta keep yer trap shut."

"Oh, I *like* to work," said Rilla cheerfully, too cheerfully, for there was a hint of a sob in the end of her words and her heart was beating wildly.

He looked at her queerly.

"Say, you *are* scared!" he chuckled, "but you needn't try ta bolt on me. I cud get a strangle holt on ya before ya cud wink yer eyes, an' there ain't no cops around these parts at this hour. They're all sleepin' off last night. Tell that ter yer big perlice-brother ef ya dare!"

Rilla remembered a story she had heard about a man who was shipwrecked on a cannibal island and who held off his would-be diners by telling them long lingoes, reciting poems and orations interspersed by excited gesticulations. That wouldn't work with this creature by her side. He could speak English and would understand what she was saying. But mightn't she use the same principle, turn his interest away from herself by saying something interesting, *any*thing, just to keep him talking until someone came along to whom she could appeal for help? She searched her mind wildly for some theme, meantime trying to make time.

"Oh, God, help me! Help! Help! Help!" her heart was crying out. She had never before been in a situation where she felt so utterly helpless, where she felt that only God could help her. This creature slouching along by her side had seemed puny and insignificant when she had viewed him from her own doorstep, as he stood by the rickety fence next door, but now he loomed large and repulsive, and his eyes took liberties with her spirit as he leered down at her. But she must not let him see this. Mad dogs and wild animals instinctively knew when humans were afraid of them. Perhaps it was so with men like this one. She must keep up her courage. She must show him she was not afraid! Oh, God! Help!

"What makes you think I am afraid of you?" she said, drawing herself to her slender height and wafting him an assured smile. "What harm could you possibly do me, even if you wanted to? Don't you know that my Father is watching you this very minute?"

She caught her breath at her own audacity, as she saw him give a quick furtive look behind him. Then she went on with confidence, a grave assurance in her tone:

"And don't you know that there are twelve legions of angels all around us this minute waiting to protect me? You can't see them, but they are there!"

A kind of wary fright came into Bat's eyes, and he turned, startled, and studied her sober young face from which all sign of fear had fled.

"You're kiddin' me!" he grinned, with yet that half-fearsome glance behind like a frightened rabbit.

"Oh, no, I'm not kidding you," said Rilla in a steady tone.

"Don't you know about those legions of angels?" Ah, she had her theme! She had been reading about it only yesterday in her morning devotions. "Did you never hear about Elisha? You know he was a prophet."

"One of these here that tells yer fortune?" grinned Bat affably.

"More wonderful than that," said Rilla earnestly, measuring the distance to the second corner where she knew the bus ought to be passing very soon. Could she keep him interested till she got there? She went on with her story.

"Why, there was a carpenter came to work on a house once and while he was cutting a beam the head of his ax fell into the river near where he was working, and he, the carpenter you know, cried out and felt very badly because the ax was borrowed. But Elisha came along and asked him where it fell, and Elisha cut a limb off a tree and threw it into the water in the place where the axhead had fallen, and the iron rose right up to the surface of the water and floated, so the carpenter got it again."

Bat's eyes narrowed as he watched her.

"No kiddin'?"

"No kidding," said Rilla earnestly. "He was a prophet, you know, a man of God, and he could do wonderful things. And there was a man named Benhadad who had it in for some of his enemies, and he planned to kill them, and he talked with some of his companions and planned how he would hide somewhere, and get his enemies as they passed by, and kill them all. And every time he planned it something happened that his enemies went some other way instead of the way they usually went, and Benhadad couldn't understand it. He thought some of his gang had turned traitor and told his enemy all about his plans, and he called them all together and asked them which of them had double-crossed him and gone over to the side of the enemy, and they all declared they hadn't, and then one of the gang told him that he knew how their enemies found out their plans. He said, 'That prophet Elisha is the one. He goes and tells your enemies every word you speak in your secret room.' So Benhadad wanted to know where he could find Elisha, and they told him he had gone to a place named Dothan. So Benhadad got all his gang together quickly and they drove by night, several cars full of them, all armed, and they came to the place where Elisha was staying while it was still dark, and they surrounded his house quietly—there were a great many of them and they made quite an army, and they all were armed!"

Rilla was talking brightly, breathlessly, and as she

talked she gave one quick look up into Bat's face, astonished at his silence and apparent absorption. He was striding along by her side, looking down at her with deep concern in his face, his eyes narrowing, his face shrewd and intent. She was talking his language now, getting right down to facts of things as he knew them. Armed gangs and raids by night. Gang wars! He was all interest, waiting to hear about this gangleader Benhadad. Unconsciously Rilla had struck a theme he could understand. There might have been a passing wonder in that shrewd searching glance he gave her, as to whether she had sighted yet the rendezvous on the dump, and whether there might be more significance to her words than appeared on the surface. But Rilla did not realize all that. She was only intent on telling her story and making it thrilling enough to get her into the safety of the bus, and the circle of decent people to whom she might appeal if Bat troubled her further.

"And in the morning," went on Rilla, drawing a deep breath of relief as she accomplished the crossing of the first street without losing the interest of her audience, "Elisha's servant went down early to get Elisha's breakfast ready. He always traveled with a servant, you know. And Elisha's servant went out to get a pail of water from the well, and there he saw the gang silently encamped around the house, and around the whole part of the city where the house was, and he was frightened. He slipped quietly back into the house before anyone of the enemy-gang had seen him and went up to Elisha's room so frightened he could hardly speak, and he said in a whisper, 'Oh, what are we going to do? Your enemies have followed us and they are all around the house, and around the city. They are guarding every door, and they've got their gunmen at every street where we could get away. I've been looking out the windows and there isn't a spot that isn't guarded. What are we going to do?'"

Rilla saw a block away that the bus was coming, and there were a lot of people in it. "Oh, God, help me! Help me!" her heart cried as she went on with her story:

"But Elisha wasn't scared in the least. He just smiled and said, 'Oh, you don't need to worry about that! We've got a lot of gunmen too. Didn't you know that? They that be with us are more than they that be with them. You needn't worry about that.' And he took the servant to a window at the top of the house where they could look out and see all around, and then he did a queer thing, he looked up to the heaven, and he prayed, 'O Lord, I pray thee open the eyes of this young man servant of mine so that he can see our army!' And suddenly as the young man looked out the window he saw them, soldiers and soldiers, armed gunmen by the thousands, all the hills and mountains about the town were full of soldiers, mounted on horses, and many on foot. And about Elisha there were horses and chariots of *fire!* All the armies of heaven there to defend Elisha and his servant, hosts and hosts of angels with their terrible swift swords flashing."

They were almost to the second corner now, and the bus was beginning to curve toward the curb of the pavement. It was going to stop! And there were quite a lot of people in it. It wasn't the bus going the right way to take her to her bank, but that didn't matter. She could change to another when she got safely away from Bat.

And Bat was not noticing the bus. His eyes were kindled with interest. There was a look of intensity in his face. The story had caught him and put him off his guard.

"You know about the angel of the Lord, don't you?" she went on, smiling a little now, and holding his attention with her glance. "'The angel of the Lord encampeth round about them that fear him and delivereth them.' That's why I'm not afraid. I fear the Lord. I fear to displease Him, and that's why I'm not afraid of things that men can do to me. It's because I know that army of angels is all round about me, with their horses and their chariots of fire. I might pray to God to open your eyes so that you could see them, but I'm not sure you could. It's only those who know the Lord and are really on His side in this warfare who can have their eyes opened to see. Well, good-by! I must take this bus now!" and Rilla like a flash turned and stepped into the bus just as the door was about to be closed. She worked her way through the crowd of people standing in the aisle, till she was far back into safety, even if Bat should follow her.

And Bat stood still on the curbing, staring after the bus and the bright vision that had told him such an extraordinary story. He stared for many minutes till the bus had vanished around a distant corner. He was seeing in imagination an army of fiery angels surrounding that girl who had left him, angels with their white wings, fiery swords and chariots! He had never heard the like before!

And she wasn't afraid!

At last he turned and said aloud to himself, "Well, I *snum!* I wonder, now—I wonder—what she meant?"

But Rilla in the wrong bus was struggling hard to keep the tears back and telling herself that she mustn't ever let her mother know this, or Thurlow either, for they would never let her go anywhere by herself again.

13

THE winter came on with a snap. Sharp winds searched the little house on Meachin Street, and Thurlow was kept busy in his spare hours chopping wood to feed the voracious little stoves that roared away all day, and sometimes all night. They had learned how to bank even these small fires and kept the house tolerably warm on the worst nights, except of course the bedrooms where the windows were open.

The inhabitants of Meachin Street just could not understand that custom the Reeds had of leaving their windows open at night. Mrs. O'Hennessy came over to see about it one morning when she smelled a particularly appetizing odor from the Reed kitchen.

"You all forgot to shet yer winders las' night," she said casually, just as though she hadn't noticed it now these three weeks, and talked it all over with the slatternly Mrs. Butts before she ventured to come and find out what could possibly be the cause of so strange a phenomenon as an open window on a cold night.

Mother Reed looked up, suddenly realizing the diligent espionage that must be kept over them by their neighbors, that such a matter should be noticed.

"Oh, no," she smiled. "We meant to leave them open. We always have our bedroom windows open at night. We think it is healthier to have fresh air while we are sleeping."

Mrs. O'Hennessy stared.

"Yer takin' an awful chance!" she warned. "I knowed a woman forgot ta shut her winders one night an' all her childer got ammonia an' died 'twoncet! They had a double fun'ral! Five childer all in one grave. Course it come cheaper. But then ya havta think o' the childer. Still some don't set much store by childer. It's all as yer raised."

Mrs. Reed tried to smile casually.

"Well, we were raised to have our windows open at night," she said pleasantly. "We've always done it and never suffered any evil effects from it yet. Indeed I don't think any of us could get to sleep without fresh air coming in, it makes so much more restful sleep, you know. Just try it sometime, Mrs. O'Hennessy, and see."

"Oh, I wouldn't dast," said the old woman, shrinking and shaking her head. "I'd get the rheumatiz. I can't stand bein' so awful cold. Don't youse 'most freeze?"

"Oh, no," said Mrs. Reed, "we have plenty of blankets, and an eider down quilt apiece."

"What's that?" asked the old woman sharply.

"An eider down quilt? Why, it's a quilt made of down, feathers, you know."

"Aw! A feather bed. Why'n'tya say so? Yeah, I know what them is. I useta hev one when I was fust married. But it got so alive I hed ta burn it up. Don't youse hev trouble keepin' the bugs outta yours?"

Mrs. Reed shuddered slightly but answered serenely:

"Oh, no, we never have bugs. We hang our things out often and air them, and we keep them very clean always."

"Aw, well, I couldn't be bothered!" said Mrs. O'Hennessy languidly. "I jus' burned mine up. Anyways the mice hed et a hole in mine an' the feathers was all comin'. out. Say, what's that yer bakin' now?"

"Why, that's gingerbread. Would you like a piece?"

"That? Gingerbread? I never seen none as purty an' shiny as that on top. Looks more like cake! You sure hev a lot o' new notions. Sure, I don't mind samplin' it. It smells mighty good. I'll try anythin' oncet."

Mrs. Reed laughed aloud as she cut a generous square of hot gingerbread.

"Well, then try opening your window some night," she said with a twinkle, "and see how much better you sleep. You know the fresh air destroys germs."

"Oh, we don't have none o' those," said the old woman with her mouth full of hot cake. "We hev bugs but we don't hev no germs. I never see one. Whadda they look like? D'they bite?"

"No, you can't see them," said Mrs. Reed, trying not to break into peals of laughter, "but they are there. They get into the air you breathe and get into your nose and your mouth and make sickness, fevers, all sorts of disease. It's a good deal like sin you know, everywhere about us. Fresh air drives out germs, and the blood of Christ washes away sin."

"Say, youse are superstitious, ain't ya? I never hold with them ideas about catchin' things. I say ef yer gonta hev um ye'll hev um, an' what's the use worryin'? I jes' wear a rabbit's foot an' don't think no more about it."

She hauled out a dirty string from about her neck with a filthy bit of fur at the end, and gave her toothless laugh.

"But the blood of Christ is not superstition," said Mrs. Reed gently. "It is something that has been done for you and me, once for all. A cleansing from sin. And you can have it just by taking it."

"Aw, well, hev it yer own way. I can't be bothered! I gotta get home an' start the stew fer dinner. Thank 'e fer the cake. It's good."

She eyed the remaining loaf hungrily, and the tender-hearted hostess could not refrain from giving her another big piece. Poor old soul! She could not understand about the remedy for sin, but her heart and her soul cried out for a little of the good things of this life, and who knew but she could be reached sometime even through a bite of cake?

"I wish you'd go with us to our chapel meeting sometime," Mrs. Reed said impulsively as she handed over the gingerbread.

"What! Me? Go ta church! Ha! Ha!" The old woman threw back her head and laughed, showing all her tooth-less gums. "Why, they'd drive me out the door. Me in these rags? Naw, I can't go ta no chapel! My time's past! Goob-by! I gotta get back! Thankee!" and she clumped down the steps and away to her shack.

The Reeds had been going regularly to the chapel all the fall. Thurlow's hours were such at present that he had most of his evenings off, and he had been fairly regular at the service, seeming to enjoy the work of leading the singing, and occasionally singing solos for them.

Sandra Cameron was usually there, and always smiled and chatted with them a few minutes at the close of the service when she was able to linger, but of late she had been hurrying away. She said her cousin was not well and was worried at her being out after dark.

Rilla looked after her wistfully one evening as she hurried away and said with a sigh as they went down the aisle:

"I do wish we lived somewhere where we dared ask her to come and see us sometime! She's lovely!"

"Well, we don't!" said Thurlow almost sharply. "She

wouldn't want to come, and I wouldn't want to put her in the position of having to refuse."

"I believe she would come," said Mother Reed thoughtfully.

"Well, she's not going to be asked!" said Thurlow almost savagely. "She knows where we live, and that's enough. It was night when she was there. Perhaps she didn't take in the dump, nor the O'Hennessy mansion. I'd rather she didn't see any more of it than she has. She's a thoroughbred!"

"She's no more thoroughbred than you are, my son!" rebuked his mother gravely. "Your grandfathers and grandmothers on both sides were cultured, refined people."

"Oh, yes," said Thurlow wearily, "the only difference being that I'm not working at it just now."

"I hope you're not dropping your refinements and culture just because, for the time being, you are directing traffic."

"Well, no, I hope not, but I'm in a pretty seamy environment right now, Mother, and the least said about it the better. I'm not complaining, but there's no need to drag any new acquaintances in on it. Miss Cameron is very nice and pleasant and we both enjoy the same services. It's good of course to know there is a girl like that, but let it go at that! Don't let's force ourselves on her."

"Of course not!" said the mother with a sigh.

"Well, we had a wonderful meeting tonight, anyway, didn't we?" said Rilla. "I thought Thurl sang the best I ever heard him. And wasn't Miss Cameron's voice beautiful in that hymn she sang? She let on she couldn't sing much, but I thought it was great!"

"Yes," said Thurlow heartily, "it is a wonderful voice. I wouldn't be a bit surprised to know she had studied with some famous teacher abroad. And yet she is so retiring about it!"

"Yes, she's so humble and sweet," said the mother. "I would certainly like to hear you two sing together!" Her voice was wistful.

"Well, don't you suggest it!" said Thurlow stormily. "If you do I won't go down here to service any more."

"Why, certainly not, Son, you know better than to think I would."

"Well, Rilla might!" said the boy half ashamed.

"Oh, certainly, blame it on me!" said Rilla a little bitterly. "I'm not to the manner born, you know. I'm not a thoroughbred, and wouldn't know any better!"

"You're just as much of a thoroughbred as she is, Rill dear," her brother said earnestly. "I beg your pardon for being so savage. I just don't want you, either of you, to do anything silly about getting me to sing."

"Of course not!" said the mother. "Now, Thurl, put that out of your head. Let's just be thankful we've got a place where we can worship that isn't too far for me to walk, and isn't too unpleasant for you two to enjoy."

"That's right, Mother! We are!" said the young man fervently. "I certainly enjoy that preacher, and I like his Monday night Bible classes too. I hope my hours don't change too often, so I can attend. I never realized before how much there was to the Bible that I didn't understand. It's getting pretty deep under my skin, in spite of all the atheism you were afraid I had picked up in college. I guess having trouble has helped me to know I needed something outside of myself."

"Thank the Lord for trouble, then!" said his mother.

Then the very next day, as he was standing in the middle of the broad avenue in the heart of the shopping district, directing traffic, Sandra came riding by in a great shining limousine, with a chauffeur in livery driving, and her pettish old spoiled unhappy cousin sitting by her side.

She was wearing a beautiful squirrel coat and a chic little hat with a tiny bright quill stuck aslant, and soft white gloves wrinkled at the wrist. The window was open beside her and he could have reached out his hand and touched the fur on her shoulder, so near she was.

She didn't see him of course, wouldn't have known him if she had. He had never told her what his business was. She would not expect him to be a policeman.

It gave him a strange feeling to have her going by so close, a thrill of something he had never felt before. She was talking to the older woman, and just as they passed in front of him and paused for the light to change, she looked up and smiled! Of course she didn't know him, and had no idea the traffic cop was anyone she knew. But the thrill of that smile lingered with him all the afternoon and lit up his heart even as it lit up her lovely eyes. Blue eyes with a true look and a smile in them, young tender lips, their natural color untouched by art, cheeks with a soft hint of rose. Hair with sunlight in its very essence, straying out from under the aristocratic little hat, waving with the lovely curves of nature, not flat and hard like some girls' waves.

He thought of the testimony she had given in the meeting the night before, how true it rang, what inner depths of communion with her God it bespoke, how yielded to the Lord she seemed. He was glad there was such a girl in the world. She seemed all that his ideal would have in a woman, if he were a young man who had a right to have an ideal woman and dwell upon her in his thoughts, if he were not a man set apart from the ordinary life that most men expected, with a family and a job to look after.

Then without any reason at all there came a thought

of Barbara Sherwood, bitterly, as if in unpleasant contrast. Barbara who had always heretofore been his ideal! Barbara who had held his heart in the hollow of her small dictatorial hand! Barbara who had gone out from his world without a regret, or a tear, with a gay smile on her lips, and a trill of a laugh, and a kiss that meant nothing at all. Barbara who had sent him a trail of post cards and snapshots from her progress round the world, and not a single real letter! Post cards with gay legends: "I swam in the pool this morning. The water was perfectly spiffy. Yours, aff. Barb." or "We did this gallery this morning. Just the type of art I love. Barbara." or "Climbed this tower today. The view is darling! Met a man on the top who was on the ship. He is taking us on his yacht tomorrow. B."

More and more impersonal they had grown, and all of them sent to his college address. Barbara didn't know yet, and he didn't intend to enlighten her. He hadn't written her at all, and she hadn't even seemed to notice the lack yet!

He sighed as he realized how far his life had gone from hers, how utterly apart they were now. Even if it were not for his change of social station, and his lack of money, and his lowly position in life, even if he did not live on Meachin Street, what would she have in common with him any more? Could he tell her about the progress he was making in patching up the picket fence nights, or in hanging paper on the bedroom ceilings? Could he describe to her the pleasant little white chapel called Grace to which his heart turned wearily when his work was done, and how he had begun to enjoy his work there, of singing messages of life to sorrowful sinners? Would she be interested if he should tell her how he hoped that poor old tramp with whom he had talked the night before had really been saved before he went out into the wind and cold and loneliness of a ruined life? Would Barbara understand when he spoke of being saved? He had always known about it himself, but not as he knew now, since he had been attending the Bible classes and mingling with these simple people at the Mission who talked in plain terms of salvation as if it were the most important thing of life. Would Barbara Sherwood be at all in sympathy with these things? Would she let him talk to her about it? He doubted it. Barbara was a member of the same church with himself. They had both joined at the age of about fourteen when a lot of their friends were joining. Had it meant any more to her than it had to him then, he wondered? He was just beginning to learn that it meant something new to him now, to suspect a sweetness in the Christian life which he had never dreamed of before. But would Barbara even understand him if he were to try to tell her about this new experience that had come to him since he in his dismay and desolation had accepted what the Lord offered him and made a new surrender of his life to his Savior?

It was just then he sighed, and perhaps some of the passing crowd wondered at the stern young face above the blue uniform, the face that was red with the biting winter blast, and stern with an air of authority, as he raised his hand or blew his whistle, and directed the throng of winter shoppers into the early twilight of the cold December day.

And just then Sandra came by again.

He would have thought that she had two presences, or that his eyes had deceived him the first time and it had not been she at all, except that she was still wearing the sumptuous squirrel coat and the chic little hat.

She had changed her white gloves for gray driving gloves, and she was in her own little car, coming steadily on toward him. Suddenly his heart gave a great thump and turned right over. She was driving slowly, in the line of traffic, obviously halting so the light would stop her, and she was looking straight at him and smiling. She *knew* him! She was going to speak to him! Perhaps even her other smile had been for him! His heart turned over once more at the thought, and then he took himself sternly in hand and was the perfect cop again.

"I was hoping you'd be here yet," she said, leaning out of her open window and smiling into his face, speaking with a low confidential voice that yet was clear enough to understand.

"Take this paper quick!" she said, holding out a small song-sheet to him. "Take it before I have to drive on. It's a new song Mr. Wheeler wants us to sing next Sunday. It fits his sermon. Will you and Rilla try it over at home, and then could you stop at my house sometime when you're off duty, and let us try it over together? I've put my address and phone number on the back and you can let me know what hour will be convenient."

He took the paper wonderingly and looked at her.

"You mean you want me to sing *with you?* You mean you think I could do it—?"

"None better!" she smiled. "I knew you'd do it for me." And then it was time for him to give the signal for her to move on. The drivers behind her were screeching their horns impatiently for attention. He flashed her a smile and put his whistle to his lips. Their two smiles darted across through traffic and disappeared in each other's eyes, and something seemed to have delayed the setting of the sun for a while for Thurlow Reed, for the very twilight grew luminous about him. Something was singing inside him that had not sung for a long time.

Yet it did not make him less alert, in the business of the hour. He swung his signals skillfully, blew his whistle keenly whenever a trespasser sought to steal through the signals, lifted a commanding hand to stay the throngs of hurrying shoppers, his every sense seemed quickened by that bright vision in the little car that had lingered a moment to speak to him. His heart was warmed, strengthened by that girl's friendliness. He was only a policeman, and yet she had wanted him to sing with her. *Her!* A girl who wore costly fur coats and rode in limousines! Things like that loomed so large just now on his horizon. He hadn't thought they meant so much before he lost them, but now he was always thinking that they meant abnormally much to other people.

Suddenly he sensed a tragedy approaching. A reckless driver, determined to run past the light with no intention of obeying signals, and a lady approaching timidly across his way. The man would never stop in time, his brakes too late were screaming but would not hold, and the lady was bewildered!

There was no time to consider. It was like a crucial moment on the football field. Thurlow dashed into the situation without an instant's hesitation, putting a powerful arm about the woman and swinging her off her feet and back into safety just in time, himself barely escaping with a bruised thigh. The lady, frightened, trembling, was set safely upon the sidewalk, and the throng surged on again while Thurlow dealt with the driver, who by this time was badly scared and only wanted to escape.

There was no time to notice the lady. If he had ever seen her before he was not aware of it, and when he turned in a moment's interval to see if she was all right he could not tell which one she was. But the singing was in his heart, and the sheet of the song was in his pocket right over his heart. It was after five o'clock and the throng were going home. His hours would soon be over now and he could go home too, and try out the song.

The incident of saving a lady's life was all in the day's work, and he had forgotten it. Only the comfortable sense that he had averted a catastrophe remained with him, as a background.

That evening about the time that Thurlow, having changed from his uniform into comfortable working garb, stood by the piano while Rilla played over the song that Sandra had given him, the George Steeles were just answering the call to dinner. It was a quiet home dinner with no guests, and the preliminaries of the meal being over Mrs. Steele looked up at her husband and said in a calm tone:

"Well, George, I nearly got killed this afternoon."

Her husband dropped his knife and fork and looked at her with blanching face. He knew it had really been an escape if she would own that much.

"Mamma!" he ejaculated tremulously, like a frightened child.

"You needn't think it was my fault." Her voice was trembling just the least little bit. "I waited till the signal was my way. Just as you said I should. I wasn't looking about at traffic at all, and I was walking quietly across the street, right in front of the library where the traffic is the worst from Forty-second Street, and the first thing I knew the grandest big young policeman with nice eyes that looked like somebody I knew, had his arm around my waist and swung me up right off the street as if I were a bundle of rags, and a great big sports car slid by us with the brakes screeching terribly! I didn't really know what was happening until it was all over, and then I realized that something big and fearful had been over me, its breath almost brushing my cheek, and that nothing could have saved me from being crushed to death if that wonderful young man hadn't risked his life and swept me out of it. I know he risked his life because there was one second when I felt that we were both in the very jaws of death and nothing could save us, and the next minute he had me out and was setting me down on the sidewalk on my feet and limping back to his place in the middle of the street."

"Yes?" said Papa Steele sharply.

"That's all, George, only he did *limp*, and rubbed his hip a little as he went back, and I completely forgot to thank him till he was back in the middle of that awful traffic again, and I *didn't dare* go back to thank him! I was all out of breath, and trembling all over. So I just took a taxi and came home. But I did remember to get his number. It was seventy-seven, George, and I wish you'd do something nice for him. He was just wonderful! And you ought to have seen him talking to the man in the sports car. I *think* he arrested him, but I didn't stay to see. But he did have nice eyes. I'm sure I've seen those eyes before somewhere. You'll do something nice for him, won't you, George?"

"I certainly will!" said the great business magnate fervently.

And then he shoved his chair back, came around to his wife's side of the table, and stooping down lifted her right out of her chair and folded her in his arms, putting his big face down in her neck and kissing her.

"Mamma!" he said. "Mamma!"

14

RILLA had gone to and from the bank for many days tremulously, watching her chance when she thought Bat was not around, stealing out across lots behind the factory building, coming home by devious ways where she could keep a sharp lookout, and not once since she left him on that street corner staring after her bus had she sighted Bat.

She was growing more and more reassured, praying daily for protection, and courage to face this matter without troubling either her mother or Thurlow. Gradually her faith was resting down harder on the God who had helped her when she called upon Him.

She was coming home late one afternoon in the winter dusk, later than she had been before on account of some extra work she had been asked to do at the bank. She was hurrying through the dark streets, hoping to reach shelter before she met any of the inhabitants of that dreadful Meachin Street. It was growing so dark that she dared not venture going through the deserted factory ground. It seemed to be full of lurking shadowy forms even in the broad daylight. So she walked quickly down the side street and turned into Meachin Street. Suddenly two bright eyes of light streamed out and pierced her vision, perhaps frightening her more than a dark shadow could have done, until she realized that it was the headlights from an automobile, and that the car was standing in front of her own home.

Breathless she paused an instant, then hurried on. What could have happened? How would a car like that ever be standing in front of their shabby little cabin?

As she drew nearer she saw that the car was a costly one, bright with chromium and expensive fixtures, and that no one was in it! Who could it belong to? Had something happened to Mother? This didn't look like a doctor's car. Or Thurlow? Had someone brought him home hurt? Oh, *God*—!

She hurried into the back door, wishing to reconnoiter before she came upon the stranger unaware. Could it possibly be Sandra's awful cousin? Thurlow had told about the beautiful car in which she had passed him one afternoon. Or—could it be that Barbara Sherwood had come home and this was a new car they had purchased?

Her heart was in her mouth as she lifted the latch of the back door, softly, wondering if Mother would have locked it. No, it yielded to her pressure, and there was a bright light within, as there had been in the living room as she passed the window not daring to peek in lest she should be seen.

There was a delightful smell of cookery going on and there were voices in the dining room. Could it be that there was company? Who could it be unless it was Barbara? Yet the last letter she had from Betty said that they were going to the south of France for a time. It couldn't be Barbara!

She stepped into the kitchen and closed the outer door softly behind her, standing there hushed, expectant, half fearful, her eyes wide with wonder, a little flush of excitement upon her cheeks.

She heard a step, a man's step. Her eyes sought the clock. It wasn't time for Thurlow yet. Who could it be?

Then a cheerful jubilant voice from the pantry door:

"Here she is, Mother Reed! I told you you needn't worry about her! I told you she knew her way about! Here she is, pretty as a peach! What are you trying to put over on us, Rilla-girl? Staying out late like this when I came all the way from college to have a nice cosy time with you and get acquainted? And I wanted to go to the bank for you, but your mother insisted I'd miss you because you were never as late as this."

Rilla stood there in the brightness blinking her eyes and staring. Was this a fairy tale or a dream? Was this truly Thurl's college friend Pat, or only a figment of her imagination? Her cheeks flamed scarlet with the joy of it all. After all these days of dreariness and sorrow and disappointment, something had happened to make a really bright spot. She caught her breath and smiled at Pat.

"She's real after all!" exclaimed the young man. "Look at her smile! It almost blinds me eyes. Mother Reed, come here quick and tell her what a bad girl she is! Find out if there's some big bad wolf outside that has tried to eat her that I ought to go out and shoot or anything!"

Rilla giggled. Somehow the burden of many days seemed to roll away from her. The earth still held some pleasant spots after all. Bat and his like were not the only contacts of a lifetime!

"It is nice to see you," said Rilla shyly.

"Now, listen at that, Mother Reed! She thinks it's nice to see me! *Nice!* I love that word! Nice! When I've been waiting here all the afternoon for her to arrive! And she only thinks it *nice!* But then I suppose I ought to be thankful for even that. Well, at least I've learned something. I've learned how to make doughnuts!"

He waved his hand toward a great platter of brown sugary discs on the dresser shelf, and another on the table near by.

"See! I fried all those in both those dishes. Didn't I do well? Your mother only fried the very first kettleful and I did all the rest!"

"Yes, he did," smiled Mrs. Reed, meeting her daughter's questioning look. "He said he enjoyed it."

"I did!" said the young man. "Had the time of my life. It was great watching them plump up and turn brown, and then fishing them out before they got too brown. It's a good game. A lot like going crabbing, only the cakes don't have such funny eyes as the crabs. Didn't we do a lot?"

He stood back surveying his handiwork with pride.

"I should say you did," said Rilla, "but—Mother, whatever will you do with so many doughnuts? You've got enough for a regiment. We'll never get them all eaten up."

Mrs. Reed gave a startled look at her child. She had forgotten that she usually had her cooking well out of the way before the children came home.

"Oh," she said with a smile, "I thought perhaps Pat would like to take some back to college with him."

"That's a great idea, Mother Reed!" said the young man. "I was hoping you would think of that. But now Rilla and I are going to eat one, just to show her how good they are. Open your mouth, Rilla!"

He plucked a cake from the platter and held it to her lips, and amid much laughter they ate the doughnut by alternate bites until it was gone.

The laughter reached out beyond the flimsy walls of the little cottage, and rang through the frosty air penetrating the shacks along the street, and more than one paused and looked toward the brightly lighted windows, wistfully, eyeing the costly car that seemed so out of place in that region.

They were setting the table together, Rilla and Pat, Rilla handing out the best china and Pat standing by to take it from her. Then when he had put the dishes upon the table he took her hands and helped her down from the low stepladder on which she had mounted to reach certain little bread and butter plates that it pleased her to use. They laughed gaily as Rilla sprang down and Pat, still holding her hands, lifted her up and whirled her around. They seemed like a couple of children having a good time. Mother Reed smiled as she came through from the kitchen. She hadn't seen Rilla so radiantly happy since her father died. Then she sighed softly to herself. She hoped her child wouldn't get any silly notions from this pleasant visit of her brother's college friend. He would go away again of course and likely not return. It was probable he had only come now to try to coax Thurlow back to college after the Christmas holidays, and of course, Thurlow wouldn't go. But it was nice to see Rilla so happy and so lovely, with her eyes bright and her cheeks rosy with the unwonted pleasure of company. It was natural for young things to enjoy young company.

Out in the frosty night Bat lingered shivering in his worn garments that were too thin and too ill-fitting to afford much comfort, slid around by the stovepipe end of his home and stood there looking across and scowling at that bright car whose chromium trimmings caught even the faint lamplight of the street and reflected it sharply and with a grace all its own. And presently Bat slid noiselessly across the frozen ground to a spot in the fence known only to himself, where the pickets tilted sidewise affording easy access to the next lot, and let himself across the slight barrier. He stole across the yard till he came and stood behind the back window of the dining room flattening his gaunt pasty face for an instant against the pane, just as Pat whirled Rilla laughing around the room. It was more like the romping of children than anything else, and for just an instant that white face with its starved wistful eyes stared into what looked to the poor sordid soul like a little glimpse of heaven, then he faded into the darkness again, standing back where he could watch and not be seen, while the merry work of setting the table went forward. So! There were people who played like that! Who could laugh innocently with a ripple in the sound! Who wore a light in their eyes and no grim sinister shadow in their faces! People who were surrounded with twelve legions of angels to protect them. Was this young man one of those? Did he have angels guarding him? Chariots of fire about that extravagant car out there, so that perhaps no bullets could penetrate its imposing beauty! He stood off and studied the new man. Who was he? Another brother? No, he thought not. Some relative? Just a passing guest? Would he go away and not be seen again, or was he another that had to be calculated upon and dealt with?

Little narrowed eyes studied from afar. Keen ears heard Thurlow come in, Thurlow in his uniform! Thurlow meeting his old friend! Hearty greetings, real joy on the big policeman's face, real admiration and joy on the face of the guest. Hand shaking! Loving slaps on the shoulder, joyous laughter in which the two women joined! It was all like a play to Bat as he stood in the depths of shadow in the cold and the dark of the moon and watched.

He could not hear all they said, only now and then he

caught a word that was called from one room to another. But he could see the rare bond between the two young men, the joy in meeting, the lighting of the eyes. He drew a jealous sigh. He had never had fellowship with anyone like this. He tried to think of Brick Etter coming in so breezily and slapping his shoulder that way, or Reds, or Slink down at the dump around a furtive fire after midnight. No joy in his friendships. Fellowships of darkness only were his. Bonds of crime, hate, selfishness! He sighed alone there in the dark with a pang of wistfulness over something he had never known existed till tonight.

Fascinated he watched on, though he was shivering in his inadequate garments, watched as they carried the dishes to the table, all helping. Saw Thurlow lead his mother by the hand, and gently, laughingly, set her down in a chair and shove her up to the table, and then go himself and carry the heavy platter to the table, the platter with a roast chicken on it whose savory smell reached out even to the back yard and made the hungry soul think: What if he were invited to that table? What if he had a right to a plate such as they were passing to that stranger? What if he had a right to sit and talk and laugh as they were doing? What if he were *capable* of doing it? He knew that he wasn't. He knew that if he were seated at that table in there he would dissolve in embarrassment. That his legs and his arms would get in the way, and he would devour his food like a wild beast, and not know how to do anything as others did. Yet his heart was bitter with a suddenly-born desire to belong in a place like that. To eat dinners of stuffed chicken with that heavenly smell, and pass plates in that quiet easy way. To receive smiles from a girl like that with eyes like the sky and hair that had caught the sunlight in its dark sheen. To have her brother clap him on the back!

But now, they were doing a strange thing! Though the food was on the table and they were all seated around it ready, still they did not eat. Instead they all bowed their heads, and he could see the young policeman was moving his lips as if he were talking to someone. A strange proceeding, yet he sensed it must be something like a prayer. There had never been a thing like that in his home. No blessing of food.

Strange thing, a praying cop! It didn't seem to fit! And yet he didn't look like a sissy either. He frowned. He must be another one who was under that strange protection his sister had talked about, those twelve legions of angels. What would it be like to be guarded that way? One wouldn't have to knuckle down to the rest of the gang if one were guarded that way.

He noticed as the meal went on that the two young men were waiting upon the mother and sister. A phenomenon, that! He always ordered his mother to wait on him. But these were waiting upon their women as if they were queens. He grinned to himself in the dark—to think of his old mother sitting at the table and himself pushing her down and insisting on going after more bread himself. What a queer way of doing! But then look at these women, all dolled up in fancy clothes, curls in their hair. He thought of his mother with her straggling gray locks and her grimy face. He suddenly wondered how his mother looked when she was young. It had never occurred to him before that she might ever have been young, or good-looking.

There was his sister Rosie. She was a looker! Selfish little beast! Always on the lookout for herself. Well, she'd got hers likely now. He hadn't seen her for two years. Yet he could remember when the sight of her had stirred something queer in his sodden breast, and he had fought a kid for using an ugly word about her. But that was when he was a kid himself.

But now he stood there shivering and reflecting upon another kind of life, wherein women were enshrined as something precious, and one was guarded by twelve legions of angels. How did one get that way? Born so probably! But that wasn't fair! God was to blame somehow. Better to blame it on God than to harbor that uncomfortable and definite fear that had haunted him ever since the morning he had walked with this queer new girl, the fear that perhaps in some far dim way he was somehow to blame for his own situation in life. It was all too deep for Bat and he was cold.

They were rising now from the table and all hands clearing off and washing the dishes. Both the men wiping dishes and putting them away! What nonsense! But having such a good time!

Wistful eyes turned away. Bat was cold! So cold! His teeth were chattering. He went home to the shack and swore roundly at his poor old mother sitting there in slatternly clothes, her hair all straggling down around her shoulders, a bottle and glass in front of her, her eyes bleary with the only consolation she knew in the life she lived. He swore at her because she had let the fire go out and he was cold!

And then, strange contradiction, he went out and chopped some wood and came in and made up the fire just as if he had been one of those softies over there next door. And then to make up for his act he swore at her again. But she only looked at him dumbly as if it were a matter of utter indifference to her, and poured herself another glass.

Then, being warm from the activity he went out, intending to go down to the dump and the furtive fire among his cronies, and forget these strange unwonted thoughts. But there was music over at the next house, and it drew him like a magnet. They were all singing, the mother too. His rubbershod feet stole near to the front windows, without a thought of the gorgeous car he might have examined at his will now that darkness would have shielded him. He came near to the window, stepping out of the pathway of light, and not even a passer-by, if there had been one, could have discerned him against the darkness. There he stood behind a friendly little evergreen that Thurlow had brought from the other house.

From his position Bat could see Rilla's lovely profile, like an angel, he thought—strange thought to have visited his bleak mind. No wonder legions of angels guarded her, when she was like an angel herself. His idea of angels had been gleaned from stained-glass windows, from the exterior of course, and was exceedingly vague, but it represented beauty in the highest sense, and he was surprised to find himself intrigued by it. He felt a strange dull ache inside him just from looking at Rilla, just from thinking about what she had said. He somehow felt himself all wrong, all full of the worst that could be, and no bitterness nor cursing could take the sense of degradation away from him. There was inside him too a terrible, wild, awful longing for something beyond and above what he had, a longing that he had never recognized nor known before.

And there was nothing that would satisfy this emptiness and all-wrongness of himself, nothing! If he were to go down to the dump and find the gang had planned a hold-up or a robbery, with himself staged for the daredevil of the whole affair—the goat he called it—and if he should go out and carry out their devilish schemes to success and get his share of the booty, that would not cure this hurt within him, this need, this exceeding new longing that had grown inside him like an overwhelming disease since these people had come to live next door and disturb the neighborhood with their strange ways, since this girl with the angel eyes had come and looked at him as if he were a mere speck of the dirt beneath her little feet!

There in the darkness Bat ground his teeth to keep them from chattering and watched the faces around the piano. The girl and the young man side by side, as if they belonged together! He was a looker too, Bat saw now with this nearer view, and he stood just above the girl as she sat at the piano playing, looking down with admiring eyes at her. They belonged together. Bat saw it, even with his untrained eyes, but it stabbed the pain deeper in his heart, and he realized still more his lack of something they had, realized that he was not fit to walk their ways nor speak to them, nor even breathe the same atmosphere with any of them.

How he loathed himself! How his past swept about him with many memories like so many devils' fingers pointing at him; hideous memories of things that he had done, never counting them sin, never knowing what sin was. Anything was lawful if one could get away with it, and Bat had so far been able to get away with a good deal. Menacing demons stole in the darkness about him and reminded him of how he had sold himself to the devil. Sins that he had often boasted of came trooping around him to separate him forever from the holiness and brightness of all things good and pure. *Sins* they were now, right out in the open, with power to weigh him down, power to keep him what he was and worse, all the days of eternity! That longing in his heart grew to bursting power. Then suddenly Thurlow's voice rang out sweetly almost beside him, just the pane of glass between. His white anxious face peered in to watch that strong young cop's face:

> *"Would you be free from your burden of sin?*
> *There's power in the blood, power in the blood;*
> *Would you o'er evil a victory win?*
> *There's wonderful power in the blood."*

Then the four voices rang out together and the words were as clear and distinct as if they were spoken directly to Bat in answer to his thoughts:

> *"There is power, power, wonder-working power,*
> *In the precious blood of the lamb."*

Bat didn't know about the Lamb. It meant nothing to him. Some hoodoo perhaps, like his mother's rabbit foot that she always wore around her neck on a string. Oh, what did it all matter? It was not for him of course.

Rilla was singing a verse now by herself, and the sweet notes of her voice stirred Bat's poor heart to the depths.

> *"Would you be whiter, much whiter than snow?*
> *There's power in the blood, power in the blood;*
> *Sin-stains are lost in its life-giving flow,*
> *There's wonderful power in the blood."*

And again the other voices joined in that chorus. It rang all around poor Bat like hovering angels, urging, insisting in his ears, but the voice of the girl had pierced his hardened young heart. It was as if that girl had told him he could be washed white like other people, like those two men beside her, her brother and her friend, and the thought of it engulfed him, devastated him with its sweetness. Something like a thin tear stole down the unaccustomed way of Bat's dirty cheek and froze there in the cold air. He was beyond shivering now, inured, hardened to heat or cold alike; he stood and faced that thought of cleanness for the first time in his life as something to be desired. Clean! Clean! He could be made clean! All the filth of his mind and body! All the stain of sin and crime on his soul—white—"much whiter than snow!"

It was going to snow in the night tonight. He could feel it in the air. The chill of it went to his soul. In the morning it would all be soft and white and cleaner than anything anywhere, dazzling clean. Clean like the look in that girl's eyes when she told him about the twelve legions of angels. Of course the whiteness of the snow wouldn't last long. The soil of the day would make it dirtier than before, till more snow came. It didn't stay white, snow didn't, not in Meachin Street. But—if Bat could ever get white, wouldn't he find some way of staying so? A sudden firmness came to the crime-marked chin and a determination to the small narrowed eyes. Clean, so that that girl could look on him once and not be afraid. Just *once* even! If he could be clean like that then maybe God wouldn't be so hard on him.

Bat stole away when the singing was done. He sensed that soon the visitor would be leaving. He did not want to be around. He had no longer any curiosity about that visitor. Something greater had come to him—a thought that perhaps he might be clean!

The blood of the Lamb. The blood of the Lamb! If that were real blood and could be bought he would get him a job, a real job, and get money enough to buy blood enough to get him white—whiter than snow. If the girl hadn't said it he wouldn't have believed it true, but there must be something in it because she sang it. It couldn't be just a song!

Bat went in, built up the fire and washed his hands. He hadn't washed his hands in a long time. The soil of years was embedded in the pores of his skin. He washed them three times, and then, finding by the light of the candle—the lamp had gone out for lack of oil—that they still looked grimy, he put on a kettle of water and washed them again. There was a piece of yellow soap on the window sill, just a small piece. He got that and washed them again, and a clean tingling feeling went thrilling up his arms. "Whiter than snow—whiter than snow!" he kept saying over to himself in a low rumble of a voice.

Then he inspected his hands again and found there were heavy black rings under each nail. He got out a cruel-looking knife and dealt with the rings severely. At last he held them out and laughed.

"Gentleman's hands!" he chuckled under his breath. "Some swell I be!"

Then another idea struck him and he washed his face, washed and washed and washed it with the yellow soap and the hot water, till he came forth so many shades lighter that he scarcely knew himself when he looked in the cracked looking glass that hung over the sink.

Suddenly he disappeared into the little outer shed and came back with a wooden tub that his mother used occasionally when, at long intervals, she washed. He stirred up the fire and put on more water to heat. He began to strip off his dirty garments. A great desire to be clean had seized him. It might not lift the burden of sin from him, but he would try it.

So Bat took a bath. He hadn't had a bath since the last warm day in September when he went swimming in the river, and the process was a work of time. He assembled water enough, and what was left of the soap, at last, and began at his shaggy hair. The problem of a towel was difficult, as the family towel had already served a month, and was quite wet with his earlier ablutions, but he found by rooting in a cupboard, a torn end of an old sheet, and at last emerged with a clean skin.

"Maw, ain't I got'ny clean cloes?" he called plaintively, opening the door of his little shed that served as the only privacy he had in this world.

The old woman had been asleep with her mouth open, snoring loudly, but now at the unaccustomed plea she roused and sat up looking about her, noting the tub, and the kettle on the stove.

"What you doin', Bat?"

"I'm gettin' me a wash," said Bat, "an' I want some clean cloes. Ain't I got a clean shirt anywheres? Not even a shirt?"

"Why, I guess yer tuther shirt is in the heap o' cloes in the shed. You lef' it there when you tuk it off las' fall. I been meanin' ta wash it, but I ain't jes' had time. It's tore. It's tore fum stem ta stern! I ain't got enny thread ta mend it yet. You might git me some thread."

She looked around bewildered.

"What you got all that tub n' all them water for, Bat?" She yawned widely and rubbed her eyes to better take in the situation.

"Why, I tell ya, I'm gettin' me a wash. Wha' daya think I'd want a clean shirt for?"

Suddenly his mother came upright on her feet in consternation.

"Ya don' mean yer bathin' ye, Bat? Not in this weather! *Don't do it!* Ye'll git yer death o' cold. Ye'll git ammonia an' die, an' thur ain't noways possible we kin bury ya, now, with the ole man in one o' his spells!"

"Aw, shut up!" said Bat, lapsing into his usual lingo. "Ain't I got a right ta bath me ef I loike? I done it, ennyhow, an' ef I got it I got it. Ain't thur ennythin' would do fer a shirt? I *gotta* hev somethin' *clean!*"

"Thur ain't a single shirt in the house," declared the old woman solemnly, "only save the one I'm savin' fer the ole man in case 'e was ta pass out in one o' his spells."

"Gimme it!" commanded Bat. "I won't hurt it. It'll wash, won't it?"

The old woman got the shirt, silenced by the suggestion of such extravagance in laundry work.

Bat, clothed and somewhat in his right mind, found himself very weak and hungry, but as there seemed nothing in the house to eat, and his mother had retired to her snoring again, he took a good swig from her bottle, lay down on the heap of rags that was his bed, and fell asleep to dream of angels. He had done his best to wash away the stain of the years.

15

PAT disclosed during the evening that he had really come down to town because he was lonesome for Thurl.

"My dad is marrying again," he said in a sad young tone, "and I don't seem to have any place that is home any more. Of course the house where I was born is mine. Mother left it to me. But it isn't home with just servants in it. Dad's new wife wants a new house and Dad is building it. I don't imagine I'll see much of them. They'll travel a lot, and Dad and I never were very close. I've been off at school ever since my mother died. Dad's all right. He came to see me every once in a while, and took me places sometimes vacations, but it wasn't home. He mostly lived at a club after Mother died."

"How long has your mother been dead?" asked Mrs. Reed sympathetically.

"Ten years," said the boy, a tenderness coming over his gaiety. "If I'd only had a sister or something it wouldn't have been so bad, but my sister died when she was only five, and there is nobody to make a home. This is great! I wish I had a home like this."

"Say, boy!" said Thurl, whirling around with a grin, "you don't know what you're saying! This hovel!"

"You've got a mother and a sister!" said the guest wistfully.

"Yes, *that!*" said Thurlow reverently. "Yes, I'm greatly thankful for that of course. But the house is not so hot!"

"It doesn't matter about the house," said Pat soberly. "Look at me! I've got a great palace of a house with all kinds of treasures in it and not a home to my name."

The mother-light shone in Mrs. Reed's eyes.

"You'll share yours with him, such as it is, won't you, children?" she said, looking from her boy to her girl.

"We sure will!" said Thurlow fervently. "I certainly have missed you more than anything else at college! It'll be great to have you coming in. We'll all enjoy it no end."

"Oh, yes!" said Rilla, with bright eyes and softly flushing cheeks.

"Do you mean it?" asked Pat, looking up anxiously and studying each face searchingly, lingering last and with a touch of gentleness on Rilla's. "I wouldn't take advantage of the privilege," he added wistfully. "I wouldn't think of intruding on Christmas or holidays or anything like that. Just week-ends now and then. Not too often you know. I wouldn't want to wear out my welcome."

"But we want you on holidays, old man!" said Thurlow earnestly. "That's the best time of all, isn't it, Mother?"

"Certainly on holidays, of course!" said the mother with welcome in her eyes. "We shall need you on holidays! It is going to be hard this first Christmas since the changes."

"Oh, that will be fun!" said Rilla, smiling.

A quick flash passed between their eyes, a warm golden look from Pat that made Rilla's heart glow.

"I'll come," said Pat. "I thank you. If you'll treat me just like the family and not make any difference for me, and let me do just what I want to." He grinned nicely at Mrs. Reed.

"Within limits," she said, smiling.

"You're the boss!" he said with a nice deferential bow toward her.

"That's settled then," said Thurlow, "and you'll come the day college closes and spend the whole Christmas vacation with us. If that doesn't cure you we'll consider you are incurable and act accordingly. But you haven't seen your sleeping quarters yet. Better come in and look them over. You'll have to bunk with me."

"It isn't the first time I've bunked with you, old man. I don't care what the quarters are, so they're with you. Anything that's good enough for you will be a palace for me. And by the way, old pal, why the uniform? Is it a play you're putting on, or have you joined the fire company, or the National Guards?"

Thurlow's face suddenly grew grave.

"I'm just a common policeman, Pat. It was the only job I could find. But I'm liking it a lot. I find there's an ethical side to it if you know how to look for it, and there couldn't be a better place to either study human nature or get experience."

"I'll bet!" said Pat. "Man, you're rarer than I thought you were! I like you a lot, and all the better that you're not above taking the first honest job that comes."

"I'm not so right sure it's as honest as I thought when I undertook it," laughed Thurlow. "I hadn't been in the service two days before I was approached and offered money to shut my mouth about something that was going on which I was put there to prevent."

"Oh, Thurlow!" said his mother anxiously. "You didn't tell me that!"

"There are a good many things I'm not supposed to talk about," laughed the son. "Mother, don't you worry! I haven't just cut my eyeteeth. And probably I'm not in any more danger than I was playing football. Isn't that so, Pat?"

Pat watched his friend with admiring eyes, and smilingly corroborated his friend's statement, but his eyes were unusually grave for Pat as he watched Thurlow thoughtfully.

Pat decided to stay over till Sunday night instead of driving back to college that night, and when the young men were in their room that night with the door safely closed, and a length of living room between them and the doors of Mrs. Reed and Rilla, Pat said in a grave tone:

"Man, you're great for what you've done! We tempted you a lot to come back to college, and I'll admit I came here today determined to force you back by hook or crook, but I'm glad I've come. I've got your angle to your duty, and I see you couldn't do otherwise. And, man, I respect you for it tremendously! But, Thurl, aren't you in a place of extreme danger! You're a hot shot you know, and anybody who monkeys with you'll find that out, I know, but, Thurl, old man, this isn't college football. You're not just up against a lot of undergraduates. You've got all hell to deal with!"

"All hell's right, Pat! I found that out before I had been a day with the service, but, Pat, there's something you don't know, and that is, I've got all heaven to protect me. I guess I may as well break the news to you now as any time. Pat, I've gone back to the God I used to know a little when I was a kid. I used to be a sort of a Christian before I went to college, but when I got out among the fellows I wasn't working much at it. Lately, though, I've come to see it all in a different light and I'm back on the job. From now on Christ is my Saviour, God's my Father, and I'm going at things from a different angle. God seems to have sent this job when I couldn't find anything else, and I figure He's going to take care of me while I'm doing His will. That may sound all haywire to you, but it's plain common sense to me, and I'm trusting God to see me through. Now, maybe that'll make a difference with you. I hope not. But I give you fair warning I'm not going to keep my mouth shut about this. I'm God's man after this, and if you don't like it we'll have to go our separate ways."

Pat's face was very grave and sweet when Thurlow finished.

"Sounds great!" he said gravely, a little sadly. "Looks like you were getting out of my class, Whirl, but I'll do my best to hobble along and not look too out of place."

Thurlow went to the Cradock residence on the avenue the next day before going home, to try over the song with Sandra. He had not been able to get away sooner, but he had telephoned her before going and she was watching for him. She opened the door herself and took him to a music room opening out of a deep hall. The room was not in the same part of the house with Cousin Caroline's own apartment. Besides Cousin Caroline was presumably taking a nap.

So the two had a half-hour together uninterrupted. They talked together a few minutes first, just about matters of the Mission, and Thurlow reported to her that he had found the famous Bat in his next door neighbor, but that careful judicious inquiry through his mother had revealed the fact that Bat's sister Rosie had permanently departed from the neighborhood.

Then they sang, and the two young voices swelled out

together and blended perfectly as if it were permitted them to share an intimacy their owners by no means dared to acknowledge.

At last Sandra swung around on the piano stool and lifted her clear eyes to his.

"Mr. Reed, you are not just a policeman, not an ordinary one. Who are you? Tell me about it please, if we are to be friends. That is, if you want to."

There was nothing of the coquette about Sandra. Not even the lifting of her eyelashes that were every bit as long and handsome as Barbara Sherwood's. She was looking earnestly at him, and he smiled and answered her with a bit of a sigh.

"Last summer I thought I was a Junior in college with a good prospect before me. Then Dad died, and the bank failed and here I am. Everything was gone and I had to get a job and care for Mother and Rilla. This was the only job I could find after weeks of searching. It's been hard for Mother and Rilla, from having every comfort to come down to rotten little Meachin Street, but I guess God had a purpose in it for us all. I know He had for me. I guess there wouldn't have been any other way to bring me back to Him. I'd gotten pretty far away in thought, if not in deed. And He used *you* to bring me back to Him. If you hadn't come to our house that night and asked us to come to Grace Chapel I wouldn't likely have ever gone to church again. I was down and out. I thought God had forgotten us. But thank God I went, partly to please Mother and partly because you seemed so interested, and I found something there I needed."

Sandra's eyes glowed.

"Oh, I'm so glad! You know I was terribly frightened that night. I didn't tell Cousin Caroline, but I was completely turned around, and I thought I saw some perfectly awful-looking men hanging around that old factory—"

"We have them," grinned Thurlow. "I wouldn't advise you to get lost down that way very often. It isn't good. I protested with all my might against going there to live, but Mother insisted, because we own the place. And there really wasn't anything else for us to do just then, after we lost our home. I hadn't a job, you know, and the money was gone. I hope sometime soon to be able to get us out of there as soon as I can see my way ahead. But I'm glad we went there just to meet you and get to know about that chapel. I've learned to know God better and to long to know my Bible, even in the short time we've been down there."

"Oh, I'm glad you came, too. I don't have many— friends—" she hesitated and lifted her smiling eyes— "not many friends who think as I—as *we* do," she finished.

"Thank you for counting me a friend," said Thurlow. "I'd like mighty well to count you that if you'll let me. I left most of my friends behind when I came down to Meachin Street. Somehow they didn't fit. And—well, *you* don't fit there either, only—I guess you understand. I guess it's because you know God so well."

Her hand lingered in his an instant as he said good-by and then she walked down the hall to the door with him, talking. She looked much younger in her simple blue home dress than she had looked at the Mission, and there was somehow a thrill in being able to talk to her about the Lord.

They stood for a moment by the door before he opened it, saying a few last words, when from the upper floor at the head of the stairs came a shrill voice:

"For mercy's sake, Sandra, what in the world is that policeman doing in my front hall? What business does he have coming in here? And who was that I heard singing with you a few minutes ago?"

Sandra's face grew suddenly white with annoyance, and she lifted apologetic eyes to his face.

He put out his hand and gave hers a quick impulsive clasp as he smiled:

"It's all right," he grinned, "I understand. Don't let it worry you. Sorry I may have made trouble for you."

"Oh, that won't hurt me," she laughed. "I have a father who understands me, and I write everything to him. Thank you for coming, and I've enjoyed it."

"So have I. Good-by. See you tomorrow night."

"Sandra, Sandra! Tell me what that policeman is doing down there? I simply won't stand for policemen walking in my house. I—"

But Thurlow was gone and Sandra shut the door and came slowly up the stairs, trying to summon patience to answer all Cousin Caroline's hateful curious questions, and interferences.

16

DOWN at the dump next Sunday morning the three men from the small cabin next above Mrs. Butts' shack lingered around the smoky fire they had made, and watched Bat slowly go up the ashy side of the hill and disappear toward the street. They had sent him on an errand just to get him out of the way, and his inner sense told him this was the case, and yet he went. There were reasons known only to himself why he went.

"You wantta watch dat guy," said Reds, the man with the auburn thatch of thick unwashed hair. "Did you take notice ta his hands? He's been washin' 'em! I never did see his hands clean yet till yestidday! When a guy gets like dat you wantta watch him!"

"Aw, shucks! He's awright!" said Slink, the shifty one. "It's that gal! Find a guy washin' his han's thur's allus a gal!"

"He's got 'im a haircut, too!" growled Brick Etter, the hard one with cruel eyes. "Somethin's come ta 'im! You don't wantta trust 'im too fur. Who is that dame anyway? Where'd she come fum? What's she down here fer? All prettied out? There's somethin' behind all this! Her brother a cop! Fer a cent I'd wipe out that guy! What's he here fer? Some game, you bet! He ain't sa dumb he don't know what it is like in Meachin Street. He might be planted here, ya know!"

"Aw, naw, you got 'im wrong," said Slink, who had the reputation of knowing a good deal about a good many people. "He's just a kid playactin', that's wot he is! He's got him a job policin' an' he's swellin' round helpin' ladies crost the street. I seen him down in the city, raisin' his hand like he owned the earth. He ain't gonta do us no harm. He's just a kid outta school. Never had no experience. You don't needta worry 'bout him. Same also 'bout that other young swell come in the nifty bus, he's just a college guy. I looked him up. He's got a swell dump out in the East End beyond Roselyn. His dad has all kinds of dough, an' the kid owns this estate. Good place ta make a haul some o' these nights. Lotta rich junk in the house an' only caretakers in charge. I'll getta line on it when I get time. Far enough away so they'd never get onta us."

"What I'd liketa know," said Reds, narrowing his eyes, "is what he comes here fer? Swell guy like dat comin' ta Meachin Street? Nothin' fer him down here."

"Same reason as Bat's hands an' haircut," explained Slink. "The skirt! He's chasin' her now. But he won't prob'ly stick long. She's too quiet fer rich guys like that. She must be a cute one, gettin' a guy like him!"

"Cute all right!" grumbled Brick Etter, the wise and cruel. "Bat wantsta watch out. She ain't his kind. Whatever she is, she ain't *his* kind. Washin' his han's an' gettin' a haircut ain't gonta do Bat no good! She's after bigger fish! Bat oughtta get wise ta that 'fore she spoils a perfectly good Bat! I'd liketa find out who she is. That's what I'd liketa know. Slink, whatcha layin' down on the job fer? Whyn'tcha get a line on that skirt?"

"I got a purty good line on her now," drawled Slink, half closing his eyes and looking off over the dump. "She works in a bank down ta Fifty-second and Lombardy Street."

"Works in a bank!" The other two pricked up their ears.

"Sure thing!" said Slink. "'Tain't a great bank, but it's got plenty o' dough. Just about our size ta tackle. Doncha be too flip with Bat. That girl might be a help ta us yet. Let Bat go after her. He might make out better'n ya think. An' we need a bank ur somethin' soon. Treasury's gettin' mighty low."

"You've said it!" said Reds. "Whaddaya know about this bank, Slink? What cops are on that beat?"

"Big Mike Harbison, an' Cranky Joe!"

"Easy combination. Daytime job. Keep yer traps shut. Let Bat get thick with the dame first. We can do a lot through her if we work Bat right."

"He might double-cross ya!" suggested Brick Etter.

"Not Bat!" said Reds. "We got too much on him an' he knows it. Hands off Bat an' watch him. We gotta be sure 'bout this. Slink, you get the fac's t'gether, an' don't notice Bat's washin'. Don't kid him none. This girl's our strong point. Get her scared an' she'll spill anythin' we want. She'll be likely ta know safe combinations an' where ta find the cash quick. But don't let her get wise ta anything! We gotta watch Bat. Give him a little cash ef he wants it. Five ur ten bucks. Don't let *him* get wise ta this yet. *Mind!*"

"Okay!" said Slink.

"Watch that guy!" warned Brick Etter. "Skirts are a pest in our business. You can't trust 'em!"

Over in the old aristocratic part of the city Sandra was having a session with her cousin.

"I must insist, Sandra, if you are going to stay in my house, that you give up this absurd slum work. I simply cannot run the risk in my state of health, of your bringing germs of horrid diseases here. I've always been most susceptible to germs, and when you go down there in that hotbed of disease you are risking my life, to say nothing of your own. I shall cable your father that I cannot be responsible for you any longer unless he forbids this slumming tendency of yours. Ever since that day when you brought a policeman—a *policeman* presuming to call upon a member of *my household* socially, presuming to dare open his lips and attempt to *sing* in my house! Having the effrontery to think that we would be willing to have the atmosphere of our quiet home desecrated by his plebeian voice! Ever since this happened, I say, I have been filled with indignation and anxiety, not knowing what may happen next. I cannot get my sleep. I waken in the night in a frenzy. There may be a gang of thieves on our doorstep, or in our private rooms. We may be shot down in cold blood in our sleep. We may even find ourselves blown into atoms by an awful bomb!"

Sandra sat quietly facing her cousin, trying to keep from laughing, trying to keep from making a sharp retort. Life in this house was daily becoming more and more impossible, and she did not know what to do about it.

When the arrangement had been made before her father went away that she was to spend the winter with her two elderly cousins, and be company for Cousin Caroline, it had seemed ideal. But it had not taken long to discover that Cousin Caroline's ideals and standards were utterly different from hers. Cousin Caroline wanted to play bridge from morning to night, and Sandra didn't play bridge. Sandra loved to go to church and Cousin Caroline said that her back was too weak to sit long in church. Cousin Caroline wanted a continuous procession of teas and dinners and supper parties and Sandra was bored to extinction with all such things. What to do under the circumstances was a serious problem.

The matter had been brought to a climax this morning by an announcement that Cousin Caroline was having a Sunday evening musicale and demanded that Sandra stay home from the evening service in the chapel where she had promised to sing, and entertain her guests.

Sandra knew what those Sunday evening musicales were. They were anything but sacred, or suited to the day.

Sandra's father was a most unusual Christian, a writer and public speaker, and his mission this winter was research for a theological book he was writing. He had brought up his daughter to serve the Lord, and had expressed his utmost delight when she had discovered a former classmate at a Christian school she had attended, living in the city and married to a most devout young minister preaching in this little mission chapel in an unfashionable part of the city.

Cousin Caroline had at first paid little heed to this obsession, as she called it, of Sandra's. It had seemed to her merely a freak that would pass. But one Sunday she had taken it into her head to go and see what it was that held the young girl's interest, and from that time forth she was all against it, and did everything in her power to invent reasons for Sandra to stay at home and keep her company.

Now Sandra was high spirited and knew it, and had spent many hours in humility and prayer laying her will and her fiery spirit and tongue at the foot of the cross, asking that she be made pleasing to the Lord; that she might be enabled to control her temper and her own wishes, and live Christ there in that home where He was not known nor honored. Therefore she endured many discouragements and unhappy hours, trying to please the unpleasable cousin.

It was better when Cousin Conrad was at home, for he was more genial, more ready to take her part and to make things pleasant for her. Often he had gone with her himself when Cousin Caroline chose to insist that the Chapel was in a neighborhood where no girl ought to go alone at night.

But Cousin Conrad was not well and had been away for two months now at a sanitarium taking treatment, and Sandra had to fight her own battles and compromise as much as possible. But sometimes it was not possible.

She listened to the tirade, praying in her heart to be guided and kept from losing control of her tongue.

"I'm sorry, Cousin Caroline," she said gravely. "I didn't realize that I had offended in so many ways. Of course if you feel that way about my work and the people I am thrown with I shall have to go away. I have no right to make you miserable, or let you worry about germs and things. And I have no right to bring my friends here, or let them call upon me if you object to the clothes they wear. It is your house."

"Object? Of course I object! Who wouldn't object to having people see a policeman coming to their house? Why, they'll have it all over town that we have been arrested. And since when did your father's daughter number a policeman among her friends? I declare I wonder what your circumspect father would say if he knew you were companioning with policemen! Singing with them! The idea! You with that lovely voice!"

"I have written Father all about everyone whom I

have met," said Sandra quietly. "He entirely approves of the things I am doing."

"Oh, he would of course, the way you write about them. You would paint everything in glowing colors. And he isn't at all discerning, poor man, so he can't understand! Just wait till I write him a few things and tell him how you are carrying on! See what he thinks then! Oh, I can't imagine what has changed you so! It must be that you are *in love* with that policeman!"

The tone in which she said "in love" was particularly offensive. The color rolled up into Sandra's cheeks and forehead in quick angry waves, and sparks flew into her eyes. She sprang to her feet as if she had reached the limit.

"Nonsense!" she said sharply. "It is time we stopped talking if you have descended to saying things like that. I don't wish to talk about this any more. I shall cable to Father at once that I am leaving, and I will go to my friends the Wheelers. Mr. Wheeler will probably have somebody in his congregation who keeps boarders. They will find me a boarding place near them and you will not be troubled with me any more."

"Indeed you will do no such a thing!" snapped the cousin, now thoroughly aroused and getting up from the chaise lounge where she had been reclining. "After all I have done for you, do you think you have a right to desert me? Go off and leave me alone in the house with servants when my poor brother is stricken and unable to come to my help!"

"Why, Cousin Caroline!" said Sandra in amazement. "You told me yourself that Cousin Conrad had been in the sanitarium the greater part of three years, and that you felt more freedom when he was away because he had to be looked out for so much and was ill so much! You said you were really better off when he was away!"

"I never said any such thing!" screamed the highly nervous woman. "And even if I did I call it highly impertinent for you to try to twist my words and throw them back to me. I am a great deal older than you and you ought to be respectful to me. You are the most ungrateful girl I ever knew. You are not in the least like your father, my beloved cousin. He was always so respectful and courteous! You must be like your mother's people. They probably hadn't much breeding! To think you would suggest going away and leaving me when I have guests and need you! And after all I have done for you!"

Sandra stood amazed and speechless. She wanted to ask her cousin what in the world she had done for her, for notwithstanding her pretentious house on the fashionable avenue, Cousin Caroline had been entirely willing to accept an ample compensation for Sandra's privilege of staying in the house for the winter. Cousin Caroline was very fond of money, and in spite of her generous income had found it altogether pleasant to have a little extra coming in. She could always use it, especially as her lawyer was rather prone to refuse advance payments from her investments. Sandra was still a full minute looking at her cousin, trying to recall a single gift or privilege that she had been given that had not been paid for in full.

"After *all* that I have done for you—!" Cousin Caroline was weeping now, and repeating this sentiment in ladylike sobbing tones.

"Just what do you mean, 'done for me,' Cousin Caroline?" asked Sandra quietly, slipping down into a chair and looking at her excited relative. "Is there something I do not know about? Did Father arrange for anything that I do not pay for?"

Her cousin took her delicate handkerchief down from her angry eyes and pierced the girl with an icy look.

"Do you have to ask?" she said fiercely. "You in this lovely home on one of the most beautiful avenues in the world, in one of the most aristocratic sections of the whole city, and in one of the most, if not *the* most, exclusive neighborhood to be found in this section of the East! And you have to ask what I have done for you? Do you think your few petty dollars pay for the privileges you enjoy in my home, meeting my friends and acquaintances? Do you think they pay for riding in my seven-thousand-dollar limousine? Do you think that the service and the friendship and the companionship I freely accord you are nothing? The privilege of mingling with my guests, of meeting distinguished people, of enjoying all the entertaining and festivity that I enjoy myself, of associating almost daily with men of wealth and culture, and of choosing for yourself a husband from the highest social circles—"

Suddenly Sandra rose again and interrupted the excited flow of language.

"Cousin Caroline," she said, and her voice was controlled and quiet, "you need not say any more. You have put your point of view very plainly, and it sets us so very far apart that I do not see how we can ever think alike. You see these things which you have named are none of them things that loomed very large to me when I came here. I was expecting to find the companionship of someone who was related to me by blood, who would have tastes and interests in life a good deal like mine, because we were born and bred to the same background. I hoped to find something a little like the companionship of the mother I have so missed. I recognized the pleasant home filled with beautiful things, the luxurious room you gave me, the service that was at my call. But these things I understood I was paying for. The other things you have named, the rides in costly cars, the invitations to places where I could not be happy because my standards of life were different from the world that invited me, the amusements I did not enjoy, the distinction of belonging to an exclusive company, do not appeal to me; and I did not come to this city expecting to select a husband. If God has somewhere in this world a companion for me I want to be worthy of the one God chooses. But I am not going about hunting for a husband. If I were choosing one, however, I should not look for him among the men I have met here. They are not the kind of men from whom I would be willing to choose my husband, no matter how wealthy and cultured they might be!"

"No!" snapped Cousin Caroline, "I suppose you would rather have policemen!"

"Yes," said Sandra steadily, "I would rather have— *some* policemen—! *Christian* policemen!" she added with a sudden lighting of her eyes, "and of course with the same degree of general enlightenment and education. Always provided I found I could love one of them with all my heart! But, please, Cousin Caroline, don't let's quarrel, not over husbands at least, for I haven't an idea of hunting a husband at present, and I don't want to quarrel anyway. I'll put it up to you. If it means enough to you for me to stay here the rest of the winter with freedom to live my life as I think I should, very well, I'll stay. But if it is going to worry you continually, and you are going to constantly invent new methods of keeping me away from my work and my friends in the Mission, then I really must go, and I think if that is the case I should go at once. I am going to my room now and you can think it over. Around noon I'll be down and stop at your door to get your decision. And it's quite all right with me whichever way you decide."

"Oh, indeed! That is your ultimatum, is it?"

Sandra looked at her half sadly with a shadow of a frosty smile on her lips, then she said simply:

"Yes, I guess that's about what it has to amount to."

With that she went her way, closing the door quite gently, and going to her own room.

But Cousin Caroline did not wait for noon to bring Sandra back. In half an hour she sent her maid, Wilma, after her.

When Sandra entered she lifted a damp and crumpled handkerchief from eyes that were swollen effectively with weeping, and exhibited a face that appeared the picture of utter dejection.

"Well, you have conquered again, you stubborn overbearing girl," she quavered, her voice like a wail of a martyr. "I cannot be left alone at my time of life, and I cannot see my way clear to laying aside the responsibility I undertook when your father left you here in my care, even if you do bring home a lot of deadly germs from your awful Mission! I will give in and humiliate myself by asking you to remain."

Sandra gave her a troubled look.

"You can't take that attitude, Cousin Caroline," said Sandra firmly. "I was twenty-one last Tuesday and have a right to order my own life. Father and I have a perfect understanding and he wants me to be on my own. I am under his constant advice, and I shall be quite all right. So if you would rather I did not stay you have only to say so."

The small willful shoulders shook fitfully and there were suppressed sobs from behind the dainty soppy handkerchief.

"I—*prefer*—you to—*stay!*" she said at last in a severe

tone as if the words came out like a tooth that was being drawn.

Sandra was very still for a minute or two watching her doubtfully, then she said slowly, thoughtfully:

"Very well, Cousin Caroline, I will stay for a while at least, that is, if you are satisfied about it. But—I'm sorry—I can't stay at home for your musicale Sunday night. I have promised to help with the song service. I'll try not to annoy you any more than I can help, but there are a few things in which I must be the judge."

A long trembling sigh from the sufferer on the chaise lounge. Then,

"I—sup-pose so!" resignedly.

"All right!" said Sandra briskly, determined to be pleasant but firm about the few essentials. She must be allowed to keep on with her work at the Mission, and she must not be forced into those ghastly social functions that were so against all her principles.

She had reached the door when Miss Cradock spoke again.

"Allessandra!"

That was what she always called Sandra when she wished to be formal and humiliating. There was arraignment in the very tone.

Sandra paused and turned toward her anxiously. Was it all to be gone over again? Her cousin had a way of stringing things out for hours.

"Yes?"

"I must make one stipulation! You really must concede this one thing, Allessandra! Won't you ask your policeman to change into civilian clothing before he comes here to call? That is if he *has* any ordinary garments. If he doesn't I would be willing to buy him a suit."

Sandra suddenly sat down on a chair by the door and

burst out laughing. She laughed and laughed, till finally her irate relative sat up and took her sodden handkerchief down from her red eyes and stared at her.

"What is the matter, Allessandra? Have you the hysterics? What could possibly be funny about my request?" Her face was the picture of indignation.

Sandra wiped the tears of mirth from her own eyes and answered.

"Excuse me, Cousin Caroline, but somehow it struck me as very funny indeed. But you won't be troubled with more calls from the policeman—though he isn't in any sense mine—not at present—for you see, he heard you the other day—and—he quite understands! But—I couldn't help thinking what he would say if he knew you had offered to buy him a suit!"

She suppressed another fit of the giggles.

"You see, Cousin Caroline, he is just out of college and as much to the manner born as—we are!"

"Then what in the world is he masquerading around as a policeman for? I don't think it is courteous! I don't like it! A gentleman would find a gentleman's job and not go out of his class. You had better tell him, Allessandra, if you insist on seeing him again, that I said—"

But Sandra had escaped to her room, feeling that her nerves had stood just about all they would for that day.

Up in her room she locked her door and went and confronted herself in the mirror, looking straight into her own eyes and asking herself a question. Was she falling in love with her policeman? If she was she must do something about it right away. She must get her emotions under absolute control!

17

THE work on the house had been going steadily on week after week. Whenever Thurlow had a few hours or even a few minutes of leisure he was making the little house more habitable.

Since the day that they had come home and found their mother had papered two of the ugly side walls in the living room all by herself the two young people had been taking lessons in the simple old art of paper hanging.

Thurlow practiced on the old kitchen which was now his bedroom, sacrificing a good part of his first roll of paper until he succeeded in getting a smooth ceiling hung at last, and then he went at the other ceilings, leaving the side walls for his mother and sister, who often had far more leisure than he did.

They were anxious to get the little house neat and well furnished by Christmas, for they were all looking forward to Pat's coming as a bright spot in the year.

"Mother, you're sure Pat isn't going to make it hard for you if he comes?" asked Thurlow one night.

"Not a bit of it. He'll make it easy. He does a lot of

things for me when you are not here. Don't worry about that. I like to have something going on to make it bright for you children. I know it is going to be hard for you both."

"Not so hard," said Thurlow thoughtfully. "I never dreamed I'd be so interested in fixing this place up as I am, but you see when spring comes I'm counting on selling it, and getting you and Rilla away to a more respectable neighborhood. It hurts me terribly to be going off day after day leaving you down in this awful dump with all sorts of people."

"Well, don't worry any longer. It's been good for me. I'd forgotten there were such people in the world, and I guess it isn't good to forget that. The Lord died for such as much as for us, and we ought to be keeping them in mind, praying for them and witnessing before them, doing for them more understandingly and more eagerly than we do. I'm getting really interested in Mrs. O'Hennessy. She's acquiring the habit of coming over when she smells the bread or the pies just out of the oven, and I've been suspecting lately that the poor old thing is half starved. Her husband had a job once, but he's drunk most of the time, and half the time in the asylum with delirium tremens. And that Bat doesn't work. I'm sure I don't know what they live on. Beer, I guess, but where do they get the beer? Maybe she makes it, I'm not sure, but what would she make it out of? It must cost something to live even on nothing but beer. And as for those seven little boys, the second door below, well, they are precious sometimes. Poor little souls. How they hunger for love and attention, and how empty their little stomachs must be. Once in a while I indulge myself a little and sacrifice a rag and wash all their faces and comb their hair. I have a comb I keep out on the back porch up under the edge of the roof. I wash it in lye after I've used it on them, but you ought to see them when I get done. I washed them all up the other day and stood them in a row. Then I took the looking glass down and showed each one how he looked. They looked and looked and little Jimmy said, 'Did God make me thataway? Is that why He loves me?' and the poor little stutterer said, 'Did m-m-m-my m-m-m-mother know I looked like this afore she died-up? I w-w-wish I c-c-c-cud s-s-see m-m-m-my m-m-m-mother. Do her have a c-c-c-clean f-f-face l-l-like me?'"

Thurlow gave her a troubled look.

"Mother, it's heavenly of you to take an interest in the poor souls but it's terrible for you to have to be living down among them. I'll get you out as soon as I can."

So the paper hanging went on, the rooms blossomed into astonishing beauty at a surprisingly small cost, and the wonder in Meachin Street grew. The women in the next block were beginning to come to borrow salt and sugar and eggs, and to ask what was good for toothache or inflamed eyes. Every woman wanted a sight of the beauties of the cottage whose glories Mrs. O'Hennessy had sounded as far as her acquaintance reached.

Mother Reed kept a jar of little cakes or cookies to pass to such guests when they came, and added to her supplies a table drawer full of little tracts, picture-pamphlets and gospels that she had found at the chapel Mission, to slip along with the cake to each one. Mother Reed was certainly doing her best to make known salvation to everyone on the South Side with whom she came into contact.

The visitors walked around and stared at the pictures and asked questions, sometimes telling their troubles and confessing their sins, and Mother Reed was quietly getting a great hold on the street, even before Christmas came.

It cost a little something to supply even a few cakes and gospels and tracts, but Mother Reed was doing well with her baking and set aside a certain portion of her gains for this work. As neither Rilla nor Thurlow were at home when all these things went on they had no idea either of their mother's business enterprise, or of her philanthropy.

For Mrs. Reed had become a popular baker, and had more orders some days than she could possibly fill.

Of course her children would have protested if they had known how hard she was working, but perhaps it was the best thing that she could have done, for it kept her from thinking of the beautiful past when she had luxuries surrounding her and loving care over her all the time. For her children's sake she would not give way to her sorrow, and therefore she worked instead, making everything bright and cheery for them at their home-coming in the evening.

The house was really charming inside as Christmas holidays drew near. Only the best of their fine old furniture was in use, the remainder being stored in the barn which Thurlow had made strong and secure. Rilla and her mother had touched up the paint in the rooms at odd times, days when the weather allowed an open window for a little while, and the atmosphere was drying rather than freezing. They mounted stepladders and painted window sashes, so that even the outside had a trimmer look.

"What would you think of asking Sandra down during vacation?" Mrs. Reed asked Rilla one evening while they were getting the evening meal on the table, and Thurlow was in his room washing his hands and getting out of his uniform.

"Oh, Mother!" said Rilla, turning delighted eyes

toward her. "But—what would Thurl say? I've never been quite sure he likes her."

"Oh, I think he likes her," said the mother thoughtfully. "We might ask him. Of course I wouldn't suggest it if he was against it. But they have seemed friendly enough, and I thought it might be nice for her. She told me the other night at church that she was very lonely sometimes. That cousin of hers isn't very congenial. But of course if you think Thurlow would object maybe we better not mention it. Only—well, even if he didn't care for having her here when he is at home we could ask her to lunch or something when he is on duty. Only you wouldn't be here then either."

"Why, I'll have some time off. They said I would. Ask Thurl anyway and see what he says."

So at dinner Mrs. Reed asked him.

"Thurl, what would you think of asking Miss Cameron to lunch or dinner or something while Pat is here?" She asked it very casually as she passed his coffee, and was surprised at the lighting of his eyes.

He cast a quick look about the pretty dining room, the cheap wall paper set off by the snowy curtains, the beautiful old mahogany, the fine old china and a few pieces of silver on the sideboard and in the corner cupboard. It was lovely and homelike and good enough for anybody. A pleased look came to his face.

"Great!" he said, "if you can get her. But I don't suppose she can come. She likely has dozens of engagements around Christmas week. That cousin of hers lives in one of those great old brown-stone houses on the avenue near the Circle. They'll have slews of guests, likely. The wonder is to me that she spares time to come to the Mission. But, ask her, if you don't think it will make too much work for you and Rilla. Pat would like her I'm sure. He's her kind."

Over Rilla's bright face there suddenly came a blank, and a thoughtfulness settled down upon her that none of their pleasant plans interrupted. The mother looked from one to the other in puzzled silence. She wondered after all whether it was going to be good to have company at Christmas. She owned she didn't understand either of her two. Perhaps it would have been better to remember that they were just poor people now, and confine their festivities to those poorer than themselves, and not try to get back to their own environment. But it hurt her terribly that her beloved son should have such a strong feeling of inferiority. Now why should he forthwith plan that Pat should like Sandra? And why should that idea have brought a soberness to Rilla's face? Was it going to bring sorrow to her girl to have Pat come? And where did Barbara Sherwood come in? Was she still to be reckoned with in the daily things of life?

The mother sighed and decided that it was all too much for her. However, Pat was already invited. It was too late to consider. He had really invited himself, and it would be just as well to ask Sandra for a meal at least.

The Christmas holidays were approaching fast and Mrs. Reed was busy all day long baking and brewing and getting her wares off to their market place. Then one day Pat arrived right in the midst of her work, asked a few intelligent questions and got the whole truth from her. No, he wouldn't tell, of course he wouldn't, but couldn't he help? It was a grand scheme and what was the use of spoiling her fun? But why shouldn't he carry her wares to the Exchange, leaving her more time to work? Why shouldn't she put him to work? Where was an apron? He could beat eggs. He could stir up sugar and butter in grand shape. He could crack and shell nuts and shred coconut, and pick over raisins. Mincemeat? He could grind the meat and apples in the meat chopper.

Why, this was going to be more fun than a cat-fight! Now, why didn't she let him take the stuff down to the city right away and then he would come back and help her get the next batch out of the way before the kids came back. That was what he called Thurlow and Rilla, the kids!

So like two happy conspirators they went to work, and Mother Reed presently saw her baking sail off in the great high-powered car with a millionaire's son keeping guard over them, as happy as a boy playing store.

She had all the materials out for the mince pies by the time he got back and he ground meat and apples, and cut citron and lemon peel, and weighed spices according to Mrs. Reed's directions, while she rolled the pie crust and deftly fitted it into the tins. Pat stood by and watched the filling put in, and the thin rich crust flapped skillfully over the top, pinched down in a neat ripple around the edge, slashed with a sharp knife in the shape of a Christmas tree, and himself carried them to the oven.

He had just shut the oven door and turned about when Mrs. O'Hennessy tapped at the door and entered with the inevitable teacup, come to borrow a pinch of sugar again.

"Yer late with yer bakin'," said Mrs. O'Hennessy.

"Yes," said Mrs. Reed. "I have some extra orders." She hurried into the pantry for the sugar.

Mrs. O'Hennessy sidled onto a chair and watched Pat, turning the meat grinder with all his might.

"This 'nuther o' yer sons?" asked Mrs. O'Hennessy affably.

"Oh, no," said Mother Reed, a trifle annoyed. "Just a friend come to spend holidays."

"Name of Patrick," said the irrepressible Pat, bowing low toward the caller.

"Thin it's Oirish ye aire?" said the caller.

"Sure thing," said Pat.

Mother Reed smiled and sensed a situation.

"I'm sorry I haven't anything to offer you to eat," she said quickly, hoping to get rid of her caller. "I've sent my finished things all to town, and I'm hurrying to finish the rest before time to get dinner." "What about one of these?" said Pat, suddenly appearing with two small tartlets Mother Reed had put on a plate for him to eat. "I'm sure the lady wouldn't want to go home empty-handed," and he presented her with a tart, one in each hand. Then he swung the kitchen door wide for her, bowing her out with a flourish, and actually sent her on her way good-naturedly. Of course Pat had to hear the whole history of Mrs. O'Hennessy's calls, and the rest of the neighborhood. The two had a beautiful time talking, finishing the second oven full of pies, and cleaning up the kitchen.

"Now," said Pat, "Lady, I'm taking these pies to market, and while I'm gone you're lying down to rest. If you don't promise me that I'll not keep your secret, see?"

"Oh, I'll promise. You've helped me so wonderfully that I'll have plenty of time before I have to set the table."

"That's the nice good little mother," said Pat, leaning over her suddenly and placing a kiss gently on her forehead.

"You don't mind, do you, Mother Reed?" he said, laughing down into her astonished face. "You know I haven't had a mother in a long time. Thurl won't mind if I borrow his for a little while, will he, just to make a Christmas out of it?"

"Why, no, you dear child!" said Mother Reed, much touched.

And then suddenly Pat stooped over, picked her up in

his strong arms and carried her over to her bedroom door, the most astonished mother you could imagine. He laid her down on her bed, and unfolding the blanket that lay at the foot, tucked it carefully around her.

"Now, you lie there till I get back, no matter if all the old-hen-I-sees in all the street come knocking at the door."

He left her still laughing at the way he had carried out his purposes, and then she heard him rushing away in his car with her last load of baking. Well, she thought, she would rest just a minute. So she closed her eyes, and the next thing she knew she heard his car coming back.

Her eyes flew open and looked at the clock on the bureau and she rose up in a hurry. It was almost time for the children to be back, and what would they think of her lying there asleep and the dinner not got yet? She would have to hurry now.

But the dinner was on the table in due time.

Pat set the table and then went out to meet Rilla.

"I don't like to have her coming home alone after dark like this," he said with a grin. "I'll go pick her up."

There were snowflakes whirling down as they drove back and Thurlow was just coming in the gate.

"Where will I put my car, Whirl?" called Pat. "How's the barn? Got room there? There's going to be a blizzard. A real Christmas blizzard! Hooray!"

Thurlow went with him to the barn to house the car, and Rilla, her cheeks glowing, hurried in to help her mother with dinner. Presently they were seated at the table, feeling that a new happiness had come to the little house on Meachin Street.

Thurlow had brought home a big turkey, the gift of a man he had helped out of a difficulty, and handed it over to his mother proudly. It was a twenty-pounder, and she drew a relieved breath. The Christmas dinner was going to be a success. She hadn't dared think about a turkey, they were so high. The best she had dreamed of was a chicken. But now they would have a real feast.

Rilla had brought home a big bunch of holly, and they found a twig of mistletoe tucked in with it. They had great fun after the dishes were done decorating the house and hanging the mistletoe. Pat captured it and hung it in the doorway between the living room and the dining room, and the laughter and chasing that ensued reached out into Meachin Street and drew Bat, poor sinful hungry Bat, through the quietly falling snow, to his old station in the dark to watch the fun. For Rilla proved to be very skillful at getting away from under the mistletoe, and it was finally Mother Reed who was caught and kissed by each one in turn. There stood Bat, his stricken white face almost near enough to be seen where the lamplight fell across the window pane, watching in amazement. Bat couldn't remember that he had ever kissed his mother.

And by and by the lights went out and it was all still in the bright cottage. Bat stole home in the dark through the soft white snow. Whiter than snow! Whiter than snow! Oh, he could never be whiter than snow! He put out his cold hand and touched it as it lay on the fence where he went through. Soft white snow, like angels' wings, the wings of the angel in the old church up on Seventh Street, the angel that stood among tall lilies beside an empty tomb. Whiter than snow! Oh, he, Bat, could never be whiter than snow!

Over by the looming brick wall three shadows passed like wraiths, paused in the drifting whiteness of the great flakes, and pointed.

"Whaddaya know about that? Whad'd I tell ya? Ya hev ta watch that guy. Now what's he ben over ta that house fer?"

Then the shadows slid along and disappeared into darkness, and Meachin Street slept, while the great snowflakes dropped noiselessly as a cloud and covered up their goings.

There were two days left till Christmas and the next morning Pat was up early and eager for work. He helped Mother Reed with her work, and drove away at half past ten with a load of good things. When he came back a couple of hours later he had a great lovely hemlock tree in the back of his car, several bundles of laurel and a lot of small packages. After he had deposited the tree in the barn he came in and draped the laurel wreaths all about the pretty rooms, till it sang Christmas from every wall. Then he hung a big holly wreath on the front door, and Mother Reed found a broad scarlet ribbon for a bow with long fluttering ends. There it hung on the cheap little door and glorified the whole street. Even in the snow it hung there, safe from the drifts because it was under a small roof that Thurlow had nailed over the front door early in the fall. And oh, what didn't that holly wreath and its red ribbon do to the Street!

Word of it got out and traveled from house to house, till even the woman with a heavy cold, and the woman who had seven children, and the woman with a toothache came out to view it in the storm. A holly wreath with red ribbons on Meachin Street was something that had never happened before!

Bat walked by, and the three evil-eyed men walked by, and looked and came back; for the way to the dump was snowed under, and their evil doings were held in abeyance for the time being.

The seven little boys ran out with seven colds, each one worse than the other, and got snow in their shoes, both from above and from below where there were holes, and snow up their flimsy sleeves of the old sweaters that were out at the elbows, and snow up their thin inadequate trousers, because they all fell down with staring. The smallest one cried, and went shivering back to the cold unhappy shelter, but they had seen the holly wreath on Meachin Street with the gay Christmas ribbon floating joyously out to defy the storm, and they went back to flatten cold little wet sorry noses against the dirty window panes, and look up into the whirl, whirl, of heaven above, and wonder what angels were like, and when would come April gold?

18

THERE was extra baking to be done that day, for the orders had come in thick and fast for Christmas, and Mother Reed told Pat she had to make hay while the sun shone. So Pat worked shoulder to shoulder with her, and the small oven was taxed to its utmost.

Pat made two journeys to town that afternoon, getting the goods delivered as fast as they were turned out, and bringing back more orders. He was as excited over the success of the Home Bakery as was his tired eager hostess. There were certain things that her children needed badly and she longed in her heart to have enough saved to buy them for Christmas. She had almost enough. Also, she had it in her heart to get a little gift each for Sandra and Pat. So she worked, bright-eyed, and with unflagging energy.

"Getting too tired, Mother Reed! Got to take a rest!" said Pat when he started on his last trip. She promised, and was as good as her word, lying down, but like a child too excited to sleep.

Pat did not return till almost dark this second trip, so she was up and at it again, making out her lists for tomorrow, doing up some trifles she had prepared for the little waifs on Meachin Street, tidying the kitchen from its hard service of the day, and doing the last things to the great kettle of soup that had been on the back of the stove all the afternoon. Supper was ready. Soup and pie. Good soup, plenty of it, with enough potatoes in it, and some tender bits of meat. Pie from the last baking, apple pie and cheese. Pat said it was the best supper he ever tasted.

And then when it was cleared away they set up Pat's Christmas tree, dragging it in merrily. Rilla brushed up the snow from the floor while the boys set up the tree in the corner of the living room across from the fireplace.

Such fun as they had trimming it! Pat had bought balls and tinsel and trinkets galore, a sweeping order giving the salesgirl carte blanche, and he was like a child unpacking them and discovering each new form of brilliancy.

They were just in the midst of it when a small runabout turned into Meachin Street, there came presently a tap at the door, and there stood Sandra on the doorstep, muffled in her squirrel coat with her gray felt hat with the cocky scarlet feather aslant, snowflakes tangled in her eyelashes, and her arms full of packages.

"Merry Christmas!" she greeted Thurlow who opened the door. "Am I intruding?"

"Intruding? No! Can the blessed sunshine intrude?" said Thurlow, his face a blaze of welcome. "Could a star intrude in the dark sky?"

"Well, I like that!" called out Pat. "Are we the dark sky? Who is this blaze of morning glory? Lead me to this star of a dark night!"

"Meet Pat!" said Thurlow, laughing and drawing Sandra into the room, with an air of recovering unexpectedly something that belonged to him.

"Oh, I didn't know you had a guest. I looked through the window and I thought you were alone."

"I'm not a guest, just a mere orphan cast on their tender mercies. Won't someone please name your lovely name?"

"It's just Sandra!" said the girl with dancing eyes. "And I'm rather an orphan myself tonight. My cousin has gone to a house party which I declined. It wasn't my style. So I thought I'd run down with a few trifles." Thurlow was lifting the mound of packages from her arms and beaming into her eyes.

"But if your cousin is away, why can't you stay with us?" cried Rilla. "We were dying to ask you to come, but we didn't quite dare, down to this little old dump!"

"Will I stay? Ask me and see!" said Sandra with shining eyes. "This is no dump. It looks like a little bit of heaven to me!" she said, looking around.

"You and me too, lady!" murmured Pat delightedly. "You're elected, isn't she, Mother Reed?"

"And, oh, what a gorgeous tree!" exclaimed Sandra. "What fun! May I help trim it?"

"You certainly may!" said Thurlow, approaching almost reverently and daring to unfasten the fur coat and lift it from her, shaking the snowflakes away that still lingered on its collar.

Rilla pulled off her gloves, and took her chic little hat and Sandra stood arrayed in a bright wool dress of scarlet, looking like a holly berry. Then the mother drew up a big chair by the open fire and pulled Sandra down into it. Thurlow was on his knees taking off her galoshes, and Pat, disappearing for a moment, returned with a large piece of apple pie on a china plate with a silver fork, and down on one knee proffered it solemnly.

It was a gay time and lonely Sandra almost wept with the joy of it.

"What about that car?" asked Pat, suddenly appearing from a reconnoiter in the barn. "There's room enough in the barn for it. No need in leaving it out in the cold. Can I put it away?"

"You don't have to go back to your home for anything, do you? I can lend you anything you need," pleaded Rilla.

Sandra smiled.

"The truth is I came down to Wheelers' hoping they'd let me park on their living-room couch for a couple of nights because it was so lonely at home, and I brought my suitcase hopefully along, but I found the Wheelers had gone to their home gathering, so I was left out in the cold."

"Good work!" said Thurlow. "There must have been an angel on the job somewhere. Now, Pat and I will go out and look after the car."

His eyes met Sandra's and a look flashed from one to the other that warmed both their hearts.

The young men went out and Sandra sat by the fire eating her pie, hovered over by Rilla and her mother, and when the two came in they all went to trimming the tree.

Once in the process they all piled into Pat's car and went whirling out in the snow to get some last forgotten things for the morrow. Mother Reed, left alone, sat for a moment by the fire looking at the tree and thinking happy thoughts about her children, wistful thoughts, a shade of anxiety in her eyes as she reflected on possibilities that might bring more unhappiness for the future. Then she was startled by a knock. The postman, getting rid of the last heavy Christmas mail. Cards from many friends, a package or two for Rilla, a fairly large one for Thurlow with a foreign postmark. She looked at it startled. Was that Barbara's writing? It did not look like it. There was a dealer's address—no, a photographer's address—given for return. Then she heard the car returning and the children stamping off the snow. They had come back. She laid the mail down hastily and went with a whisk broom to help brush them off, and forgot the package until they were all in again.

They came in laughing and talking as if they had been friends for years. Mother Reed noted the happy look in both her children's eyes, and suddenly she wished she had put away that package with the foreign stamp. It seemed a false note in the bright evening. Christmas Eve, Barbara Sherwood's gift perhaps, and Thurlow happy with another girl, having a good time. Why let him see it until later when the others were gone?

But it was too late. Rilla had spied the pile of mail and was already sorting it out.

"Oh, a letter for me from Betty!" she cried. "And a package for Thurl! Oh, that must be from Barbara Sherwood! That's where they've been staying. See the postmark!"

Then suddenly Rilla wished she had bitten her tongue out before she said that. She looked up at her brother as he reached out a quick hand for his package, as if once in his hand he could obliterate it. The light had gone from his face and he wore a heavy frown.

"Open it!" said Thurlow's mother quietly. "That's our rule, you know, all things that come in the mail can be opened before Christmas, the rest of the things wait till morning."

Mrs. Reed had a feeling that if there was any ghost here it had better be laid at once and put out of the way. Nothing could be harmed by bringing it out in the open. It was better so, perhaps, than to have bright hopes rise only to be withered later, if there were any such possibilities either way.

Thurlow looked hesitantly at his mother, and then with another frown broke the string with his fingers and tore the wrappings away, saying:

"Oh, well, get it out of the way. It won't be anything much. Some trinket likely!"

But a square thin box came to light from the foreign wrappings, and then a picture in a handsome leather frame!

Thurlow held it up to view and there was Barbara Sherwood's engaging smile and lovely dimples, Barbara's amber-flecked eyes twinkling gaily at them!

Thurlow stared at it a full second and then flung it on the table carelessly among its wrappings with no comment and went back to work on the tree.

Pat looked at him quizzically and then went and picked up the picture, holding it under the light where they all could get a good view of it.

"Some baby!" he commented gaily. "Looks like a movie star! Gaze on those lamps! She certainly knows her audience, doesn't she? I beg your pardon, Whirl! Hope I haven't hurt your feelings. Say, isn't she the baby doll you brought up to college once?"

"Did I ever bring her up?" said Thurlow with elaborate carelessness. "Yes, I guess perhaps I did. That's Barbara Sherwood. Didn't you meet her?"

"Well, I should say I did!" said Pat, gazing on the picture speculatively, "and I didn't care for her. She's a looker all right, but I never thought she was your type."

"Type?" said Thurlow, still with that studied indifference. "Just exactly what do you think my type would be?"

Pat looked at his friend and then about the room. "Well, brother," he said with comical thoughtfulness, "since you have asked, I should say your type would be more like—well, like these two girls here." His look lingered on Sandra, and suddenly she felt the color flame into her cheeks. It was vexing to her that her color behaved so outrageously sometimes. But she smiled and bowed low with a "Thank you," and Rilla followed her example with a sweeping curtsy and a "Thank you, kind sir!"

Thurlow's glance darted keenly about the little circle.

"Well, you see, discerning friend, I couldn't bring my sister to the prom because she was too young then. Mother didn't let her go out to parties. And as for Sandra, I didn't know her then. Besides"—he straightened up from his work and let his glance go slowly from face to face of his little, somewhat breathless audience— "besides, Barbara *asked* to go! I couldn't very well help it, could I?"

Rilla gasped.

"Thurl!"

Mrs. Reed looked startled, puzzling just what state of mind could have forced Thurlow, always such a gentleman, to speak so almost bitterly, of even just a friend. And Barbara had been surely more than just a friend to Thurlow! Or hadn't she? She was puzzled to know. There was an instant's tensity in the air.

But the irrepressible Pat broke into the gap in the conversation.

"All is then well," he said solemnly, "and we shall lay the lady on the table and proceed to the business of the hour!" And amid the half-nervous laughter of the girls he laid the handsome picture face down on the top of the piano, covered it elaborately with a bright rainbow scarf that lay across the back of a chair, and turned away. The scarf happened to be Sandra's.

It developed presently that Thurlow's beat had been changed for the period of the holidays, and that he was to go on duty at midnight.

"Oh, Thurlow!" said his mother in dismay. "You didn't tell me!"

"No, Mother-Mine!" said Thurlow with a tender smile, "I didn't want to spoil the party. Haven't we had a good time?"

"Yes, but—how long have you known?"

"For almost two weeks."

"But Christmas Eve!" said Rilla unhappily.

"Christmas Eve is about over, isn't it, little sister?" And Sandra couldn't help thinking how tenderly he spoke to his sister.

"But we were going to sing carols!"

"We'll have time to sing 'Silent Night' after I've changed to my uniform," he said, looking at his watch, "and the rest of the carols can wait till morning. I'll be off at five and I'll get back in a hurry!"

"But when will you sleep?" asked Sandra, wide-eyed.

"You don't need sleep when you're having a good time!" said Thurlow happily, and his mother drew a sigh of relief. But Thurlow gave Sandra a look that made her forget that picture lying face down on the piano under her rainbow scarf.

"Well, can't we at least take you to wherever it is you have to go?" asked Sandra. "My car is small and easy to get out, and it's snowing pretty hard now."

"Thank you, but it wouldn't be good either for you or me. No, don't worry. This is real Christmas weather, and I'll be all right!" He gave her another smile that made her cheeks glow, and made her glad that Cousin Caroline wasn't around to look into her heart now, nor see her cheeks burn.

"Oh, I do hate to have you out all night in the storm. Christmas Eve, too. So many dreadful things can happen. So many people drunk!"

"Now, Mother-Mine, that doesn't sound like you.

Remember those angels you are always talking about. Don't you think God can take care of me Christmas Eve as well as any other night? I'll have to serve nights a lot of the time, of course, and we mustn't worry! God is there!" He kissed her and went away to get ready.

But when he came back from his room arrayed in his uniform, looking so big and stern and capable, Pat turned around from where he was helping Rilla fix a string of silver balls and spoke.

"Take your time, officer, we're going to sing all the verses of 'Silent Night,' see? For I'm taking you as near your destination as you think it wise to let me go. So, now, Rilla, let's go!" and they began to sing.

"Silent Night! Holy Night!—" the rich sweet voices rolled out, and huddled listeners at open doorways marveled, wondered what was the light that shone out from the cottage, where queer things were always going on, and some braved the storm to go and see.

They did not see the big cop and the other man go to the barn, and were startled as Sandra's little car slid out through the snow bearing Thurlow to his duty, but just as they heard the car start a strange thing happened to the little cottage, where the lamps had been turned low while the singing went on, leaving only the colored tinsel-twinkle on the tree for light. But now, suddenly, as the car came forth from the barn and turned into the road, a great bright star blazed forth, just above the door.

The watchers could not possibly know that Rilla and Pat had arranged it all, and that Rilla had attached the star-cord to a battery at just the right moment as a surprise to Thurlow.

Then, following the vision of the bright star, came voices.

Rilla and Sandra, warmly wrapped, stood on the doorstep beneath the star, the light drifting down into the whiteness of their faces, making a halo of their pretty hair, the large softly falling flakes of snow weaving a veil over the picture, as they sang:

> *"Joy to the world, the Lord is come!*
> *Let earth receive her king;*
> *Let every heart prepare Him room,*
> *And heaven and nature sing."*

The frowning furtive amazed group of shadows stood and listened, withdrawing into the deepest darkness, a mere part of the blackness of the great factory wall that stood out against the whiteness of the white, white world.

> *"No more let sin and sorrow grow,*
> *Nor thorns infest the ground;*
> *He comes to make His blessings flow*
> *Far as the curse is found—"*

The car had stopped abruptly as it came in front of the cottage and the men in the shadows could see the men in the car lift their hats as they listened to the singing. Then as the voices of the girls died away, the two in the car took up a strain, and the words smote the hearts of the sinners cowering there under a gospel to which they had never listened before:

> *"O holy Child of Bethlehem,*
> *Descend to us we pray;*
> *Cast out our sin and enter in;*
> *Be born in us today.*
> *We hear the Christmas angels*
> *The great glad tidings tell;*

O, come to us, abide with us,
Our Lord, Emmanuel."

The voices ceased, and then the young men cried out:
"Good night! That was great! *Mer-ry Christ-mas!*" and the car dashed away into the whiteness and rounded the corner with the echo of Merry Christmas in the white air.

"Well now, whaddaya make o' dat?" said Reds.

"Ain't that the limit!" said Slink.

"You wantta watch them guys!" said Brick Etter. "Singin' cops ain't ta be trusted. They mebbe got us on the spot!"

"On the spot with God, p'raps," said Slink, and snickered.

"Where's Bat?" asked Brick Etter sharply. "You wantta watch that guy. And who's that other dame?"

Then they passed on into the white darkness, looking back with strange mingled fear and wistfulness toward that great white star that kept vigil alone over the cottage, where the songs still seemed to hover in its beams.

Rilla and Sandra nestled warmly into the big soft bed and talked a few minutes, just hovering on the edge of things they would like to say and didn't quite dare. At last, after a pause, Sandra said in a sleepy tone:

"Who is Barbara Sherwood?"

Rilla roused to answer, tried to be casual:

"Oh, she's just a girl that used to live across the street from us. We all went to school together. She's in the south of France with her family this winter." Her voice trailed off sleepily with intention and Sandra asked no more, but she lay thinking until she heard her car returning with Pat, and then she too closed her eyes in sleep. After all, there was tomorrow, and the south of

France was a long way off. And tomorrow was Christmas Day!

Then they all slept, and only Bat was awake, stealing forth when the rest were all gone, and standing alone across the street, keeping white vigil with the great blazing star, vaguely connecting it with the lamb of God whose blood would wash one white as snow.

19

THURLOW had not opened all his mail on Christmas Eve. He hadn't even glanced at it to see what it was, and it lay there on the table beside the piano when he got back on Christmas morning.

Pat had not let him come home alone on Christmas morning. He had slipped out into the rose and gray of a new dawn, with the snow all fallen and the sun arising in great shape, and brought Thurlow back. He was bleary-eyed for want of sleep, but wore a radiant face and fairly beamed when he recognized Pat in his big car at the corner where he had been dropped the night before.

They came stealing into the house, but were not ahead of the girls, who were waiting to surprise them with the first cry of Merry Christmas that morning.

It was after the breakfast of real old-fashioned buckwheat cakes and sausage and maple syrup that Thurlow discovered his letter and opened it, and out of it dropped a check for a hundred dollars.

In amaze he stooped, picked it up and looked at it dully! What on earth could this be? Then he turned to the letter.

Mr. Thurlow Reed,
No. 77 in the City Service,
Care of Station No. 4,
Harvey and Cook Streets, City.

Dear Mr. Reed:

At this joyous Christmas time I feel that among other gifts for which I am duly grateful, I want to thank you for a very great service rendered to me a few weeks ago when you saved the life of my dear wife from being crushed out beneath the wheels of an oncoming car.

I know that no words are adequate to express my gratitude, nor is this trifling check which I enclose a fitting repayment for so great a service, but it will perhaps serve to show you that I recognize your bravery and my indebtedness to you for the dearest on earth to me.

Be assured I shall not forget what you have done for me, and may God grant you a joyful Christmas Day.

Yours very sincerely,
George Steele

Thurlow stood dumbfounded gazing at the check and then he handed the letter over to his mother.

"I shall not keep it of course," he said dazedly. "I was only doing my duty. But wasn't it nice of him?"

"I don't see why you shouldn't keep it!" said Rilla after the letter had been read aloud. "You earned it. You risked your life."

"The city pays me for risking my life, every day, little sister. I was only in my line of duty. You understand, don't you, Pat?"

"Oh, yes, I suppose I do, old man. Still, I wish you'd

keep it. It's a sort of prize, or a medal like the croix de guerre."

"What do you think, Mother?"

"It's just possible you might hurt him by returning it. Why don't you go and see him, Thurl? Maybe you could tell. I'm sure whatever you decide will be the right thing." She smiled her perfect confidence.

The look in her boy's eyes was reward enough for her faith in his decision. He folded the check thoughtfully and put it in his pocket.

"I'll see," he said. "I'll pray over it," with a sudden illumination in his face. "I've just been discovering what a wonderful relief that is, putting the responsibility on God."

His eyes sought Sandra's. He seemed to be speaking to her.

"Isn't it!" she said softly, with an answering illumination in her eyes.

Pat stood there silent, looking at the two thoughtfully, respectfully. These two had something he didn't understand. Then his eyes sought Rilla's and he saw that she too understood this magic language.

"I guess you folks'll have to let me in on this secret society you seem to have, sometime. If you can get all lit up like that over a few words, I'd like to know the secret."

There was a wistfulness about his words that touched them all, but it was Rilla who answered:

"Oh, we will! We will! It will be wonderful to have you in it too!"

"Okay! Then let's get to work opening these packages. I absotively can't wait any longer. Here, Mother Reed, you begin."

Such a beautiful time as they had opening the presents, which had begun in such a humble way several weeks before, when Rilla drew the first thread in a handkerchief she was hemstitching for her brother. But somehow there had been ways to get other necessities too, that they knew each other needed. And then Sandra had added her lovely expensive trifles, that yet were so dainty and so fraught with loving thought that they could not be refused. And then came Pat with several gorgeous presents, without regard to price.

"You know you told me, Mother Reed, that if I came I might do as I pleased," he reminded her, when she remonstrated with him for the beautiful pearl breast pin which he had given her.

"Within limits, dear boy," she said gently.

"Yes, well, that was my limit this time. I wanted to give you something real to show you how much I appreciate your having taken me in this way. I thought that would look nice on you so I got it, but if you don't like it I can change it for something you'd prefer."

"I love it!" said Mother Reed suddenly. "Of course I'll accept it and wear it every time you come to visit when I dress up for dinner."

"That's the right answer!" sighed Pat with relief. "I was afraid you were going to spoil the day for me."

For Rilla there was a set of books Pat had heard her say she longed to read, and for Thurlow a wonderful watch that would shine the hour in the dark. For Sandra there was a great box of candy, and both girls had Christmas roses, only in Rilla's there was one gorgeous white rose in the midst.

Rilla had been saving up a little here and a little there ever since Pat had said he was coming for Christmas, and her gift to him was a small, clear type, beautifully bound Bible. At the last minute she had weakened on giving him such a gift when he might not even believe in it, and had selected a fountain pen as her gift to him. But after what he had said about letting him in on their secret understanding she had slipped into her room and brought the package from where she had hidden it last night when she substituted the pen, and put it among Pat's other things. And Pat, when he found it, opened to the fly leaf and read the inscription, then lifted his eyes to her face with a beautiful look. Afterwards he followed her into the kitchen when she went to baste the turkey and standing beside her as she rose from stooping over the oven, he slipped his arm about her gently and looked down into her sweet flushed face.

"I'm glad you gave me just that, Rilla" he said earnestly, and then he bent over her and reverently kissed her forehead.

Mother Reed was coming so nothing more could be said then, but Rilla came back into the living room looking as if she had received a benediction, and all day long her eyes continued to shine in a lovely faraway glory that illumined her whole face.

They had a party that afternoon for the seven little boys who lived the second house down the street. They came slicked to the last hair, their faces washed as far as the ears at least, and with an assortment of raiment that would have broken the hearts of real mothers. Mrs. Butts came also, a trifle out of breath, hurrying in with the family handkerchief which she said "Jimmy would need." Once there she stayed, entranced. Mrs. O'Hennessy just frankly came without any excuse but that she wanted to see "how the childer took the Christmas tree."

Thurlow was asleep in his back bedroom for a while, but he had told them to go ahead and not mind him. He'd like to see the poor little devils get their fill for once, and he'd be out by the time they fed them.

So they sat for a time and just looked their longing

little souls out at that wonderful tree, and little Jimmy wanted to know if that was the kind of trees they had in heaven. By this time he had called at the Reed home often enough, and conversed on religious themes enough, to be fairly sure there was a place called heaven, and a way to get there.

Then they played some games, and Pat and Rilla and Sandra played with them. "Going to Jerusalem" was a game utterly new and charming to the poor little hoodlums of Meachin Street. They played "Drop the handkerchief," and "Blind man's buff," and "Hide the thimble," until one little urchin was discovered trying to secrete the thimble permanently in his ragged bottomless pocket.

Then Rilla sat them down in a row and told them a Christmas story, making pictures with chalk on a sheet of brown paper, a picture for each of them, with a tiny Bible verse on each, which she made them say over until they seemed to understand.

When they grew restless Sandra grouped them around the piano and taught them Luther's cradle hymn, "Away in a manger," and the little piping voices caught it quickly and shouted it out with a vim. After that Thurlow appeared on the scene and helped dish out the ice cream which Pat had insisted on getting. The girls passed the cakes and candies, and gave out some little simple presents, having hastily improvised two gifts for the elderly uninvited guests, two colored pictures that Rilla found in the desk drawer.

Then for a grand finale the guests grouped around the piano and sang their song again, and the four young people sang two or three more for the elders, Christmas messages with salvation made plain in them.

The little boys were allowed by Pat to go up to the tree and each select an ornament for their very own, and then, clutching their precious booty, they went outside in the white world where the gathering darkness was dropping down, and stood in a row while Rilla connected the great star.

They all stood breathless, huddled there in the snow, till, at a signal from Pat, who had been whispering to them as they came out, they all shouted "Merry Christmas!"

With many a look backward, so that they frequently fell over in the snow because they wanted to watch the star, they went back to their desolate shacks, and the party was over. Mrs. Butts seemed thoughtful and a bit effusive as she said good-by, and Mrs. O'Hennessy wiped away a weak tear and said she wished Rosie could have had a party like that.

At last the Reeds and their guests were alone, and they sat themselves down and laughed long and loud, and then almost wept as they recalled certain pitiful remarks of their young guests, and the quaint appreciation of them all.

"Great cats!" said Pat, "that was hard work! But I like it! I'd like to do it again, many times, and I mean to. That's a use I can put my big house to sometime. Just wait till I get out of college and I'll be tellin' ya!" And just then the turkey cried out from the oven that it was done and wanted to get out right away this minute, and they all scurried around and put the wonderful dinner on the table, the dinner that had fairly got itself ready all day.

Thurlow mashed the potatoes that his mother had put on to boil as soon as the guests departed, mashed the turnips, and skinned the beets. Rilla made the coffee and got the bread and butter and cheese and olives and nuts, while Sandra whisked the table into shape in no time, and Mrs. Reed made the gravy and took up the turkey.

Such a dinner as they had! It took almost two hours to eat it because they took things in a leisurely way. They had sat down at five and didn't get up till seven. And then suddenly it was time to go to the chapel to the Christmas service. Pat didn't know about the chapel but he went along, taking them all down in his car, and heard a Christmas testimony and prayer service, and then a ringing Christmas message. He sat beside Rilla holding the hymn book when they sang, and then stood up with Thurlow and Sandra and Rilla to sing a quartette that the minister requested. Pat enjoyed it all. But then perhaps Pat was in a state of mind to enjoy almost anything just then. Nevertheless on the way home, sitting beside Rilla in the front seat of the car, he told her that he liked it and he wanted to go again. He said he never knew there were churches like that, nor ministers like that, and he wanted to get in on it. Rilla was very happy about it. It seemed an answer to a very earnest prayer of hers that had been in her heart all day for Pat.

Then they turned the grim corner into Meachin Street and there was the star, shining away into the night, and there across the way in the shadow of the great brick factory wall there seemed a whole populace, who shrank and faded into nowhere as the car came sweeping up to the gate of the Reed cottage.

They gathered around the piano again and sang, hymns and carols, and sweet old songs, till Thurlow had to go again to his job and night came down, Christmas night in a greatly stirred Meachin Street.

"You'll come and see us again?" asked Thurlow anxiously as he stood in his uniform by the door, ready to go, and talked to Sandra alone for a minute.

"I'd like to. It's been wonderful!" she said, meeting the look in his eyes with another like it. "It's the first time I've felt at home since Father went away. I'll write him all about it tomorrow and he'll be so glad I've found some Christian friends."

"Oh, that's great!" said Thurlow, holding her hand in a close clasp. "But won't he mind that one of them is a policeman?"

"Not my father!" said Sandra proudly. "He'll say it is great that there is a Christian policeman. He'll say he wishes there were more of them!"

The clasp of their hands grew stronger for an instant and then Thurlow turned and tramped down to the car where Pat waited for him, and Sandra stood in the door and watched him away, the big good-looking policeman with the gun and the steel bracelets hidden away about him, and a night full of adventure and possible peril before him. Her heart contracted with a sudden fear, till she remembered what he had said to his mother last night about God's angels taking care.

And Rilla stood at the window and watched Pat guide his beautiful car away into the night, thinking how wonderful he was, and how her heart had thrilled when he kissed her so gently. Then she looked at Sandra's face, gentle and sweet in the light of the great star. The mother watched both girls and prayed in her heart that God would give them His best.

So Christmas was a new beginning of many things.

20

THURLOW went to see Mr. Steele the next day and told him he did not feel right about taking that check, that he had only done what he would have done for anybody, what he was paid by the city to do for anyone in need.

The big man sat back in his armed mahogany chair with the tips of his fingers touching and looked at the big boy in the uniform and smiled.

"Well, that's a nice feeling for you to have, young man, and I honor you for it, but what about me? I feel a great gratitude to you for what you did for me personally, whether you had a personal interest in me and my family or not, and it eases the overwhelming burden of gratitude in my heart for me to give you a little token of my esteem. I'd like you to take that check and use it in any way you see fit, just to remember that I'm grateful. Get something you've always wanted, or get anything you like, but take it. You see, my wife asked me when she came home to do something for you, and I promised I would. This isn't it, this is my own personal symbol of gratitude that she was spared to me. I'm keeping my promise to my wife a little later. You'll hear from me again, but this is just a little Christmas gift to one who did a great thing for me, whether he knew it or not."

At last Thurlow was convinced that he must keep the check and a great pleasure stole over him as he rose to leave. It was good to have so much ahead and know he had a right to it.

"I'm leaving for the sunny south tonight," said the man as he followed Thurlow to the door, "but when I get back I am going to send for you and I want to talk something over with you. Aren't you the young man who came to see my wife about selling a house to her woman's club? I thought so. Then you're the son of my old friend Reed. Well, I want to have a good talk with you when I get back. I'll send for you some day. Good night!"

And Thurlow walked on down to his beat whistling as he went: "Thanks be to God!" out of the anthem he and Sandra had sung a few Sundays ago.

So the happy holiday passed. Sandra went back to her whimsical cousin, and Pat went back to his college. Life settled down to the daily monotonous grind. Sometimes Thurlow was on duty at night and sometimes in the daytime, and Rilla had learned to walk staidly to the bank without looking for furtive figures at every corner. Bat hadn't been near her since, and of course she had been foolish to be so frightened.

Much of her courage, too, came from having her mind so filled with happy thoughts. Pat was writing to her almost every day, although twice a week was all he was supposed to write. He was telling her all about himself, his past, and the everyday happenings in college. That gave her a great deal to think about, and she wrote often to Pat. She was always thinking pleasant thoughts to write to Pat. Pat would be coming again at Easter vacation, and he wanted them all to come to him at Commencement. Thurl thought he might get off for the day and take them. Life was looking bright indeed to Rilla. She had taken a Sunday School class in the Mission and coaxed the seven little boys to go with her, and that made many amusing incidents to relate. Oh, life was taking on a new look for Rilla and she was almost happier than she had been when she was a carefree girl back in the old home. If Father were only here now she would be perfectly content, she told herself. Father would love Pat, and Pat would love Father.

She was walking along one Monday morning thinking her happy thoughts, when she saw Bat come out of a street just ahead of her and turn his head her way.

But she wasn't afraid of Bat any more, she told herself. She knew his queer old mother, and understood his background better. Poor Bat! She was in a mood to feel very sorry for everybody else, she was so quietly happy herself.

Then, too, Bat had been at the chapel last night. Sitting in the back seat in the shadow, chewing on his endless quid of gum, narrowing his eyes at everybody and everything, watching and listening with a strange hungry look in his face, as hungry as those seven little boys had been for the cake and ice cream on Christmas Day!

Rilla had sat at the piano where she could see his face without seeming to watch him, and once she thought she saw a tear trickle down his cheek. He had brushed it quickly away, but when the prayer came she noticed that he bowed his wild thatch of a head, and later, when Mr. Wheeler asked if anyone would like to accept the Saviour tonight, or would like their prayers, she had been certain that Bat had raised his hand. It only went up halfway and then was jerked down hastily and Bat had lowered his head and look shamedly at the floor, but she had been quite sure. The minister told her afterward that he thought so too. Perhaps Bat would really find the Lord! Wouldn't that be wonderful? Poor Bat!

So it was with an altogether kindly feeling that Rilla approached the corner where Bat was standing, and looked up with a pleasant little impersonal smile to greet him.

But Bat's face was not smiling. He was frowning and he looked furtive and almost as frightening as the first time she had seen him. She shrank away as he slouched along by her side.

"Say, you, are you still got them twelve legions of angels you was tellin' about?"

"Oh, why, yes, of course!" said Rilla, suddenly getting her breath again and trying to talk quite cheerily.

"Well, say, could anybody get 'em too? Anybody else 'siden you?"

"Why, yes, of course," said Rilla, taking courage now. Perhaps Bat wanted to ask her how to be saved and didn't know the right words to use.

"I heard ya singin' 'bout the blood of the Lamb washin' sins. Have they got any o' that thar blood down at the Mission? I'd work an' I'd pay fer it ef I cud get some, enough to wash me white like you sung once."

"Why, you don't have to pay for the blood of the Lamb!" said Rilla. "It's free! The Lamb is God's Son, Jesus Christ. He is the one who paid His lifeblood to take away our sins. His blood is free and washes us white."

"You mean it don't cost nothin'?"

"Not a thing. It's free for the taking."

"How d'ya make that out?"

"Because God says so in the Bible. He says: 'Though your sins be as scarlet they shall be as white as snow, and though they be red like crimson they shall be as white as wool.'"

"Ain't that grand! But how d'ya get it? Say, ef I come ta youse house some night will ya tell me how ta get white?"

"Of course!" said Rilla, elated but a little frightened at the prospect. "And my brother will tell you. He knows how to tell people about those things."

"He's a cop. He wouldn't wantta talk ta me. I b'long ta the gang!"

"Oh, yes, he would," said Rilla earnestly. "He was glad you were in the meeting last night. He said so."

"Well, I'd sooner talk ta youse ef you don't mind. I ain't sa shamed like ta talk ta youse."

"All right," said Rilla. "I'll be glad to tell you how Jesus Christ died in our place to save us from the penalty of our sins!"

They had come to a street corner where the traffic was thicker, and Bat suddenly stared ahead and stopped short. Then he ducked behind a tree.

"I gotta beat it!" he said in a scared voice. "Say youse work in a bank?"

"Yes," said Rilla, feeling a sudden grip of fear about her heart again.

"Youse goin' thar now?"

"Why, yes," said Rilla, wishing instantly she hadn't told him. Wondering if she couldn't unsay it somehow.

"Well, doncha go! See? 'Tain't good fer ya ta go taday, see? I'm tellin' ya. See that thar bus comin' down ta this corner? Youse get in it an' go back home. Things is agoin' ta happen an' you mustn't be thar, see? An' don't youse go doublecrossin' me neither. Youse get in that bus quick. See, it's stoppin'! Go home an' stay tahum an' dontcha say I said so neither, ur I'll get mine, an' I gotta fin' out about that blood first! S'long!" and Bat turned the corner with a sudden slithering motion and vanished among a crowd of people getting into a trolly car.

Rilla stood on the curb looking after him, frightened, shaken and bewildered. The bus was standing there and people were crowding into it. Should she obey? What ought she to do? What was it that was going to happen at the bank? Why did he want her to stay at home? Of course she wouldn't do it, but what had he meant? Ought she to seem at least to obey him? She could get off at the next corner.

The door was just about to close and Rilla swung up the steps and was safe inside, trundling along back over the road she had just come, trying to think her way through.

Then it all came to her what it must mean. There was some ill intended toward the bank! Perhaps a hold-up planned, and Bat knew about it and was trying to give her a hint. Trying to save her from danger. What should she do? If she could only get in touch with Thurl! But how could she do that? Would he have reached the police station yet? His hours were in the morning now, and he always went to the station first. He had a motorcycle now, and belonged to the motorcycle corps.

The bus stopped and she got off and flew up a side street where she knew there was a public telephone. How could she tell Thurl anything so that he would understand, and yet not give Bat away? She had a feeling somehow that she must protect Bat. He had tried to save her.

And would Thurlow just laugh at her perhaps? Oh, how could she make him understand? And then she must fly back to the bank and warn them before it was too late! Perhaps it was too late even now. Bat had looked suddenly white and frightened as if he saw someone who startled him. Perhaps a hold-up was on the way even now! She ought to telephone the bank first perhaps! She entered the telephone booth trembling, but when she tried the bank number they told her it was busy. All the bank telephones were busy. What could it mean?

Then she called the police station and asked if Thurlow Reed was there yet, praying God that he would be there, and almost at once she heard her brother's voice.

"Thurl!" she cried in relief. "Something is going to happen at the place where I work. You know. Can't you send somebody quick? I can't tell you who told me, but I'm sure it is something. Couldn't somebody go there quick and kind of hang around? No, not you, somebody they wouldn't know, to see what happens."

There was a moment's silence at the other end of the wire. Then:

"You are sure of this, Rilla?"

"Oh, I don't know," cried the girl desperately. "I was just told to go home quick and stay there, that something was going to happen."

"Where are you, Rilla?"

"I'm on my way to work," said Rilla breathlessly. "Good-by!" and she hung up.

"Rilla! Rilla!" her brother called. "Operator, get me that number again, please!" But he was answered only by a jangling of wires and voices, and he slammed the receiver in place and turned to his chief excitedly.

Five minutes later five plainclothes men silently slipped away from as many quiet hideaways and made their way by separate roads toward the bank where Rilla worked. And Rilla herself was breathlessly hurrying along by her usual route toward her morning duties, late and breathless and frightened. If any watchers saw her they were satisfied that she would be in her place when they arrived, if they intended to arrive.

Rilla, as she rushed along, began to wonder whether she had not made a mountain out of a mole hill. Perhaps Bat was playing a joke on her. Perhaps he only came to the meeting for a joke. Perhaps all he had said about the blood of the Lamb—! But no, that could not have been a joke. Bat had been too much in earnest! And there was the tear she had seen. That was genuine she was sure.

The blood was pounding in her temples, and her lungs hurt as she breathed. It was not that she was walking so fast. It was that her inward turmoil interrupted the natural action of her heart. And she began to pray, "Oh, God, keep me calm. Send help if there is danger!"

Then she entered the bank and all was as usual. The busy workers were all in place, and the work of the day was going forward as usual, only that she was ten minutes late. She felt a sudden shame! Had she created a situation out of absolutely nothing, just because Bat had warned her not to go to the bank? What ought she to do? Ought she to go and confess to some official what she had done, or would Thurlow do something about it? Suppose he and three or four policemen rushed in without warning and she were called upon to explain? And if she did explain she would have to reveal who had told her. Oh, she had been a fool to pay any attention at all to a creature like Bat. Perhaps he was half-witted. And now perhaps she would lose her nice job, when she had just received a tiny raise, and was enjoying her work so much! They would likely think her awfully officious. And yet, come what would of it, she ought to tell someone what she had done.

She looked around, trying to decide what to do. Should she ask to see the president a moment? Would they grant her such a request? Or would it be some lesser official who would have such things in charge? There was a quiet elderly man at a desk outside the window writing a check. There was another talking with one of the cashiers. All things looked as they should at this time of the morning. There wasn't a sign of a sleuth outside in the street, just a few passers-by. An excellent time for a hold-up, perhaps, but how could she know? If she only knew what she ought to do.

She stood hesitating, looking toward her place and her usual work, and then she saw the cashier signal to her. She walked fearfully toward him, wondering if he was the one she should tell. But he spoke first:

"Miss Reed, will you show this man through to the president's office, and wait there for further orders?"

The president's office. Then perhaps there would be opportunity for her to tell the president. She must get it off her mind somehow before she went to work or she would make blunders all day long. Oh, if she had only waited long enough to ask Thurlow what to do! But then he would have told her to go home. She was morally sure he would have insisted that she should not go down to the bank until he was positive everything was all right.

She led the way behind the great safe down the corridor that led to the president's office, and the president himself opened the door. He seemed to be expecting them.

He greeted pleasantly the man she was escorting.

"Good morning, Mr. Bramley, you have some kind of a line on us?" he said, smiling.

"I believe we have. At least one of our young sleuth-hounds seems to think he has a lead. They've been watching a certain gang for some days. They think they have reason to believe they are about to strike somewhere, and on account of a warning they've received we're covering the vicinity today from hidden stations. We're ready to protect you if anything should happen, but we don't want to be in evidence lest we may alarm the criminals and they may put off their plans indefinitely."

"I see. Well, what do you want us to do?"

"Look after your money. Don't have much in evidence. See that your safe is protected. But don't let your natural routine be interrupted. Let everything seem perfectly natural. Warn your men if you want, and perhaps the girls too. You'll know best about that. Send the women home if you think best."

The president looked thoughtfully down at Rilla.

"You've heard what this man says. Do you want to go home, Miss Reed?"

"I'll stay!" said Rilla. "Of course, unless you feel I'll be in the way."

"Thank you, Miss Reed. I appreciate that. We'll do our best to protect you from any possible danger. Now, captain, suppose you give your orders."

The work of the morning went quietly forward and nothing happened. All the morning Rilla kept looking up now and then toward the door, but only the usual people came and went, and she began to think there was nothing to all this. Thurlow would certainly have it in for her when they both got home! If they had sent five men and perhaps a posse of police to guard that bank all day because of her foolish excitement she would never get over it. She would never be able to lift up her head again.

It was near the end of the month and they were preparing statements for their depositors. Rilla found herself making mistakes and having to go back and correct them. This would not do. She must work more carefully. She must not be so excited.

She glanced up at the clock. It was almost half-past twelve. There wasn't a soul in the place except the regular workers. Nothing had happened yet! Why could she not be calm and do her work? In a couple of hours more the bank would be closed, and then a little later she would be out and free, on her way home! Free from the awful thought of—!

And suddenly the thing happened, the thing for which she had been waiting all the morning.

She had her hands full of the statements she had just finished and was on her way to the bookkeeper's desk across the room, when the street door opened and she saw Brick Etter enter and walk to the cashier's window holding out a check.

Her heart seemed almost to stop beating and her knees grew weak beneath her. This was the moment for which she had been planning all the morning and now she felt so utterly helpless!

She took the two more steps to the bookkeeper's desk calmly as she had planned to do. And even as she turned to get back to her place, trying to walk as if nothing was happening, unable even yet to be sure anything really was, the door opened again and she saw a huddled group of figures enter, like grim shadows, and though she could not distinguish their faces because of the flood of sunshine at their backs, the slouch of their walk was strangely familiar. That surely was Reds and behind him Slink, heading the band! And even as she thought it she saw they had disguised themselves with red bandanna handkerchiefs tied about their heads just below their eyes. They were actually inside the bank, and no one seemed to know yet. Where were the men set to guard them? Had Thurl sent his men back to the station? Oh, was there nothing she could do?

And now there flashed in Brick Etter's hand something dark and sinister. It was pointed straight into the face of the cashier. Rilla, partly through terror, and partly because her brain was functioning as she had tried all the morning to teach it to do, dropped to the floor beneath the desk. With a wild idea of warning the president in his room and any policemen he might have with him, she crept warily across the three feet separating her from the corridor that led to the president's office.

But, lo, the corridor was full of armed men, almost stumbling over her! And one caught her up and pushed her hastily back out of sight, so forcefully that she fell again and lay there on the floor trembling and white as the men tramped by her and swarmed into the bank. Had that been Thurlow who told her to keep back? Oh, had Thurlow gone into danger? What would they do if anything happened to Thurlow?

A shot rang out! Two! Three! A whole volley! Shots from all over the bank it seemed! She lay there huddled where she had fallen, too frightened and weak to get up, not able to think where to go.

There were more shots and confusion. Calls! A command! Feet tramping away! The clanging of the police siren! The gong of a hospital ambulance, and Rilla rose to her knees, then stumbled to her feet, her eyes wide with terror.

There were footsteps coming down the corridor, a lot of them. They were bringing someone. Was it—it *was*—Thurlow! She could see the dark waves of his hair above his forehead, and his eyes were closed! "Oh, God! Not Thurlow! Please! Don't take Thurlow! Take me if you must, but not Thurl! For Mother's sake!"

And then she slid softly down to the floor at the very feet of the men who were carrying Thurlow to the president's office.

When she came to herself she was lying on the leather

couch in the president's room herself, and Thurlow was sitting in the president's big chair with his coat off and a bandage about his shoulder, smiling at her.

There were a lot of men in the room, some of them policemen, and a doctor was standing over her with his hand on her wrist.

But she was not looking at the men. Her eyes were on her brother, and she was remembering what had happened. Fear grew in her eyes.

"Thurl! Are you hurt? Did they get you?" she cried out.

"Only a scratch, Rill," he said with a grin. "Lie still a bit and get your bearings."

"But you are hurt! You have a bandage on your shoulder!"

"Nothing serious, little girl," said the doctor, turning toward her. "Lie still and rest up a bit. You've been through quite a strain, you know."

Then the president stepped to her side.

"Yes, lie still, Miss Reed! You've done great work and you've earned a rest." His voice was husky with feeling. "We appreciate—what you've done—for the bank! You were—a brave girl! You've probably saved several lives by warning your brother in time—as well as property. But—more than that, those men were killers, and *my son* was out there at the window when the first man drew his gun!"

"Oh!" said Rilla, turning her gaze on the president, and then toward Thurl. "Did they get him? Did they get them all?"

"They caught Slink and two underlings," said Thurl, "but I'm almost sure Brick Etter and Reds were in this, yet we couldn't find them. They made a slick getaway if they were here."

"They *were!*" said Rilla decidedly. "I saw them, all

three! It was Brick Etter who came in the door first and tried to cash his check. I saw him when he first opened the door!"

"Are you perfectly sure about that, Rill? You're sure Brick Etter was here?"

"Perfectly sure," said Rilla with conviction. "I saw him come in the door, and Slink and Reds were just behind him."

"Then I'd better get busy!" said Thurlow, springing to his feet. "I know what to look for now. They'll be hiding out—"

"Steady, boy," said a big policeman, coming up to Thurlow and pushing him gently back into the chair from which he had risen in his excitement. "We've got a taxi coming and you're going home for a good sleep. We'll need you later in the day, you know, and you want to get your nerves in good shape."

"I'm all right! I couldn't sleep!" protested Thurlow. "I've got to get down to the station at once. There are things I ought to tell the chief. I didn't have time before I left."

"All right, if you think that's necessary," said the other, "but we're taking you, see? No monkeyshines!"

"I haven't time to be taken!" said Thurl. "Give me my coat. My shoulder isn't serious. No, I'm going to have my coat on!"

They helped him into his coat finally, and in spite of them he sailed off on his motorcycle.

Rilla stood in the door and watched him away proudly. Her color was beginning to come back and she looked less ethereal.

The president insisted that she should go home at once in his own car.

"Oh, thank you, but I couldn't!" said Rilla firmly. "My mother would be frightened if I came home that way, and early. And there's no reason in the world for her to know anything at all about it. I must go in the usual way or she will know something has happened."

So Rilla had her way too, and went off home alone when the time came, although she never knew that the president's car trailed her half a block away and kept her in sight till she had turned the corner into Meachin Street.

Rilla drank a glass of milk and went about the little daily task that she usually performed when she got home from the bank, but she kept glancing out of her window and her mind was not at rest. She was trying to think back and remember whether she had seen Bat among the robbers. Now and then she hummed a bit of a tune lest her mother would notice her uneasiness and question her.

> *"He will hide me, safely hide me,*
> *Where no storm can e'er betide me,*
> *He will hide me, safely hide me,*
> *Neath the shadow of His wing."*

she sang, and her mother looked lovingly toward her and thought how sweet and strong her girl was growing.

Thurl came home just as the dusk was beginning to drop. He told his mother he might have to go on duty later in the evening and he had come home to snatch a wink of sleep. He asked for coffee and Rilla made it for him, strong and hot with plenty of cream as he liked it. He sat by the table drinking it.

"Have you seen Bat?" he asked her in a low tone.

"No," she said anxiously. "Do you think he was in it?"

"I'm not sure. It was he of course who warned you?"

"How did you know?"

"I was sure. I've been watching him," said the brother evasively. "I believe Bat has been trying to pull away from the outfit for several weeks past. But it's a hard thing to do, you know. I think he was genuine last night, don't you?"

"Oh, I do," said Rilla. "I could see him from where I sat and he really looked—"

"I know. I was watching too."

"Oh, I wouldn't want him to think I'd told," said Rilla in distress, "after he risked his life, maybe, to tell me. He said they'd get him if they knew!"

Then the mother came in from the kitchen and they said no more.

Suddenly a shot rang out, and then two more! Thurlow put down his coffee cup and sprang to his feet, his eyes alert, listening.

"They've got him!" he said. "Rilla, call the station and tell them I'm on the trail. They'll take the river road. Call quick!"

He was out the door and astride his motorcycle before Rilla got to the telephone.

"Oh, Thurlow, my son! Don't go out alone!" called the mother wildly.

But Thurlow was thundering along into the dusk, down the bumpy street and under the railroad bridge toward the river road, after a couple of the most desperate characters in the city.

He had no idea as he tore along, after those pitiless fleeing neighbors of his, with possible death lurking behind every shadow, that his keen instinct and his quick action would result in the capture of two criminals whose whereabouts had long been a mystery that the Department of Justice was trying to solve. Much less did he dream that his own name as a hero would be blazoned across the front page of the papers. Yet so it proved to be.

And Bat was lying crumpled on the floor of the little cabin that was his home, with his dull-eyed mother bending over him stupidly, frightened and bewildered.

The policemen arrived almost immediately, with a fleet of motorcycles, noisily booming into the street that was all agog with horror over what had happened among them—children and grown folk milling around, asking strange wild questions, getting underfoot everywhere, standing in frightened curious groups.

The officers made quick work at Bat's home, asking a sharp question or two of the bewildered old woman, giving a knowing look at the crumpled figure on the floor, then they streamed away thunderously into the darkness, leaving two of their number behind to guard the premises.

Then Bat's mother appeared at the Reed door, the tears streaming down her face, pitiful in her distress, like a broken ship without a rudder. She was wringing her hands.

"Come! Come quick!" she cried to Rilla who opened the door. "Bat's dyin' an' he wants ya!" she ended in a great heart-rending sob.

"Oh, I'll call my mother!" cried Rilla with a frightened look behind her.

"Naw, it's youse he wants. He said, 'Bring her *quick!*' Youse *gotta* come. They got my Bat, an' he wants youse, and youse *gotta come!*"

The old woman seized Rilla's hand in her own dirty one and with a fierce strength born of her need, literally pulled her along to the house.

Fearfully Rilla entered the house where death was waiting to claim its own, and came to stand beside Bat, there on the floor.

"You tell me—how ta get—that there blood?" he pled, his dying eyes lifted piteously to her face. "I—shan't need—them angels. De gang got me—an' I'm goin'—fast. But you make a prayer—ur somethin' quick, an'—get me—that blood! I—gotta—get—my sins—washed—white—like snow! I ain't fitten—ta die till I git 'em washed!"

Rilla dropped down on her knees by the dying boy and took his cold claw of a hand in hers.

"Listen!" she said earnestly. "Jesus Christ, your Saviour, shed His blood on the cross, to make it safe and sure that any sinner might be saved who would believe on Him. Will you let Him be your Saviour, Bat?"

"Sure—I will!" gasped Bat. "What I—gotta—do?"

"Only believe!"

"But—I ben—awful—bad!"

"Of course. But Jesus Christ took all your punishment. He forgives everything! He washes all the sin away. The Bible says He is able to present you faultless before the presence of His glory without spot or wrinkle or any such thing, if you'll just trust yourself to Him, your Saviour. Will you?"

"Sure!" said Bat simply.

The two policemen stood there solemnly on either side, watching the scene, strangely stirred, as the young girl bowed her head and prayed a few words.

"Dear Lamb of God, that takest away the sins of the world, wash poor Bat and make him white. Take him Home to be with You forever! Make him know how You love him, and help him not to be afraid any more. For Christ's sake we ask it."

The doctor had come in with a curious look at the beautiful girl kneeling there beside the dying man, and stooped to put a finger on Bat's wrist.

"It's too late—Doc!" Bat's breath was almost gone.

"They—got me! I double-crossed—'em—this time an' that's one sin—He didn't hev—ta wash—away!"

Suddenly Bat threw up his arms, and bright drops appeared on his lips.

"See! See!" he cried out, gasping. "Them angels! He's sent 'em! I—ain't gonta need trouble youse no more! I thank 'ee! Goo'-by!" and Bat was gone!

Pat came down the next day for the weekend and stepped into the situation with tender sympathetic efficiency.

"Oh, I donno whut we're gonta do fer a clean shirt ta bury 'im!" wailed the poor bewildered mother. "He would put that un on when he had him his bath, an' now it's got blood all over. It ain't fitten!"

"Never mind, Mrs. O'Hennessy," comforted Pat, "you leave that to me. I'll look after that."

So Pat went out and got him clean and decent things, and when Bat finally lay in the coffin and the Reeds and Wheelers and Sandra gathered for a simple service, with the assembled curious multitude of Meachin Street, he was clothed decently, better clothed than he had ever been in his sorry sinful lifetime. Also, he wore a dignity in death that had never been his in life. The neighbors came and stared and wondered, and listened to the prayers and the simple gospel message of salvation which perhaps they had never heard before, and were entranced while the two girls and the young men sang:

> *"What can wash away my sins?*
> *Nothing but the blood of Jesus."*

It was an impressive service. Bat's mother was there dressed in a neat black dress and hat that Mrs. Reed had given her. Bat's father, back from his last spree, sat beside her in a new suit that Pat had bought him, and which he would probably pawn tomorrow morning. Bat's sister was there, sick and frail, the ghost of the beautiful girl she used to be. It would not be long before she would go down into the dark valley herself. Did she get anything from the message that would help her to get ready for that day?

But it was left for Pat to put the final touch to Mrs. O'Hennessy's pride in that death and burial of her son. Pat promised her that he would put up a stone at the head of the grave, and when that stone was ready there was cut upon it this inscription:

WILLIAM O'HENNESSY
WASHED WHITE IN THE BLOOD
OF THE LAMB

But the neighbors couldn't understand why the William when his name had always been Bat.

21

THE April gold had come at last!

For weeks the seven little boys from the second house below had hung around the picket fence and watched the green sabers of the daffodils appear, and shoot up and develop. For days they had counted the buds, and watched the sun and the rain, and all with a view to the great day when the April gold should be ready and they would go to Mrs. Reed's party and have cakes.

For weeks Thurlow and Rilla had been at work painting the house in their leisure hours, getting up early in the morning, and rushing home late afternoons, using every spare minute. Rilla had worked on the windows and lower boards, and Thurlow had taken the higher work. The shutters they had painted inside the kitchen one at a time, so they were ready to hang as soon as the house was finished. The fence they all worked at, a few pickets a day, even Mrs. Reed coming out now and then and taking a hand. At last the house stood there in glistening white, with its lemon-colored shutters, and its moss green roof, and the fence surrounding the house in sharp white pickets, white that covered up its ugly roughnesses and mended places, and made it seem a new wonderful fence, with its fringe of green at the foot.

Day after day the street had walked that way, several times a day, some of them, to see how the work was progressing. Mrs. O'Hennessy was heard to remark that if poor Bat was only here he would do the same for his home, that he had been saving up to repair the place for a long time. And some of the neighbors when they heard it said to each other, "Oh, *yeah?*"

But Mrs. O'Hennessy went right on idealizing Bat. How surprised Bat would have been if he could have known.

Rosie was home now, occupying Bat's shed room, going in and out with her haunted look, and frightened eyes, coughing all night and growing thinner day by day. Mrs. Reed had her over often and tried to point her the way of the cross, but she wasn't sure that Rosie listened.

Mrs. O'Hennessy came over the afternoon the fence was finished and stood there looking at the completed picture, the white, white house, the soft green roof, the lemon-colored shutters, the white fence with its fringe of green and the golden daffodils just bursting. The forsythia had smiled out the day before in its golden bells, threaded on thin brown branches.

"It is my April gold at last!" Mother Reed said, winking back the sudden tears that misted her eyes.

"Ef my poor Bat cud only be here now!" sighed Bat's mother, gazing in wonder.

"But where he is there are much more beautiful houses," said Mrs. Reed. "There are many mansions up there, and golden streets, and the glory of the Lord is there, God Himself, you know."

"Maybe," said the poor stupid thing, "but I'm sure there's nary a house like this one up there! This is different somehow. An' I ain't sa sure I'd loike gold shtreets. They'd get all shcratched up with men's shoes, an' wouldn't it make a lot o' schrubbin'! I'd loike a good asphalt better, ef you ast me! An' as fer God, I think I'd be afraid o' Him."

Mrs. Reed smiled pitifully and turned back to her home, to gaze out again and again at her April gold opening down the borders of the walk, and all around the fence.

The little boys got up unnecessarily early the next morning and fought for the tin basin, washing their faces quite hard, and even their ears, to be sure and be ready. For the party was to be at three that afternoon, the April gold party!

The Reeds were lingering at the breakfast table unwontedly that morning. Thurlow had worked all night and had not yet gone to his sleep. He had been walking about the yard with his mother to view her April gold. And Rilla happened to have a holiday. So they sat there chatting and full of thankfulness as the sun poured through the bright windows, and the daffodils nodded and swayed in the spring breeze.

"We've a great deal to be thankful for," said the mother with a smile upon her lips.

"Yes, haven't we?" said Rilla, with joy-lights dancing in her eyes, as she nestled her hand about a letter in her apron pocket that had come last night and she couldn't bear to let it far from her yet.

"I never thought I'd actually be getting fond of this dump!" said Thurlow with a grin, "but we've had some grand times fixing it up!"

It was just then it happened.

They heard someone open the living room screen door. The inner door they had left wide open to the sunshine. They heard a step across the floor, and looked up and saw in the doorway Barbara Sherwood.

"Really?" she said, arching her eyebrows that had somehow lost their old comeliness, and were threaded to a mere pencil line. "What's the little old idea?"

She looked about the room recognizing pieces of furniture, paintings and china. She looked at the three sitting there so contentedly in a shack in old Meachin Street on the dirty abandoned South Side! Decent economy in hard times Barbara Sherwood could understand and tolerate—in others, and bemoan with them, but this was glorified penury and she resented their evident content.

For an instant the four looked at one another in a growing dismay. Queer things were happening in Thurlow's heart. It was turning a somersault and righting itself astonishingly. Here was Barbara Sherwood, the ideal of his heart, the girl who had brought bitterness into his life with her indifference and her flirtations, and he had thought that if she would once come back and show that she cared to come near him again it would be the utmost bliss that he could ask. But now that she was here he somehow resented her presence. She didn't look the same at all. What was it about her that had changed her so? Her lips were too red. Was that the difference? Barbara with painted lips! He had never thought she would do that. And there was a hard bright unnatural finish to her face, that used to have such a fresh soft look, like blush roses. And those queer eyebrows! She didn't look like herself. Why had she taken on such styles?

She was wearing a garb of bright colors, and when she turned a little in the doorway her back was practically bare to the waist save for a couple of slender straps. And she was stouter, and coarsened, and less attractive. Something told him she was not the same in any way. And as if to emphasize the change she produced a tiny gold case from her trifling handbag, took out a cigarette, lighted it, and began to smoke, surveying them all in a supercilious amused way as if they were children to whom she was condescending.

Thurlow checked the smile that had been dawning on his face and arose gravely, looking very tall and impressive in his uniform which he had not stopped to change before breakfast.

Barbara looked at him in detail now, and frowned.

"For heaven's sake, Thurl! What have you got on? Is this a masquerade?"

Thurlow gave an amused glance down at his uniform.

"No," he said gravely. "You see I have the honor to be in the city service, and this is the uniform we wear. I flattered myself that it was rather neat and becoming."

But Barbara did not smile. Instead she curled her lip in scorn.

"I suppose you call that funny!" she said sharply. "Well, I don't! If you really mean that you are a policeman, I think it is an insult to all your friends!"

Thurlow's chin lifted a bit haughtily.

"Not to my *friends!*" he said significantly.

"Yes, to your friends!" reiterated Barbara. "What is the meaning of all this anyway? Here I try to call you up on my arrival and a stranger answers me. Three days I search for your whereabouts and find you in the slums in a uniform! I should think you would have a little regard for your station in life, and the people in your social set. What on earth is it all about anyway? Have you turned socialist or Bolshevik or something?"

Mrs. Reed suddenly rose with dignity and drew forward a chair.

"Won't you sit down, Barbara? I will try to explain. You see we lost our money. It happened just about the time you went away. We lost our house, too, because of the bank's closing, and this place was the only solution at the time. We happened to own it. The explanation is very simple, after all. Just necessity. But we've managed to have a very pleasant time fixing up this little place, and we're quite comfortable. Won't you draw up to the table and have a cup of coffee with us? I think it is still hot."

"For heaven's sake!" said Barbara, rudely ignoring the chair and the invitation. "Why on earth didn't you appeal to Dad? He would have done something about it, of course. I'll speak to him right away."

"Don't trouble your father with our affairs, Barbara," said Thurlow sternly. "We are getting along very nicely and don't need any assistance."

"We won't discuss it!" said Barbara sharply. "It's all very distasteful to me and I'd rather not hear any more about it, not until things are set straight anyway. What I came hunting you for is that I know it's almost commencement time at your college, and I want you to invite me as your guest. A man I met in France is to give the baccalaureate address and I thought I'd like to hear him, and of course class day and all the rest is very interesting after one has been away awhile. You'll ask me, won't you? I've made all my plans to go. I had no idea I should have such a time to locate you."

Thurlow looked at her steadily an instant, and then spoke pleasantly.

"I'm sorry, Barbara, I'm not in college any more."

She whirled upon him.

"You're not in college either? You mean you've left college? How utterly *silly*! Well, really, I think it's high time you had a keeper or something. I never supposed you had as little spirit as that. Well—" She paused and looked out of the window unseeingly, as if she were studying a way out, and then she whirled back to him. "I suppose you can take me to commencement day exercises anyway, can't you? If I pay the expenses? I shouldn't like to put you to any expense of course since you are hard up, but I certainly want to go and I can't very well go alone."

The color receded entirely from Thurlow's face. He was ashen white, and haughty now.

"I'm sorry," he said coldly. "You should have told me before that you wanted to go. I'm taking another girl! Perhaps, however, you would like to go *with* us!"

"With you?" said Barbara, her voice fairly shaking with anger. "What are you trying to do, Thurl, insult me?"

"No," said Thurlow steadily, "although I guess you were trying to insult me when you said you would pay the expenses. You must know that isn't pleasant."

"When one puts himself in such a position as you have done he can't always expect everything to be pleasant. Well"—Barbara whirled about and started for the door—"I'll get busy in your behalf and see what can be done."

She slammed out of the front door before her sentence was finished, leaving the three sitting at the table. It was all very quiet in the room till they heard the car drive away. Thurlow had risen and gone to the window to look out. He saw the girl he used to think he loved stride down the walk without a look toward the gold of the daffodils and get into her car. The car was a new model and very showy. She was sitting in the back seat alone, and the car was chauffeur driven. The whole outfit was rather ostentatious, and unlike what the Sherwoods used to affect. Had Barbara changed her whole nature?

He watched till the car whirled out of the street and then turned back to his family.

"And that's that!" he said, smiling quietly.

The next day there came a letter from Mr. Sherwood, brief and to the point, kindly and brusque as he always was. Thurlow wondered if Barbara had inherited some of his excellent business qualities. He had never noticed it before, but perhaps it was so. The letter read:

Dear Thurl:

Barbara informs me that you have been unfortunate financially and have taken a temporary position with the Public Safety Service.

It is commendable in you of course to be willing to take any job for the time being to support your family, but of course we cannot allow your father's son to stay in any position like that. I am therefore asking you at once to offer your resignation to the Service, and get ready to make a change. It seems most unfortunate that you have stopped your college course.

If you will drop in on me during the course of a few days, at my office, between the hours of three and four in the afternoon, we can talk the thing over, and see what is best to be done for you. I am not prepared off-hand to offer you anything definite, but I am quite sure, if it seems wise, that I can make a place for you with us after a few weeks as bond salesman for our firm.

Barbara tells me she is asking you to dinner with us tomorrow night, so I shall be seeing you soon.

It is unfortunate that you have lost your house. I wish that you had had the foresight to inform me sooner before it was too late to save it. I was shocked to find building going on there so near our home. It seems that you might have been more considerate than to bring a public hall into our exclusive little neighborhood, but I suppose you did not realize how we would feel about it. How-

ever, we may be selling our own place soon, and
then of course it will not matter.

Yours sincerely,
Guerdon Sherwood

Thurlow read the letter through twice and then he sat
down and wrote:

Dear Mr. Sherwood:

I thank you for your kind interest in our affairs,
and for taking the trouble to write and offer assistance. But I am afraid Barbara did not quite understand the situation. I am not looking for a position,
being quite satisfied with the one I have at present.
And the outlook for the future seems very good.

God has been very good to us and we are
enjoying our pleasant little home, though it is not
quite as palatial as our former home, but it was a
haven to us when we had to leave the other house.

I am sorry that inadvertently through us you are
suffering inconvenience through the Club Auditorium that is being built, but it was not a matter of
choice with us, the selling. The place was being
stolen from us that a large apartment house might
be erected. I felt gratified that I was able to sell it
in an honorable way to such a respectable organization as the Woman's Club.

I thank you for your suggestion that you might
have helped us in our extremity, but we all felt that
we could not think of burdening you with such a
perplexity, especially while you were on a vacation.

I thank you also for your kind offer to make a
place for me with your firm, but am glad that I do
not have to put you to such trouble.

It is unfortunate that I will not be able to accept your kind invitation to dinner tomorrow night; I shall be on duty at that hour, and it would be impossible.

Thanking you for your friendship and kindness in the past,

Sincerely,
Thurlow Reed

"There," said Thurl, bringing the two letters and laying them in his mother's lap, "and that is *that!* Now, have I enough clean shirts to go to commencement? They are going to give me four whole days off, and we're going to have a real lark. Pat phoned me this morning that he is coming down in his car to get us. I suppose Rilla already knows, however, and so it isn't news to you. I'd like it if you and Rilla would ask Sandra to stay all night with us the night before we start. It will make it easier to get off early."

"Of course," said the mother. Then after a minute: "Thurlow, are you quite sure you want to break entirely with Barbara?"

Thurlow turned a radiant face to his mother.

"Quite sure, Mother-Mine! Are you regretting it?"

"Not in the least!" said Mrs. Reed with decision. "I'm very glad about it."

"So am I," said Thurlow happily.

The night before they went to commencement George Steele sent for Thurlow. He looked annoyed when he received the message.

"That *would* come tonight of all nights!" he sighed. But then it wasn't quite so bad as it might have been if Sandra had been spending the night with them. She had found she had to do penance playing for some of Cousin

Caroline's guests, so she wouldn't be there, and he knew that Pat and Rilla were quite sufficient to themselves just now, so he might as well get this over now as any time.

Mr. Steele took the big policeman into his library and sat down to an hour of pleasant converse, touching on every question of the day from politics to religion, adroitly finding out Thurlow's opinions. At last he said:

"Well, young man, I've been watching you very closely for the past six months and I've come to the conclusion that you are the man I want if you are agreeable.

"Your admirable work in discovering and capturing those gangsters in that South Side bank affair gave the final weight to my decision.

"In our business we have a large department of investigation and justice, and I've been looking for some time for the right man to train for manager of this in the not too distant future when our present man retires. I know you are young, and you may not turn out to be the right one; I'm not making any promises. But I am offering you a chance to try for it and you can say whether you are interested or not."

For the next two hours he went into details, laying the whole plan of the organization before Thurlow, watching him keenly as he talked. And Thurlow was watching Mr. Steele. More and more as he talked he respected him, both as a business man and as a personality, and when he came away he carried with him a contract which he had promised to go over carefully, and bring back, signed or unsigned, at the end of the week.

Thurlow walked home that night to Meachin Street with his head among the stars.

They started out the next morning on their long drive in Pat's great beautiful car.

Cousin Caroline sighted it from her window as it drew up at her door.

"Sandra, Sandra," she called as Sandra was shutting her suitcase and hurrying to be absolutely ready when they came, "look out of the window and see who this is in this gorgeous car in front of the door. Now, if you were going away to commencement in a car like that I wouldn't object. It's an honor to have a car like that drive up at my door. And who is the stunning-looking man in the back seat with the smart gray-haired woman?"

Sandra cast a glance out of the window and smiled impishly.

"Why, that is the car I'm going in, Cousin Caroline, and that stunning man in the back seat is my big policeman. I'm so glad you like his looks!" caroled Sandra.

"Your policeman!" said Cousin Caroline blankly. "Now, Sandra, you are joking. You are always joking!"

"Not a bit of a joke, my dear. The lady in the back seat is my policeman's lovely mother. Some day I want you to meet her."

"But how could a policeman afford a car like that, unless he's accepting bribery?" said Miss Cradock offendedly.

"Well, it isn't his car, it belongs to the young man in the front seat, with my policeman's sister, Rilla. If they aren't engaged they soon will be. But you needn't worry about cars, my policeman will have a car as good some day, you'll see, and he isn't accepting bribery either. He's a Christian, Cousin Caroline. Good-by. Have a nice time with your friends and don't worry about policemen!"

The commencement was all it promised to be from start to finish, even if Thurlow did discover that Barbara was there with a freshman he had never seen before. She stared haughtily at Sandra when they met, and barely acknowledged the introduction. It was so annoying to find that the girl who had taken her place wore just as expensive imported clothes as she did, even if Thurlow was a policeman living quite beyond the pale of respectable society.

But neither Sandra nor Thurlow minded in the least. They were much too absorbed in one another, and were only on the outer edge of the great audience when honor was done to Thurlow by his class.

Sandra's hand stole softly up and into Thurlow's, and a pink glow came into her cheeks, and a light in her eyes as she looked up to him and smiled her gladness in the honor. Thurlow looked down and held her hand close, his eyes full of delight in her. And then, as soon as the speech was ended, he led her quite away from it all, to a place in the woods that he knew. A place where he had at one time thought to bring Barbara, but never had, and now he was glad.

There among the quiet trees, away from all the world, Thurlow told Sandra how he loved her.

"I have loved you ever since I saw you," he told her. "But I thought there wasn't any chance for me, a poor young man, even if you don't object to policemen."

"*Christian* policemen, remember," said Sandra, nestling close. "Go on! I surmise there is more!"

"Sweet!" said Thurlow, stooping and laying his face against hers. "Yes, there is more. Last night George Steele, the oil magnate, sent for me and offered me a position—" He went on to give the details which didn't matter in the least just then to Sandra, since she had Thurlow Reed's strong arm about her, and his love assured to her. Even the substantial salary that went with the offer did not take her off her feet. She felt that her policeman was worth a big salary, but she would have loved him just as well without a salary at all, even if she had to live on Meachin Street.

They emerged from the woods as it was growing dark, and came forth in a double radiance all their own, so luminous that their friends knew at once that something wonderful had happened.

It was not until they were on the way again in Pat's car that Thurlow told them. He told his mother and said the rest might hear. Told her first about himself and Sandra and that they were going to be married soon, and then followed it with the news of the wonderful new position.

Mother Reed reached around and kissed her new daughter tenderly, and said: "I'm so glad—for you *both!*" and nobody noticed the two in the front seat nudging and winking at each other. Sandra had been saying a lot of nice things about how she missed her mother, and how she was going to enjoy having Thurl's mother for her own. And then Pat spoke up:

"Talking about mothers," he said, "how about letting *us* under the mother-bird's wing too? Maybe you don't know it, but Rilla and I are going to be married at once, as soon as we get back. You may think we're too young and all that, but I don't see having Rilla off in that old hold-up bank, nor walking late in the dark through those streets, and I want a chance to take care of her. Also I don't want my mother-in-law baking and brewing for other people to piece out a living, and—yes, I know I promised not to tell, but time's up, Mother Reed! I'm graduated and we're going to be married! And if Thurl and I can't take care of you, who can?"

They all laughed and gasped and looked at Mrs. Reed.

"Yes, Mother, you thought you had put a lot over on us, didn't you? But I knew it all the time!" said Thurlow.

"I'm not a detective for nothing. I didn't say anything at the time because I had my hands pretty full and you seemed to enjoy it, but I didn't mean to let it go on long, at that. However, it's as Pat says. We're going to take care of all of you from now on, aren't we, Sandra?"

"We certainly are!" she said, patting Mother Reed's hand that lay in her lap.

"Well, now, to proceed and continue on," said Pat when the laughter had subsided. "You all don't know where we are going now. You think you are going home to Meachin Street, and Cousin Caroline, and so on, tonight, but you're not! You're visiting me at my home-mansion tonight, and we're heading straight for it, and no kidding! If anyone objects let him speak now or forever after hold his peace, or—jump out and run home! Try and do it!" and Pat put his machine at seventy-five miles an hour, for a brief space. Then slowing down somewhat he drew Rilla's head down upon his shoulder and kissed her, right there before them all.

It was late afternoon when they turned into a broad drive that wound about a spacious velvety lawn that looked almost like a gold course in its smooth loveliness. Behind great screens of hemlocks and pines and rhododendrons appeared a fine old house, white pillared, broadly terraced, with an air of having been there always.

"Behold! The ancestral mansion!" said Pat, with a flourish of his arm. "I only hope you all like it, folks, because I do! And I thought for the time being maybe we could all bunk here together, at least till Thurl and Sandra get too high-hat for us!"

"Say, old man, I never realized all this!" said Thurlow gravely. "What I don't understand is, how did you ever stand Meachin Street?"

"Well, you see, *you* were there, Whirl, and then *Rilla*

was there—that seemed to make *quite* a difference, somehow—" Rilla blushed and giggled in the darkness—"and then Mother here made home! And I like to be at home! Oh, I love Meachin Street. Don't misunderstand me. But there are a few reasons why I'd think this might be more convenient. Of course I could have a pump put in if Mother here prefers it—" He turned a mischievous eye back at the rest of them.

"But say, folks, while I'm talking I may as well get it all off my chest. What would you think of my buying the old factory and letting the Wheelers have it as an annex to Grace Chapel? They could take care of no end of people there, kind of a rescue home, you know, and carry on what the Reeds have begun in the way of transforming Meachin Street. I'm worried about those seven boys growing up. I only wish we'd been in time for Bat and Rosie. But better late than never. And I was thinking, if Mother isn't too much attached to the little white house, what about my buying it and letting the Wheelers live there close to their work?"

"How about our *giving* it?" said Thurlow eagerly. "Mother, what about it? Wouldn't we want to do our part?"

"Certainly!" said the smiling mother. "I can't think of a better way to use my April gold."

So they entered the fine old mansion and went around in sweet amaze, looking at the home that had belonged to Pat's mother's people years ago, studying her sweet young face in a wonderful painting on the wall, touching delicately the things that had been hers, Pat's mother! They would know her in heaven, for Pat had said she loved the Lord. He told how she used to sit and read her Bible in those last days before she went away.

It was after the dinner, which had been cooked and served by good old servants who had been with the family since Pat was a baby, that they all drifted out on the terrace to watch the setting sun.

"Do you like it here? Could you be happy here, Mother Reed?" asked Pat anxiously.

"Happy!" said Mother Reed, laying a gentle hand on Pat's arm. Why, it would seem like the ante-room to heaven! And I feel that I have a dear new daughter, and a dear new son!"

"Okay!" said Pat, trying to bluff the tears back from his eyes. "Then, this week-end, Thurl, you and I start planting those bulbs for next year's April gold for Mother!"

About the Author

Grace Livingston Hill is well known as one of the most prolific writers of romantic fiction. Her personal life was fraught with joys and sorrows not unlike those experienced by many of her fictional heroines.

Born in Wellsville, New York, Grace nearly died during the first hours of life. But her loving parents and friends turned to God in prayer. She survived miraculously, thus her thankful father named her Grace.

Grace was always close to her father, a Presbyterian minister, and her mother, a published writer. It was from them that she learned the art of storytelling. When Grace was twelve, a close aunt surprised her with a hardbound, illustrated copy of one of Grace's stories. This was the beginning of Grace's journey into being a published author.

In 1892 Grace married Fred Hill, a young minister, and they soon had two lovely young daughters. Then came 1901, a difficult year for Grace—the year when, within months of each other, both her father and husband died. Suddenly Grace had to find a new place to live (her home was owned by the church where her husband had been pastor). It was a struggle for Grace to raise her young daughters alone, but through everything she kept writing. In 1902 she produced *The Angel of His Presence, The Story of a Whim,* and *An Unwilling Guest.* In 1903 her two books *According to the Pattern* and *Because of Stephen* were published.

It wasn't long before Grace was a well-known author, but she wanted to go beyond just entertaining her readers. She soon included the message of God's salvation through Jesus Christ in each of her books. For Grace, the most important thing she did was not write books but share the message of salvation, a message she felt God wanted her to share through the abilities he had given her.

In all, Grace Livingston Hill wrote more than one hundred books, all of which have sold thousands of copies and have touched the lives of readers around the world with their message of "enduring love" and the true way to lasting happiness: a relationship with God through his Son, Jesus Christ.

In an interview shortly before her death, Grace's devotion to her Lord still shone clear. She commented that whatever she had accomplished had been God's doing. She was only his servant, one who had tried to follow his teaching in all her thoughts and writing.

Don't miss these Grace Livingston Hill romance novels!

Mail your order with check or money order for the price of the book(s) plus $2.00 for postage and handling to: **Tyndale Family Products, P.O. Box 448, Wheaton, IL 60189-0448.** Allow 4-6 weeks for delivery. Prices subject to change.

The Grace Livingston Hill romance novels are available at your local bookstore, or you may order by mail (U.S. and territories only). For your convenience, use this page to place your order or write the information on a separate sheet of paper, including the order number for each book.